FINDING FINN

FOREVER LOVE BOOK TWO

CHARLIE NOVAK

This one is for Carly, who continues to inspire me.

CHAPTER ONE

Gem

THE LOST WORLD'S three-year anniversary party was in full swing, and the tiny bookshop was packed to the rafters, which, considering there was two feet of snow outside the door, was no mean feat. Winter had turned Steep Hill into a skating rink, and I'd been worried we'd open the shop and spend the whole day by ourselves with a mountain of cake and signed books. But it seemed like nothing would stand between our regulars and the prospect of free food.

I was currently shoving more stock onto the shelves while the store's owner, Jay, chatted to a few people and Edward, his best friend and Lincoln's walking fae prince, manned the counter. Both of them were in their elements, and a small nugget of pride lodged in my chest to see the store packed with people. I'd been coming here since The Lost World had first opened, and over the past three years I'd watched it go from strength to strength.

While the start might have been rocky, at least according to Jay, it was now a thriving indie bookstore with a long list of regulars and a strong online shop that kept the pair of us incredibly busy. I hadn't been sure what to expect when I'd started working for Jay part-time just over eighteen months ago, but since then the shop had pretty much become my whole world. Especially since the game design business I'd been trying to get off the ground for the past ten years still showed no signs of taking off. At that point, it seemed dead in the water, and I was starting to wonder whether it might be better to call it quits just to save myself the heartache of watching my dream slowly decay.

"Hey, Gem," said a familiar voice from behind me. I stood up from where I'd been bent over a drawer, retrieving a couple of fantasy novels, and turned, a frown already etched onto my face. Standing there, and not looking at all sheepish while holding the hand of another man I didn't recognise, was the guy I thought I'd been dating. Jesse.

Thought was the operative word because the bastard had ghosted me two weeks ago and now I knew why.

And after I'd bought him a really nice fucking Christmas present too. There was thirty quid I wasn't going to get back, and the epic blow job I'd gotten when he'd unwrapped it felt like a cheap distraction instead of the gesture of affection I'd assumed it to be.

"Jesse," I said, trying to sound casual and like I wasn't upset by the fact the man I'd given half of the last year to stood there cosying up to someone new. Like it didn't feel like a situation I'd lived a thousand times before. Like I didn't really feel surprised. "I didn't expect to see you here."

"We thought we'd surprise you." He smiled at me waspishly, and I knew he was trying to provoke me. Why I'd hooked up with him in the first place was something I still couldn't figure out, given the mile-wide mean streak it turned out he possessed, but these days anyone who showed interest in me was enough to make me jump. Apparently my self-esteem really was that low.

"We?" I glanced between the pair of them and raised an eyebrow. "I'm assuming this is your new flavour of the week?"

"This is Link," Jesse said, ignoring my comment. "We met at New Year."

That made sense. I'd gone back to Scotland to see my family and indulge my nephew, and apparently not giving Jesse enough attention for three days had made him find someone else who would. I sighed internally. What was it about me that made me pick men who couldn't seem to function unless I was worshipping the ground they walked on twenty-four-seven? Was I really that desperate?

That wasn't a question I wanted to answer, at least not right now. Even if I already knew the truth.

I glanced at the other man. He was your traditional tall, blond, and handsome with bulging muscles and tiny clothes that clung to every part of him, despite the freezing weather. He was the complete opposite of me, and Jesse was staring at him with a hungry expression.

"Link? From *The Legend of Zelda*?" I asked, still holding my stack of books.

"Ocarina of Time," Link said with a wide smile. I wondered if he realised what he'd been dragged into—he looked too sweet to be malicious. "Mum played it a lot when I was born because I didn't sleep much."

Christ on a fucking cracker. How fucking old was I? This guy was at least eleven years younger than me given that reference. Which was probably why Jesse was drooling over him. Young, sexy, muscular—he probably had stamina for days, and if there was one thing Jesse loved, it was sex.

The more I thought about it, the more I wondered how the fuck Jesse and I had even made it to six months. My closest guess was that nobody else had been available or that I'd been one of several men Jesse was stringing along for his own amusement. I was such a fucking sucker.

"It's a good game," I said, trying not to smile at the fact that talking to Link was clearly pissing Jesse off. It was like he'd been expecting a different reaction, but if he thought I was going to cry and scream, he had another thing coming. I wasn't going to give him the satisfaction of knowing I was hurt. That could come later when I was alone with a decent bottle of whiskey, and even then I'd be more upset that I'd once again been used rather than nursing a broken heart. "I used to play it a lot at university."

Jesse rolled his eyes. "Fascinating."

"Oh, I'm sorry. Am I bothering you? Is there something I can help you with?" I heard the sarcasm and disdain dripping off every syllable. Usually, I'd never speak to someone like that, but I figured I could make an exception for this prick.

"No, we were just passing by," Jesse said as he grasped Link's arm. "We should go."

Link looked almost sad for a second, and I watched his eyes wander over the bookshelves and the stack of epic fantasy novels we had on display on a tiny table in the centre of the room. Poor bastard probably didn't know what the fuck was going on, and I wasn't angry at him for getting suckered into whatever Jesse was doing.

"Hey, listen," I said, unable to resist the temptation to fuck with Jesse. "If you've got five minutes, I can get you some cake, and I saw you looking at our fantasy display. I can give you some recommendations if you like." I held my breath for half a second, wondering if my gamble would pay off. If not, I'd just look like I was doing my job, but if it worked, it might lessen the ache in my chest a little. I could be a spiteful bastard when I wanted to be.

"We're fine," Jesse said and turned to leave, but Link stayed still, his eyes fixed on the books.

"Er, you go ahead," he said. "I'll meet you there."

"What?" Jesse hissed. "I can't go by myself."

"It's fine," Link said, not looking at him. "I'll catch up."

"How dare—"

"I think it's time you leave now," I said, stepping forward before Jesse threw a screaming fit in the middle of the store. I still didn't know what I'd seen in him, and I probably never would, but I didn't want him to make a scene. If it was my shop, I'd have let him get on with it, but The Lost World was Jay's baby, and today was a celebration of three years of hard work, and I wasn't about to let this bellend ruin it.

Jesse looked me up and down. "I don't know why I bothered. You're pitiful."

"Yeah, well, the feeling's mutual." I tilted my head towards the front of the store. "There's the door. I suggest you use it."

Jesse huffed and stalked off towards the exit, and I let out a breath. Link was looking at me with a curious expression like he was thinking something through. "So how do you and Jesse know each other?"

I burst into laughter, the sudden sound causing a few people to turn as I shook my head. "We were… together? I don't even know if that's the right word come to think of it."

"Fuck. I didn't know." Link looked absolutely crushed, and like I'd predicted, the poor bastard hadn't had a clue. "Jesse told me you were someone he worked with." He frowned. The expression looked almost painful. "But that doesn't seem right."

"Don't worry about it," I said. "But if I were you, I reckon I'd stick well clear." Link nodded, and over his shoulder, I saw Edward looking at us curiously. He was both the first and last person I wanted to get involved—because while he was definitely as spiteful as me, Edward was more likely to act on it. Although he'd mellowed out a little over the past few years. I nodded to him, hoping he'd get the hint and wander over. While Link was a sweet guy, I didn't really want to deal with him.

"Is everything all right?" Edward asked as he appeared behind Link, his platinum hair rippling under the lights. Edward's clothing was somewhat legendary, and today, he wore a heavy blue-and-gold brocade frock coat that fell to his knees with a ruffled cravat and knee-high laced boots that elongated his perfectly shaped legs. The first time I'd met him, I'd been a little in awe. And a little turned on. But Edward only had eyes for one man—his partner Izzy, who knew just how to temper Edward's exuberant personality.

Link turned and stared at Edward, his mouth practically hanging open. "Hello," he said quietly, a pink tinge suddenly appearing across his nose. Aww, bless the wee lad. Not that I could blame him, Edward had that effect on a lot of people. "I'm Link."

Edward looked between the pair of us, and I tried to give him a look that said I'd explain later. He must have gotten the hint because he slipped on a charming smile. "Hello, darling. Would you like some cake?"

"Yes, please."

"Perfect. Why don't you follow me?" He turned and walked towards the stairs that led down to the shop's basement where we'd set up cake and drinks. Link followed him like a lost puppy.

That was that then.

I sighed and looked down at the stack of books that were still in my hand. They needed to go on the shelves. As I began to put each one in place, the reality of the situation hit me. Here I was again—thirty-six, single, and working a part-time job while trying to resurrect a dead business. All I'd ever wanted was to be a game designer. When I was younger I'd dreamt of designing the perfect role-playing game, something that would become the next Dungeons and Dragons. But despite my best efforts, nothing had worked.

The feeling of failure that lived in my chest stirred, reminding me of its ever-growing presence. These days, I tried to think of it as a monstrous pet I was forced to carry around me like some sort of kraken with hooked tentacles that sank further into my flesh with every passing day. And not in a good way.

I shoved the last book onto the shelf with more force than necessary, looking around for more gaps to fill. At least if I was busy, I wouldn't have to talk to anyone. There was only one person I wanted to be around right now, and that was Finn.

Finn and I had met last year when his brother Lewis, who was Edward's personal assistant, had introduced us. I'd been looking for some test players for my RPG in the vague hope that running some live sessions would kickstart some interest in the game, and Lewis had dragged Finn along. He'd been quiet at first, but when he'd settled into it, I'd discovered there was a sharp, witty side buried beneath his quiet exterior.

We'd ended up going out for food a couple of times and had hit it off as friends. Now, I was closer to him than anyone else and considered him my best friend.

Finn had never said anything about Jesse, but having seen the pinched expression on his face whenever I'd mentioned him, I didn't think he'd be too surprised when I told him what had happened. I didn't think he'd rub it in. He'd probably just offer me food.

The heavy ache in my chest intensified. I pulled my

phone out of the inner pocket of my tweed jacket and fired off a message, hoping Finn would be free to help me wallow in self-pity. Then I bent down to open another drawer, hoping the rest of the day would pass without any more surprises.

CHAPTER TWO

Finn

I WAS HALFWAY through a sentence when my phone lit up on the desk beside me. Normally, I'd ignore it, but as soon as I glanced at the screen I realised how long it had been since I'd taken a break. I really needed to get better at limiting my recording sessions or at least scheduling in breaks so I didn't work for nine hours straight.

Pausing the recording, I slid my headphones off and grabbed my phone before the call ended, noticing how numb my butt was from sitting still for so long.

"Hey, Chantelle," I said, leaning back in my chair and letting myself relax for the first time in hours. A wave of tiredness washed over me, and I knew I wouldn't be going back to work after this. Perhaps I needed to start setting timers.

"I swear to fucking God, Finn, I swear to. Fucking. God. Why the fuck did I sleep with Ryan?" Chantelle's bouncing

London accent carried the same level of anger it always did when she talked about her ex-boyfriend and father of her child. I assumed Ryan had fucked up royally again and that Chantelle was calling me to vent, because that's what best friends were for. Her timing couldn't have been more perfect, though—it was like she magically knew I needed a distraction.

"Because he has a big dick," I said with a wry chuckle as Chantelle sighed.

"Don't I fucking know it. I swear, Finn, I'm swearing off men. Well, straight men. They're all wankers." I tried not to laugh. Chantelle and I had known each other since the first day of university when we'd moved into the same flat and she'd decided we were going to be friends. I wasn't sure *why* she'd picked me, considering I was a quiet, nerdy, anxious mess, and she was loud, fierce, and took no shit, but she had. Ten years later, she was one of the people I was closest to, and I loved her to bits.

"What did Ryan do?"

"Where do I fucking start? Hang on." I heard her turning away from the phone. I smiled to myself as I listened. "Kelsey, get off the sofa please. I don't care that your dad lets you jump on his sofa. You're not jumping on mine. Get down. Thank you."

"Everything okay?"

"Honestly, don't get me wrong, I love Kelsey to bits, but she's doing my fucking head in today. She was at Ryan's last night, and she's come back exhausted, hopped up on sugar, and telling me all the shit he lets her do. And he gives zero fucking shits because it's not his problem!"

Chantelle exhaled loudly like she was trying to calm herself down. I wished I could reach through the phone and give her a hug. Being a single mother to a five-year-old sounded exhausting, especially when Kelsey's dad was more interested in finding his next hook-up than being a parent.

"Oh, and guess fucking what?" Chantelle continued. "Ryan's gone and knocked Lissa up too. I saw her in Tesco last week while I was getting a cake for my mum's birthday. She didn't even fucking know he already has three kids. She knew about Kelsey because she was at Ryan's when Lissa was round one day, and that's when I met her, but he'd forgotten to mention Cole and Sierra. And, apparently, he'd fed her the same fucking bullshit he fed me and the others about how he promised to be a good dad, and they'd be a family and all that bollocks. That man needs to be fucking neutered."

"I'm sorry," I said, wishing even harder that I could give her that hug. "I can't imagine how stressful that is. And you're right, Ryan's a wanker. If you wanted, I could hold him down and you could remove his testicles with a spoon?"

"It's not even that I'm pissed for me. It's so fucking hard to explain to Kels that the reason she doesn't get to see her dad more is because he's a dickhead who can't keep it in his pants. He keeps making her all these bloody promises I know he won't keep, and it's going to break her fucking heart when she realises." I heard the sadness and frustration welling up in her voice. "And work is driving me fucking bonkers, and my mum is too. It's just all…"

"Shit?"

"Yeah. Exactly. It's all shit." She chuckled weakly and sniffed. Chantelle very rarely cried—she had a core of steel—and the fact that she was even considering it showed how much she trusted me. But we'd been that way for years. We didn't have any secrets anymore.

And that was both a good and bad thing considering what she'd talked me into.

"Why don't you two come here for a weekend?" I asked, spinning around in my chair and stretching my legs out, rotating my ankles until they popped. "The weather's a bit rubbish, but we can have a couple of days out. If you don't mind the wind and rain, we can always venture up to Skegness."

"Are you sure?"

"Positive. Kelsey will love it, and then I could give you a hug in person."

"I do miss my Finn hugs," she said. "I'll have a look at some trains. Maybe in a couple of weeks? Depends when I can get something cheap."

"No worries, just let me know. It's not like I do much with my free time anyway."

"God, you are such a fucking sweetheart," Chantelle said with another sniff. "If only you didn't feel like my fucking brother." I snorted. We'd tried sleeping together once when we'd been drunk and lonely. We hadn't gotten far because it had been awkward as all hell, and we'd vowed never to try it again. "How many of your sibs are single?"

"Not many these days," I said. "They keep pairing off."

"Bollocks."

I laughed, and from the other end of the line I heard a crash and then wailing. "I'll let you go."

"Yeah." Chantelle sighed wearily. "Thanks for the vent."

"Anytime," I said. "I love you, and give Kelsey a hug from me."

We hung up, and I stretched again, scrolling through my phone as I spun my chair around slowly. There was a string of messages in the family chat about lunch tomorrow, and my brother Eli had sent me an endless list of TikToks. I had five siblings—four brothers and one sister—who were generally loud, intrusive, and very loving. I counted myself very lucky on the family front, even if I wished that they weren't quite so overbearing—especially my brother Oscar, who still treated me like I was Kelsey's age. He'd sent me some pictures from his latest trip, though, and it was nice to see his face against the backdrop of white sand and lush vegetation from whatever beautiful corner of the world he'd been in.

There were also a couple of messages from Gem. I read them as I stood and let myself out of the small, stuffy recording booth my sister, Jules, had built for me a couple of years ago in the second bedroom of the tiny flat I rented.

GEM *Guess who turned up at The Lost World today with his*
new toy?
GEM *I'll give you two guesses.*
GEM *Fancy pizza and whiskey?*

"Bugger," I muttered to myself as I retrieved a giant hoodie from my bedroom and headed for the kitchen to make myself a cup of tea. I wasn't at all surprised Jesse had dumped Gem for someone else because he'd always given me that sinking feeling. Whenever I looked at him, it always felt like something was off and that it would end badly. I didn't want to say I'd been right because I'd never mentioned it to Gem out of politeness, but I got the feeling Gem already knew how I felt.

I'd always had a knack for reading people and for being able to see the things they tried to hide. It made me a good judge of character, but I very rarely told people what I thought. Partly because I was far too anxious to interfere and partly because I knew most people didn't want to hear it. I'd tried once when my oldest brother, Richard, had brought a girlfriend home from university. I was sixteen and had immediately gotten an uncomfortable knot in my stomach, but Richard had said I was imagining things and to stop being silly.

After their incredibly messy breakup two weeks later, when she'd locked him out of his flat and thrown all his possessions out his bedroom window, I'd resisted the urge to say *I told you so* and instead never mentioned it again.

I flicked the kettle on and leant against the counter as I replied.

FINN *I'm sorry. That's so rude of him!*
FINN *I'll order pizza, you bring drinks.*

Gem was very particular about his whiskey, so it was easier to let him bring what he wanted. Even so, I did have a couple of different bottles in a cupboard in case of emergency. It was another thing I'd never mentioned to him because I thought that might cross a line. Gem and I were just friends, and I didn't want to make anything complicated. Crushing on him wasn't going to get me anywhere.

GEM *You're a legend. Be with you in about an hour.*

I smiled to myself and finished making my tea, trying to ignore the little flare in my chest as my brain registered that Gem was single again.

"No," I said. "I can't say anything. That would just be rude."

Jesse might have ghosted him two weeks ago, but the final nail in the coffin hadn't been until today, and despite the bravado I was sure Gem would put on, he was bound to be hurt. Besides, I couldn't see him wanting anything with me anyway. I was a nerd's nerd—the sort of man most people instantly dismissed. It didn't help that I was rather gangly and awkward, and I was also painfully shy around people I didn't know.

It made making friends nearly impossible, so finding a partner would be like reaching for the moon. The only reason I knew Gem was because my brother Lewis had introduced us last year, even though he'd practically had to drag me out of my house by the ankles. I was glad he had because Gem was nothing short of amazing. At least in my eyes.

I just wished other men could see what I saw. Gem deserved everything, but he seemed ready to settle for the first man who showed interest. Even if that man was an undeserving prick.

That made me sound very bitter, and perhaps I was. Over the last six months my feelings for Gem had escalated from friendship into unrequited pining without any conscious input on my part, and it was sometimes hard to live with. Mostly because I knew I'd never stand a chance and was doomed to spend all eternity dreaming over him from afar.

Picking up my tea, I headed through to my living room and settled on my sofa. I took out my phone to order us some food, knowing how busy the local Domino's got on a Saturday night, and once that was done, I began to flick through some of the notifications for my side project.

Writing and narrating audio porn hadn't been something I'd ever expected to do, but it had come around after a slightly drunken night a couple of years ago. I'd been lonely and horny and had somehow found myself heading down an interesting rabbit hole. Since I'd been drunk, I'd made the mistake of sending a link to Chantelle, who'd immediately jumped on the idea and convinced me to do it alongside my regular voice acting and narration work.

Now, I had a thriving side hustle, but it was one I did more for fun than money.

It was almost funny when I thought about it—around most people I was quieter than a mouse, but put me in a recording studio, and I became a different person. I'd always wanted to be an actor because there was something about inhabiting another character that made everything so much easier, but I struggled with auditions and being in front of humans. One of my teachers at university had suggested narration and voice acting and had gotten me some time in one of the music department's recording booths. As soon as I'd started, I'd realised I'd found the place I belonged. And while it had taken me a while to get established, I now had a thriving narration career with more projects in my diary than I had hours in the day.

The side hustle was similar but in a totally different world. It allowed me a freedom of expression I never would have thought to explore.

As I looked at my profile, I realised I was due to post something. Luckily there was something already edited and waiting to go on my laptop, it just needed uploading, and I could easily get that done before Gem arrived. Then I wouldn't have to worry about it, and I could come back to the comments tomorrow.

Taking my tea with me, I headed back to the booth and my computer, leaving the door open this time. The video was ready to go with its simple text background and the nondescript logo of my anonymous persona, and I'd already written a little blurb to go with it. I slipped on my headphones and began to click through things to get the upload going. It didn't take long. I hit the Play button to double-check the audio quality, the deep, soft voice I used for these projects echoing in my ears.

"Hello, baby. Have you been good for me today?"

CHAPTER THREE

Gem

"I HONESTLY DON'T KNOW what to do next," I said, sipping the coffee Finn had brought me as I pondered my fate and leant over the counter, staring darkly at the floor of The Lost World.

"In general, or after the campaign wraps up?" Finn asked as he perused the new releases shelf and sipped his hot chocolate. It was the Tuesday after the anniversary party, and I'd dragged Finn to Lincoln to discuss the last session of the campaign for my role-play game, which we were due to play this week. I wanted to be enthusiastic about it, but my heart just wasn't in it.

When we'd started this, I'd had the vague, if somewhat ambitious dream, of it turning into a social media sensation like *Critical Role*. I'd at least hoped it would boost interest in my game, and I'd see an influx of sales.

Suffice it to say, neither had happened.

We'd had a few regular watchers, and it had been shared around a little, but it was nothing to write home about despite Lewis's best attempts on the social media side. Our subscribers seemed more interested in watching us play than doing it themselves. It was why we were wrapping up our campaign well ahead of when I'd originally planned—there was no point continuing with something that just wasn't working. The only problem was, I didn't know what *would* work.

"In general." I sipped the coffee again. "What the fuck am I doing with my life?"

Finn made a soft, distressed noise, and I heard him padding across the floor towards me. "You can do whatever you want. You're so talented, and you know so much about games. You're passionate too. I know you'll find something."

"Thanks." I looked up at him, and Finn smiled softly. Something in my chest twitched. I frowned and reached for it, rubbing the sore spot. That was new.

"You okay?"

"Yeah, just a muscle spasm. Probably just stress."

Finn nodded sympathetically, and my chest twitched again. "The last session will be fun. I promise. I'm sure Edward has plenty of tricks up his sleeve, and Lila mentioned something about bringing in some cupcakes. Even if it hasn't been as successful as you hoped, it's still been fun." He paused and then said quietly, "And I got to meet you, so that was nice."

He looked almost nervous to admit that in public, and that made me grin. "Yeah, you did. And your life changed for the better. I mean who doesn't need a sarcastic, ageing, single man with no prospects for a friend."

Finn chuckled. His laughter always surprised me because it was so much lower than his voice. It was the sort of soft chuckle that would be dangerous on another man. "Don't be so hard on yourself," he said. "Please."

There was something so earnest in the way he said *please* that I couldn't ignore it. "Fine. For you."

"Thank you." He smiled, and I had the sudden feeling I'd just been manipulated. The weirdest part was, I didn't mind.

The door to the shop opened, and Jay walked through with Rupert, an adorable if slightly ragged-looking Staffie, who was wearing a thick, knitted jumper over his blue fur. "Afternoon," Jay said as he leant down to unclip Rupert's lead. Rupert immediately pottered over to me, rounding the counter and leaning against my leg. I reached down to rub his single ear before he climbed into the padded bed tucked at the other end. Jay sighed as he heard the sound of Rupert's paws on the cushion. "Honestly, you'd think he hadn't spent all day asleep already."

"Such a hard life," I said with a chuckle. Rupert huffed in agreement. He was one of two rescue Staffies Jay and his fiancé Leo owned, and they each took one to work with them. While Rupert spent his days asleep behind the bookshop counter, occasionally emerging for snacks, his sister Angie went to Leo's flower shop, Wild Things, just down the hill.

"Very." Jay wandered over to the counter to dump his bag. "Do we have many orders from the weekend to fill?"

"Yeah, a little over two hundred. I think that discount code you offered for the anniversary helped."

Jay stared at me. "Two hundred?"

"And three, if you want to be technical. I think we've got stock for most of it, but it's going to take some time."

"Yeah… I'll go and make a start," he said, running his fingers through his hair. "By the way, did you see one of the shops farther up is for let? Next to Pimento where that little gift shop was."

"Oh? They finally put a sign up for it then." The place had been empty for about three months, and we'd casually wondered whether the owners were going to sell it off, convert it, or put it back up for rent again.

"Yeah, it's up for commercial, same as here. It looks quite small from the plans I could see online, but I think it's got an upstairs and a stockroom at the back."

"You thinking of moving?" I asked and raised an eyebrow. Finn gave me a quizzical look. I had no idea why Jay would be looking at a property that was smaller than the one he had now. It wasn't like he was struggling to pay rent.

"No," Jay said. "But I have an idea that would be perfect for it." He grinned at me, his eyes lighting up behind his glasses. "You should take it and turn it into a games store."

"What?" I stared at him in disbelief.

"I'm serious! You'd be great at it." He began to list reasons off on his fingers, fizzing with energy as he spoke. "You love board games, and you have this encyclopaedic knowledge of them. You're friendly and funny, which means you're great with customers, but you're super level-headed, which means you'll make great business decisions. Plus, you've been practically running this place with me, so you know all the ins and outs of ordering, even if you'd be using different suppliers. And I can give you a rundown on running costs, bills, and taxes. I can also give you my business plan too. The one I used when I first started out. It would be enough to get you a start-up loan, and I could totally help you finesse it. I bet Tristan could give you some good advice too."

I looked between Jay and Finn, unsure what to say. Jay was beaming, and he'd clearly given this some thought, and Finn was giving me another of his gentle, encouraging smiles. Deep down, I knew it might be a reasonable idea. Jay wasn't wrong when he said I loved games, and I had a fairly good idea of how to run a business given how much he'd involved me in The Lost World over the past couple of years.

But my initial reaction was a stubborn one.

I didn't want to run a game store. I wanted to be a game designer. It was what I'd always wanted, and just because I hadn't succeeded yet didn't mean I had to write off my dream. Being thirty-six didn't mean I was past it. Then again, hadn't I just been moaning to Finn about my life? But it was one thing to choose to do something and another to have the idea thrown at you.

My thoughts were becoming more and more tangled by the second, and I didn't know what to do.

"I'll think about it," I said finally. It was the one answer that would buy me time. "It's not a no, but it's not a yes either."

"Fair enough," Jay said. "It's a big commitment. I just wanted to throw it out there because I know you'd be great at it!" He looked at me, then checked his watch and pulled a face. "Shall I start packing up orders? We could do with getting some out before the post office closes."

"I already made a start," I said. "There's a list upstairs in the stockroom. You'll see what I've marked off."

"Amazing! I'd have started already if we hadn't had this ridiculous fitting appointment to go to." He sighed. Jay and Leo were getting married in a couple months, and Edward had volunteered to make their suits as a wedding present. Edward had, as predicted, gone over the top.

"Did you talk Edward out of the capes yet?" I asked, happy to have an easy way to change the subject.

Jay rolled his eyes, and Finn chuckled. "Just about. He keeps muttering about how my ideas are boring. The suits look lovely though. I just wish I didn't have to listen to him bitch about how I won't let him have any fun." I snorted. "At least the books won't tell me I should consider something more interesting than black. I've already agreed to the patterned lining. What else does he want?" Jay began to head towards the stairs, calling over his shoulder. "If Edward appears, I'm not here! I've moved."

I watched him go and went back to the remains of my coffee, which was just about drinkable. Finn watched me carefully. He hadn't said anything since Jay had arrived, but that didn't surprise me. He'd been listening, though, and I was sure he'd offer an opinion if I wanted one. Which I did. Finn was the most sensible person I knew, and he was good at looking at things from different perspectives.

He was also the one person whose opinion I'd consider listening to.

"So," I said into the silence that was broken only by Rupert's snuffled snores. "A game store."

"A game store," Finn repeated quietly. "How do you feel about that?"

"Honestly? My first reaction is to say no, but I'm also aware that might be kind of stupid of me."

"It's not," Finn said as he walked over to the counter. "It's a big undertaking, and it's not for everyone. Running a small business is hard work."

"There's a *but* there. I can feel it."

Finn smiled. "But I agree with Jay. I think you'd be very good at it. You are very good with people, and you're sensible. I know it's not what you wanted to do with your life, but this would still keep you involved with games and gaming." He looked at me fondly, and the damn muscle in my chest spasmed again. "And I'd be happy to help. As much as I can anyway. I think Jay was right about deferring to Tristan for financial matters."

I hummed in agreement. Tristan was Finn's brother Eli's boyfriend, and also the best friend of their oldest brother, Richard, which had led to some interesting circumstances, considering Eli and Richard didn't exactly get along. But Tristan was an independent financial adviser and, from the couple of times I'd met him, seemed to have a good head on his shoulders. If I did consider this ridiculous scheme, he wouldn't steer me wrong.

The fact that I was already thinking about that should

have worried me because clearly I wasn't rejecting this hare-brained notion outright like I should have.

"You're wavering," Finn said teasingly.

"Stop encouraging me," I said. "I shouldn't be thinking about this."

"Why not?"

"Because…" I thought for a second. "Well, for one, it'd be really fucking expensive, and I can barely keep a roof over my head as it is. I'm not sure a bank would consider giving me a loan or any sort of assistance. Two, I'm not sure whether I'm actually interested or just intrigued by the idea because it's new and sounds better than my life is right now. And three…" I sighed. "I don't know if there is a three. I mean, I keep saying I want to be a designer, but we both know how that's turned out. Maybe it would be better if I just put that idea to bed."

"Why would you have to give it up though? You do it as a side project now. Why couldn't you do it while running your own business? And that way you'd potentially have a willing pool of test subjects. You could even make it a thing—a sort of designers' tester evening. Everyone can come along and bring the game they're developing and test things out on each other, and if anyone else wants to join in and test some games then the more the merrier."

Finn had a point, and it was a good one. I did both now, so why couldn't I keep doing both in the future?

"Stop being so reasonable," I said grumpily, although I was smiling. "You're making a good point."

"I know." He moved a little closer, and I suddenly realised just how gorgeous his face was. Finn was happy to blend into the background, but when I got up close to him, he was more handsome than I realised. Maybe more than even he realised. He had a strong jaw, soft hazel eyes, and lips that had a deep cupid's bow. They were the sort of lips that looked very easy to kiss. "I'm good at being the voice of reason."

I swallowed, tearing my eyes away from the swell of his mouth. Finn was my friend, and it wouldn't do me any good to get caught up in the shape of his lips. "So does that mean I'm going to look at this place, then?"

"I don't know," Finn said with a wry smile. "Does it?"

CHAPTER FOUR

Gem

"YOU KNOW, when Jay said smaller, I didn't think it'd be this small," I said, looking around the room that comprised the front of the shop currently up for rent. It had only been two days since Jay had first suggested I take a look at the place, and I was already standing in it. I still wasn't sure if that was a good or bad sign. "You could barely swing a cat in here."

Finn hummed in agreement while the letting agent who'd agreed to show us around launched into a customary spiel about it being cosy, and welcoming, and the perfect size for a start-up, despite the fact that the reduced size didn't mean the rent was any less than Jay paid for The Lost World. And I knew that because I'd discussed it with him before I'd come to look around.

I ignored the letting agent and wandered through towards the back room, trying to focus my mind on what I could do with the space. *If* I went ahead. Despite my internal protestations, my brain seemed to have already decided we were doing it. The room at the back wasn't a bad size. There'd at least be room for some shelves of stock, and there was somewhere I could plug in a kettle.

"Could you give us a minute?" I heard Finn ask the agent. She agreed, and then I heard Finn's quiet footsteps on the wooden floor. "What do you think?"

"I don't know," I said as I turned to look at him. He stood in the doorway, wrapped in his thick winter coat with a woolly hat on his head. It had a little red pompom on the end, and for some reason that made me smile. I shook my head, trying to get my thoughts back on track. "The main space is smaller than I'd anticipated, and there's no step-free access so I'd have to invest in a ramp. And while there's an upstairs, those stairs are pretty steep." I pointed to the set of stairs in the corner.

"Have you looked upstairs?"

"No, I was too busy considering all the problems with the downstairs."

Finn gave a soft chuckle—the low, dangerous one that made something inside my stomach twist. "Let's at least go and look at it before you dismiss this place outright."

"There you go being sensible again."

Finn's lip quirked, and he gave me a pointed look that made something twist in my chest. Like heartburn but not. "I know. It's good for you to have someone sensible." The words hung in the air for a second, and then Finn's nose tinted like he'd suddenly realised what he'd said. But I wasn't sure why he was embarrassed. "Come on. Let's go and have a look."

He directed me towards the stairs with an outstretched hand, and I found myself going willingly. The upstairs turned out to be a bit bigger because, while the downstairs had been split into two rooms, the second floor had been left as one. It had a bay window at the front that looked out over the street and was currently covered in some moth-eaten lace curtains. The whole place needed a good scrub and a lick of paint, but it wasn't in terrible shape. The steepness of the stairs worried me, and there wasn't enough space to run board game or play test evenings. But Jay already ran those at The Lost World… Maybe there was some way we could do it in partnership?

Since he'd suggested this in the first place, I didn't think he'd object. And The Lost World's game nights were popular and well attended, so it would make sense to leave them there.

I rubbed my chin and squeezed my cheeks, frowning as I looked around. There was definitely potential here, and my brain was already imagining where I might put things. I was getting ahead of myself, though, because I didn't even have a business plan let alone money for a deposit, rent, and bills. Even if I did want to start a shop, there was a good chance this place would be gone before I managed to get everything together.

But even just starting to picture everything made me feel… something.

"What do you think?" I asked Finn, wondering if his assessment matched mine.

"I think it's got potential." He looked around, his eyes running over the chipped paintwork. "It needs cleaning up and repainting, and you'd obviously need some furnishings, but I don't think it's terrible. Yes, downstairs is small, but this space is good, and you'd have space for a variety of games and accessories, and you could also offer to order things for people like you do at The Lost World. I agree the stairs are steep, and you'd need a ramp to make the place accessible, but I think it's a good location, not terribly priced, and it would be easy to maintain. You could do a lot worse."

"I agree," I said. "And I was thinking I could ask Jay about partnering up to run the board game nights since there's no room for them here."

"That would be a good idea." Finn's eyes settled on me, and it felt like he was peering into my soul. Not that he'd find much there he didn't already know. "Does this mean you want to do it then?"

"You know, I'm not sure I could say no at this point," I said with a chuckle. "My brain has already decided for me. I don't think I really get a say in the decision." Finn laughed and made a soft, little hiccupping sound at the end. "I'll think about it for a couple of days, just to be sure."

"I think that's a good idea. Maybe make a list of pros and cons. I find that quite helpful sometimes." Finn smiled at me, and my worries began to fade away. I wasn't sure what it was about his smile that made me feel calm, but it seemed to possess this magical quality that made me feel better. It was a gift of his.

I looked around the upstairs again, imagining it filled

with shelves, each one packed with games. The idea struck a chord deep inside me, reigniting a passion I thought I'd lost. "Yeah, I might well do that."

I spent the whole of the afternoon lost in my head as I went back and forth on the game shop idea. My brain kept getting stuck on the most ridiculous little details, like what I would call the place, but I thought it was probably to stop myself from getting stuck on the big things like how employment law worked or how I'd pay taxes.

I knew there were a lot of people who'd be willing to help me figure it out if I asked them or paid them, but that meant I had to commit to the idea in the first place. There was a mental roadblock stopping me from crossing that final hurdle and saying yes, but I couldn't figure out what it was. It might have been fear that this would be another thing I'd inevitably fail at. Normally, spite would have motivated me to do it anyway, but this time, I was being more cautious. Maybe because of the amount of money involved.

This wasn't something I could just give up if it didn't work. I'd have to make a real commitment to it.

"Get outta your head," I muttered to myself as I stared at the laptop in front of me where the cursor blinked on a blank document. I'd been trying to make a list of pros and cons and questions to ask myself, but so far the exercise had just succeeded in driving me further into my head. I needed a break.

Grabbing a pair of earbuds—because my flat's walls

were ridiculously thin—I stretched out on the sofa and opened the browser. I needed to relax, and there was one sure-fire way for me to do that. I stuck my earbuds in, unbuttoned my jeans, and began to click through MyFans to find what I wanted.

I'd discovered audio porn about a year ago when I'd been aimlessly scrolling through PornHub and had immediately gotten hooked on the content produced by one specific user, Fantasy and Filth. He had this amazing voice that sent shivers across my skin every time he spoke, and if I closed my eyes, it felt like he was beside me, whispering delicious things into my ears. It was familiar and alien all at once like an echo of someone I'd heard before. I'd never followed that rabbit to find out who it reminded me of, because it felt like a dangerous path to follow, but it had only taken three videos for me to know I needed more, so I'd quickly signed up for his fan subscription.

He always produced at least six audios a month and often added some fun bonus content like Q&As, sex toy reviews, or the occasional picture or video of him recording —but always from the chest down. I had no idea what his name was or what his face looked like, but the anonymity of it added to the fantasy. This man could be whoever I wanted him to be, and there was something delicious about that.

As I scrolled through his content, I noticed he'd uploaded a new video since I'd last checked. Since the site mostly hosted videos or pictures, the audios just had a black background with a text overlay that explained the scenario and whether it was aimed at men or women, since he produced content for both, although I just tended to pick whichever scenario sounded hottest to me.

I debated between finding one of my favourites or trying the new one, but I figured if the new one didn't quite work I could always find another. I clicked on the title, *Reminding You to Be Good*, and read the full description posted below the video, which had some tags in it. It had things like domination, praise, cock sucking, anal play, anal penetration, rough sex, and creampie all listed, and my cock was already getting hard at the thought. I loved the idea of giving up that power to someone, even just for a short while. My own life felt chaotic, so it was nice to get out of my head for a while and just be.

I hit Play, put the laptop on the floor, and slid my hand down towards my dick.

"Hello, baby. Have you been good for me today?" the deep, soft voice asked, making my cock jump. "Did you do everything I asked when I left this morning?" There was a pause, and I imagined him coming home, coming here, and realising I hadn't done anything I'd planned… anything that he'd asked me to do. I swallowed, wrapping my hand around my thickening cock.

"No?" the man added, a dangerous note in his voice. "What did you do instead? Did you do anything you promised?" I groaned, sinking farther into the sofa and awkwardly trying to push my jeans over my thighs. The audio lasted for sixteen minutes, but I didn't think I would. The man's voice dropped low, and my cock dripped precum onto my fingers. "I'm very disappointed in you. And after you made me a promise. Do you need a reminder, baby? Do you need me to teach you how to be good for me?"

"Yes," I said, twisting my hand over the head of my cock. "Teach me. Make me yours."

The voice gave a low chuckle, the sort that made my chest tighten and my stomach flip. It was a noise I'd do anything for. "I don't know, baby. You haven't even apologised yet." There was a deep noise and another chuckle. "And now I've got my fist in your hair, so you're not going anywhere. Every move you make, everything you do is for me. So tell me you're sorry and then"—the voice dropped to a deadly, sweet whisper—"I'll remind you you're mine."

"I'm sorry. I promise. I'll do the list." I knew nobody could hear me, but I was already lost in the fantasy. "I'll make the decision."

"Thank you," the voice said with a gentle sincerity that made me moan as the sound of kisses filled my ears. "Thank you for apologising. I forgive you, and I know you'll be better next time. You know what to say if I get too rough, don't you? Or if you don't like something? Good. Remember to use your words for me." I groaned, unable to stop myself from stroking myself faster as my other hand reached down to roll my balls between my fingers. I knew I needed to let go of my cock or this was all going to be over way too soon. Gasping, I forced my hand away, squeezing the sofa cushion as my cock throbbed and dripped onto my abdomen.

"Now get over here," the man continued. "And show me just how good you can be. I want you to worship my cock... Oh fuck. Mmm, yes... just like that. God, that mouth." Wet, sloppy sounds joined his words, and I knew the narrator was working his cock. He let out a deep grunt. "Mmm, fuck, I love your mouth on my big cock. You've always known how to suck it… Now, look at me. Good boy, that's it, look at me as you take my cock into your throat."

He groaned, and my resistance melted away. I spat into my hand and grabbed my cock, my moans melting into his as I began to jerk myself fast and hard. There was something about his voice that made me come undone so easily. The wet, messy sounds continued as the narrator moaned, then added, "Fuck, that's it. Deeper, I want it all the way into your throat. I know you can take it. Mmm, take it, baby. Let me pull your hair and push you deeper… because sometimes you need to remember who's in charge. I want you to enjoy yourself, but… mmm, fuck… I want you to know you're mine, and you're here to make me feel good. And I love how it feels when my cock hits the back of your throat. Fuck, just like that… It feels so good when it gets all wet and messy when you gag on it."

"Fuck, shit… yeah, please," I said, random words falling out of my mouth. I was so close, and I couldn't hold on for much longer.

My other hand slid past my balls to tease the furled skin of my hole as the narrator said, "Let me look at you. Fuck, look at how hard you are for me, baby. Your cock is so hard, just like mine. I bet you need it, don't you? You need me to fuck you?"

With a deep grunt my cock shot across my stomach, hot cum painting my skin as I tipped my head back and panted through each breath, slowly working my cock through the aftershocks of my orgasm. By the time I'd started to come back to myself, the audio had moved on to the fucking part, and as tempted as I was to keep listening, it was too much. I hit Pause, knowing I'd be coming back to listen to it again soon. I really needed to know how it ended.

I sighed to myself, looking at the mess I'd made. First, I needed to clean up, and then I needed to make that fucking list. I'd made a promise after all, even if it was to someone I didn't know.

CHAPTER FIVE

Finn

As was the norm for a Sunday lunchtime, my mothers' house was the personification of chaos. I loved them more than anything, but my siblings wouldn't know what being quiet meant if their lives depended on it.

There were six of us in total, five boys and one girl, and although I was only related to two by blood, I'd never considered any of them anything less than my siblings. Perhaps it was because I couldn't remember my life without them in it. I hadn't been quite three when my mother, who we all called Mimbles, had confessed her love and moved in with her best friend Miranda, who we virtually all referred to as Mum, and created a giant blended family in an old cottage in the middle of the Lincolnshire countryside. Then Miranda's ex-husband, Terry, had bought the house next door and added his partner, Paul, and since my own father had died when I was very small,

Terry and Paul had been happy to step in as surrogate dads as we'd grown up. They'd never insisted that Oscar, Jules, and I call them that unless we were comfortable with it, but since Terry had been around for as long as Miranda had, I'd always called him Dad because I'd never seen him as anything else. In fact, the only one who didn't was Oscar, but that was because he still had strong memories of our father.

It meant I'd grown in up this enormous queer family, who showered all of us in love and support, but it could be a tiny bit smothering at times.

Currently, I was seated at the kitchen table while Paul and Mimbles were out in the garden talking about plans for their shared vegetable patch, despite the fact it was only January. Mum and Richard were upstairs looking for something, I'd missed what, and Dad, Jules, Lewis, and his boyfriend, Jason, were all in the living room watching *Labyrinth*. I knew I should go and join them, but I was enjoying the rare moment of quiet. Also, I'd volunteered to put the potatoes into the oven, which gave me an excuse to lurk in the kitchen and finish reading through the book I was due to start recording towards the end of the week.

The front door slammed, and I heard the exuberant call of my brother Eli. He was probably the loudest of us all, and the most dramatic, but he was also the one who wildly encouraged me in everything I did and bought every single audiobook I narrated, even if they weren't to his taste.

"Hello? Where is everyone? Are you avoiding me?"

"Yes!" I heard Jules call. "Fuck off."

"Charming! I shall find someone else who loves me

then," Eli said as he stuck his head around the kitchen door. "See? Finn is here. He loves me."

"Do I?" I asked, looking up from my phone and smiling sweetly at him.

Eli gasped dramatically, clutching his chest. "You wound me, dearest brother. And after I thought you were the only one I could trust." He walked over to me, wrapped his arms around my neck and kissed my cheek loudly. "Never mind. I shall forgive this hideous betrayal."

"Who betrayed you?" asked another voice, this one belonging to Eli's boyfriend, Tristan, who'd appeared in the doorway. Looking at them, you'd never have seen a couple more mismatched. Eli was a brash, demanding drag queen with wild curls and a sharp streak a mile wide, dressed in ripped skinny jeans, an old AC/DC t-shirt, and a vintage shearling coat, while Tristan was a quiet and careful Prince Charming in jeans and a green fleece, looking like he'd just stepped out of *Country Life* magazine. But I'd never met a pair of people more suited to each other. Tristan's solid presence tempered Eli's fire while Eli sparked new life in Tristan.

"Finn. I don't think he loves me anymore," Eli said, not letting go of me.

"Oh well," Tristan said with a wry smile. "I'm sure you'll live."

"I might not. I might expire on the kitchen floor. The only solution is Finn telling me he still loves me."

I sighed, half tempted to tell Eli I didn't just to see what happened. But I didn't because it wouldn't be the truth, and I didn't like lying. "I do."

"I knew it!" He kissed me again, then released me so he could slide onto the bench next to me. "Did you hear the terrible news?"

I raised an eyebrow. "It depends what you consider terrible news."

"Dick is going to ask Ruby to marry him," Eli said with the most horrified expression I'd ever seen him produce. "I'm going to have to go to a *straight* wedding! It will be terrible! There will be boring, straight people everywhere talking about boring straight people things like... I don't know... the stock market or when Ruby will get knocked up."

I couldn't stop myself from laughing, and Eli grinned at me triumphantly. I knew I shouldn't be encouraging him, but if that was the worst reaction we'd get from him about our oldest brother getting married, then that was an achievement. Eli and Richard had never gotten along, but their relationship had mellowed slightly after an incident last year when they'd had a punch-up in the middle of the lawn.

"I don't think it will be that bad," I said. "Ruby's quite alternative, and I'm sure you can be on your best behaviour for one day." I looked at Eli and then at Tristan, who was looking at Eli with a mixture of fondness and exasperation. Clearly, they'd had this conversation before. I almost felt sorry for Tristan because he was Richard's best friend and would probably hear this a lot over the next few months.

"I know. And I will be—for Ruby, though, not Dick. She doesn't deserve to have her wedding ruined just because she'll be marrying the most boring man alive." Tristan coughed pointedly, and Eli sighed. "Which will be her choice, and I'll be very happy for them. And I promise to be as good as I can and not make any snide remarks to Dick's face." He lowered his voice conspiratorially. "I'll save them up and make them at home."

"You're a menace," I said.

"I know. But a loving one." He smiled at me, his eyes roaming over my face. "How're things with you, then? What are you working on at the moment? Tell me everything."

I began to tell Eli and Tristan, who'd joined us on the bench, about the book I was about to start and what I had coming up after that. In truth, I'd never be able to tell them everything. My side project would always be a secret because, despite how nosy my family was, we needed to have *some* boundaries. Luckily, none of them had found out yet, although I had worked hard to conceal my identity. There was very little chance anyone who knew me would be able to identify me from the videos, even if they did find them. I never showed my face, I used a different voice, and I always made sure anything remotely identifiable was removed from the background. The fact that most of my work was just audio helped too.

"Tristan," I said as I came to the end of my point about work and remembered the rest of my week. "I did want to pick your brain about something financial. Not for me. For Gem. He's looking at potentially opening a small business, and I wondered if you'd be open to helping with some financial planning."

"Sure," he said. "I can do that. What sort of business?"

"A game shop. Jay suggested it to him earlier in the week since one of the units near The Lost World has come up for rent, and I think he's seriously considering it." I knew Gem was still unsure, although every time we spoke he seemed a little keener, but I was hoping if I could get Tristan to agree to assist, then it might help Gem decide.

I thought the idea was a good one, even if the commitment was sizeable, and it wasn't what Gem had envisioned for himself. I knew he needed a challenge and something to sink his teeth into. Gem loved working at The Lost World, but games were his passion, and this seemed like the ideal opportunity to combine the two.

Gem seemed to think setting up the shop would mean he could never design another game, but I knew that wasn't true. I also knew he was stuck in his head about the fact that his last game had failed to launch, and I was worried the longer he dwelt on it, the further he'd sink into a spiral of unhappiness.

I didn't want to force my opinion on him, but I was sure the shop idea would be great for Gem. I just had to hope he came to the same conclusion, and if necessary, I'd nudge him along a little without forcing him. There was a delicate balance between encouragement and obligation, and I didn't want Gem to think he had to do something because everyone thought he should.

Which was why I'd made a quiet promise to myself to never offer my opinion without being asked for it.

"That would be amazing," Tristan said, his eyes lighting up at the idea. "What sort of games? Board games? RPGs? Miniatures?"

"You just want somewhere close to work that will supply you with more minis," Eli said with a wry smile.

"I mean… it doesn't hurt just to look."

"It is your money, Mr. Rose. If you want to fill your office with toy soldiers, you're very welcome to." Eli leant over and gave him a soft kiss, and I pretended not to notice the way he squeezed Tristan's thigh. "Besides, if you do that, you can't complain about my make-up, shoes, or wigs."

Tristan chuckled, and it was hard to miss the amount of love pouring out of his gaze. "Done." He kissed Eli again, then looked back at me. His face tinted as if he'd suddenly remembered they had an audience, and he coughed. "Sorry. Um, yes, I can help you. It's not my area of expertise, but it shouldn't be difficult for me to figure it out and make suggestions. Does he have a business plan yet?"

"No. He's still not sure whether to proceed or not."

"That's understandable. It's a big investment both financially and timewise. But if he does decide to go ahead, you've got my number. Just drop me a message, and we can grab a coffee."

"Thanks," I said. "I really appreciate that."

"Isn't he wonderful?" Eli asked as he looked at Tristan with a heated look I wished I hadn't seen. "You can talk to them while I'm on tour."

"Does that start soon?" I asked, trying to remember what Eli had said about dates. The problem was, since I often booked things very far ahead for work and my diary was almost overflowing, I lived in a perpetual time soup. The only reason I knew what day it was outside of work was because I'd set my Alexa up to remind me about things like lunch with my family.

"Yes! Next week." Eli beamed. He'd been invited to take part in a variety show tour hosted by a well-known drag queen and had spent the past six weeks flitting between rampant enthusiasm and quiet fretting. The fact that he'd been quietly nervous rather than dramatic about it meant Eli really was worried, and Jules, Lewis, and I had all done our best to reassure him whenever he came to us. It had been hard to get Eli to admit his fears, and I'd discovered the best way to go about it was to approach it sideways and let him get to it in his own time, but eventually, he'd told us about how worried he was that he wasn't going to live up to people's expectations.

Despite the fact that Eli gave off a very *no fucks given* vibe, underneath he cared very deeply—almost too much at times—and all we could do was reassure him of his own brilliance and hope he believed us. But, given the fact that he was practically bouncing in his seat, I assumed today was one of the days he felt very excited about the whole thing.

"Our first two shows are in London next weekend. Then we're doing Cambridge the Wednesday after, and—"

"Next weekend?" Jules's head appeared around the kitchen door with a deeply suspicious expression written across it.

"Yes, why?"

"What the fuck, dickhead. I thought it was ages away. I need to look at your car before you drag it up and down the country," she said. "There's no way that heap of junk will survive otherwise."

"Excuse me! It's not a heap of junk," Eli exclaimed, even though we all knew that was a lie. Jules had brought Eli's poor car back to life more times than I could count, each time with progressively stronger mutterings about pushing the boundaries of what automotive engineering was capable of.

"You could take mine," Tristan said. "I'll be fine to run around in yours for a few days."

"You're very sweet, but it's fine. Besides Indy and Solo won't fit in mine, and they'd miss going up to the woods. They're only two seconds away from moving in with Alexis as it is." Eli smiled, but the firm set of Tristan's lips suggested the conversation wasn't over.

"Did you at least bring it today?" Jules asked.

"We did actually," Eli said, his eyes dancing, and I had the suspicion he'd planned this.

"I'm going to go get my stuff," Jules muttered as she turned towards the front door. "Come and open it up for me. Let's see what you've done to it."

"Could you be any more of a lesbian?" Eli asked as he climbed over Tristan to extricate himself from the bench.

"I don't know. Could you be any more of a bitch?"

"And that is why I love you," Eli said, leaning over to give her a kiss. Jules grinned at him fondly, ruffling his curls. The pair of them had always had this snarky, sassy banter, but it was built on a rock-solid foundation of love and respect. They'd snipe at each other, then two seconds later be curled on the sofa eating a mountain of chocolate with Jules's legs stretched over Eli's lap while they watched some ridiculous, campy horror movie. "You still need to let me find you a girlfriend. When was the last time you got laid?"

"If you buy a new car, then you can set me up," Jules said. "On one date."

"Harsh, but fair." They continued talking as they walked out towards the front door. Tristan shook his head and chuckled fondly.

I looked down at my phone. There was a new message from Gem.

Gem *You don't happen to know anything about business plans?*

"Tristan," I said. "About that advice? Do you think we could start now? And perhaps with the basics of a business plan?"

Tristan grinned at me and pulled out his phone. "Okay, so first of all…"

CHAPTER SIX

Gem

I STARED down at the mess of papers spread out across the coffee shop table in front of me, frowning as I sipped the large latte with an extra shot I'd ordered when I'd arrived. For this, I was going to need all the caffeine I could get.

"Are you ready?" Finn asked, pouring himself a cup of tea and giving me an encouraging smile. Warmth kindled in my chest.

"I suppose so," I said. "You know, when I asked for your help on this I didn't expect you to give up your whole afternoon. Don't you have projects to work on? Not that I don't want you here, it's just..." I fumbled over the words. I didn't want Finn to think I wasn't grateful for his help because I really was. I knew he was my best friend, but I hadn't expected him to volunteer his entire afternoon to help me write this bastard thing. I'd been expecting him to throw me some ideas or look it over when I was done. But that was Finn—generous to a fault—and it made me realise how lucky I was to have him in my life. I'd never meet another man like him.

"It's fine." Finn looked at me with something I could only describe as fondness, which made the feeling in my chest burn hotter. "I've got a day or two before I start recording, so I figured you might like some help. Besides, this gets me out of the house for once."

"I can't believe you're giving up your chance to play *Final Fantasy* for two days."

Finn chuckled. "Me either. It shows how much I care." He looked pointedly at me and the papers. "Come on then, you can't put it off forever."

"I know." I sighed. When I'd finally decided over the weekend to at least write a business plan and see how I felt afterwards, I hadn't expected the thing to be such a mountain. It was probably because I'd made the mistake of mentioning it to Jay on Saturday, and he'd promptly pulled out a bundle of old documents and begun to talk me through his. He'd even sent me a copy with comments about things he'd recommend changing or didn't think would apply to me. It had been helpful if a bit overwhelming. "I didn't think it would be so complicated. Did you ever have to write one of these?"

I didn't know much about how Finn's narration business worked, only that he was really fucking good at it. He had this uncanny knack for being able to turn his voice to anything—whether that was cosy mysteries with disastrous detectives, rich romances with sex scenes that would make most people blush, or high stakes thrillers with clocks ticking down to the end of the world. Finn seemed to be able to do it all, and even though I'd only managed to listen to snippets of his work, he enraptured me every time.

There was something magical about his voice like it could easily lead me to dangerous places and I'd follow without question.

Finn shook his head as he stirred sugar into his tea. "No. The narration business was almost accidental, and while there are certainly things I'd change looking back on it, I never set out with a coordinated plan. Although it might have been a good thing to have. You don't have to stick rigidly to this if you find that things change—you're not carving it in stone—but Tristan said if you want to secure financing, you're going to need a solid business plan to convince lenders you're serious."

I hummed. Jay and Leo had both said the same.

"All right then, let's get this bastard done." I opened the notebook I'd brought with me and picked up my pen. I'd always liked writing things out on paper first because I felt like I could get a better feel for the idea. It allowed me to explore, follow my thoughts, and see where I went. "Where do we start?"

Over the next three hours, another round of drinks, and some large slices of cake, Finn and I began to draw up the shape of the plan. Some of it was still rough, and there were bullet points and questions all over the place, but it was something. Finn had pulled out his phone to look for other similar businesses in the city. I knew there were a couple of game shops, but they all seemed primarily focused on video games, and although there was a board game café at the other end of town, their focus was on getting people in to play games and buy food and drink, rather than retail.

"You know," Finn said, picking at the last crumbs of his chocolate orange cake. "If you wanted to do some market research, you could build a quick Google form and ask Jay to share it on The Lost World's social media. And you could ask people who attend the board game nights to fill it in too. Maybe take your laptop with you so people can do it then and there rather than hoping they'll remember when they get home. Even just having a hundred responses would be good, and you could include the data in your plan. Plus, if the respondents are people who already attend the board game nights, you'll know they're local to the area and thus more likely to be potential customers."

"That's not a bad idea." I sat back in my chair and rubbed my face. My brain was starting to turn into mush, and everything in front of me was a jumble of numbers and letters. I was nearing the end of my rope, and I didn't think I'd be able to do much more today. Not if I wanted it to be legible afterwards. It needed to stew overnight, and hopefully my subconscious would fix some of the issues by the next time I looked at it.

"You okay?" Finn asked.

"Yeah, just tired. I think my brain has melted." I dropped my pen onto the table and reached for the last of my coffee, not realising it was stone cold until I'd swallowed half of it. I pulled a face, and Finn laughed.

"Shall we call it a day then? It's probably for the best since they're starting to close." He looked around the shop, and I followed his gaze, realising that the staff were busy wiping down the empty tables. We were the last customers there, despite the fact it wasn't that late. Outside, the winter sun had set, leaving Lincoln blanketed in darkness.

"What are you doing now?" I asked as I began to gather everything up and slide it inside an old folder I'd brought with me. I didn't want to spend my whole afternoon working on something only to lose it all.

"I don't know. Maybe I'll go home and play some games? Since I'm here, I might see if Lewis is around…" he shrugged. A sharp tug had pulled at my heart. I didn't want Finn to go.

"Or you can come back to mine," I said quickly. "We can make some food and play a game or something?"

"You're not bored of board games?"

"No." I grinned. "I don't think that's possible. Besides, if we want to be technical, we can count this as research."

Finn laughed, and his eyes crinkled the way they always did when he was really happy. I suddenly realised Finn could fake a good smile, but if I looked carefully I could tell between the real one and the fake one. And the fact that I'd noticed that made me weirdly… happy? Finn was my friend, so I guessed I should know. But Finn didn't seem to let many people get close to him. It was like there was an invisible barrier that you only realised was there when you bumped into it and were quietly diverted. But being able to tell the difference between his smiles made me feel like I could see through the barricade.

"Okay," he said softly. "That sounds fun." We packed up and began to head out, wrapping up against the cold. "What sort of food do you want?"

I frowned. I didn't have a lot in. I hated that at thirty-six I still had to live on such a tight budget—it was another thing that made me feel like I'd failed. I racked my brain thinking of something I could make or what I might have in the freezer. "If you don't mind waiting a little, I could make a sausage casserole."

Finn's eyes widened. "That sounds amazing. I haven't had sausages in ages."

"You know," I said, giving him a wry smile as we began to walk towards where Finn had parked his car. "I'm sure there's a joke in there somewhere."

"I'm sure there is." His lip twitched into a smile, something I hadn't seen before dancing in his eyes. When I'd first met Finn, I'd thought any sort of dirty joke would be enough to make him turn scarlet. Then I'd met more of his family, and I'd realised he'd probably heard it all, especially since he'd grown up with Eli. "You can make it if you want."

"Nah, I feel like it would be too obvious now. Kinda ruins the effect."

"Next time then."

"Are you saying you're going to set me up for more dick jokes?" I teased.

"Maybe," Finn said, his smile growing. "You'll have to wait and see."

Two weeks later, on Valentine's Day of all days, I found myself sitting on my sofa with a cheap ready meal while I trudged through the process of applying for a business loan. I hadn't actually expected myself to get this far, but the further I ventured into writing the business plan, the more excited I got.

I'd tried to tell myself it was just because it was something new and the shine would inevitably wear off, but it was hard to believe my own arguments when I found myself getting lost in forecasting, budgets, and predictions. Finances weren't exactly exciting—in fact they were a bastard-coated bastard of bastardness—but if spending hours staring at spreadsheets hadn't dampened my enthusiasm, nothing would.

The final nail in the coffin had been when I'd found myself awake at three in the morning, scrolling through Pinterest for internal decoration and layout ideas while tossing names and branding around in the back of my head. If it was going to keep me up at night, then I'd better fucking do it, otherwise I was going to spend the next six months wondering why the fuck I hadn't.

That, and the dismal numbers for December and January on my own games, and the notice from my letting agency that my rent was going up, persuaded me that maybe it was time to look for new options.

Tristan had kindly looked over my finished business plan and double-checked all my numbers, giving them the occasional poke. He'd even given me a list of banks to apply to and another of other potential funding sources, so I had a vague hope that everything would go smoothly. I just had to spend my evening filling in this bastard web form, which seemed to go on for fucking ever.

It wasn't like I had any other plans. Although maybe I'd

treat myself to a long wank with a nice dildo as a reward. I was pretty sure Fantasy and Filth had promised to upload a couple of Valentine's specials, so maybe I'd use one of those as a treat for all my hard work.

My phone flashed on the table, and Finn's name popped up. I picked it up and opened the message, chuckling to myself as I read.

FINN *Remind me why I agreed to go to Eli's show again? I'm the only single person here apart from Jules—except she's flirting with at least two of the staff.*
GEM *I'm sorry. I should have come with you. Or you could have come here. I can offer Tesco spinach and ricotta cannelloni and sadness.*
FINN *That sounds better than being surrounded by drunk, horny couples. Is it terrible if I secretly bet with myself over who'll be the first to leave? Mind you, I can't believe they're all here in the first place! I wonder what Eli threatened them with to make them show up?*
GEM *Violence? Glitter? Glitter-based violence?*
FINN *Probably. Either that or he knows all their secrets and has resorted to blackmail.*
FINN *Or he got Tristan to ask them. It's hard to say no to him. He's just too charming and polite to turn down. Tristan could ask to murder me, and I'd probably tell him I'd be delighted.*

I snorted and shook my head, shoving another forkful of cannelloni into my mouth. One day, I'd have to learn to make this from scratch. I didn't think it would be too diffi-cult or expensive. I felt bad for Finn though. He'd asked me if I wanted to come with him to The Court's Valentine's Day spectacular, but I'd declined because the idea of being surrounded by couples or hearing jokes about being single was enough to make me heave. It sounded like Finn hadn't had much say in the matter, but then again his brother was performing, and Finn would always be there for Eli if he asked, even if Finn wasn't keen on it.

That man was so fucking selfless it was unreal.

Sometimes I wished he'd say no or stand up for himself, but deep down I had a suspicion if he really hadn't wanted to go, he wouldn't have. I knew he'd declined to go to the Halloween event last year because he and I had already had plans. Maybe this was Finn's way of making up for that, especially because Eli was going to be spending so much time on tour this spring.

GEM *Is that how they got you to go?*
FINN *No. I'd already promised Eli I would. I'm sure I'll enjoy it when it starts.*
FINN *What are your plans? Apart from the cannelloni and sadness.*
GEM *Since it's Valentine's I have a hot date with my laptop and the Lloyds Bank business loan application.*
FINN *Sounds sexy lol.*
GEM *Unbelievably so.*
GEM *Maybe if I'm lucky I'll get to do something fun afterwards.*

I stared at the message, horror dawning, as I realised what I'd just said. It wasn't technically flirting, and if I was lucky, Finn would just look at it as me making a bad joke. I didn't know why it bothered me so much because it wasn't as if I hadn't made those sorts of jokes before. But there was something squirming in my stomach that made me pause.

Was it because I wanted Finn to brush me off as usual? Or was it because I wanted him to ask me what *something fun* meant?

FINN *I hope you get a chance to. You deserve a reward.*

The squirming in my stomach intensified. I'd never thought about Finn like that before… or maybe I'd never allowed myself to. He'd been so shy when we'd first met that I hadn't wanted to scare him off, and by the time we'd gotten closer, I'd met Jesse.

But now things suddenly felt complicated. Finn was my best friend, and he did so much for me. I didn't want to push our friendship into anything that would make him uncomfortable, and Finn never really talked about his own dating life beyond a couple of casual mentions about previous partners. Even so, there was a new, niggling feeling worming its way into my chest, and I couldn't pin it down long enough to know what it was.

FINN *The show is starting so I'll speak to you tomorrow =D Have a good evening!*

As I read the message, I realised the aching sensation crawling through my heart was the feeling of wanting more. It was whether I'd be willing to risk our friendship to get it.

CHAPTER SEVEN

Finn

"Are you ready?" I asked, breaking into a smile despite the icy wind trying to freeze my face in place as I watched Gem fumble with a set of keys.

"I suppose so." He pursed his lips as he looked at the shabby grey front door of the shop like he was wondering what he'd gotten himself into. Then he put the key into the lock and turned it. The door opened with a squeak, and we stepped into the dusty interior that was lit only by the lingering daylight of the cold, February afternoon. "Fucking hell," Gem said. "It's freezing in here. Might as well be in the fucking Arctic."

He walked across the shop towards the little back room and found a light switch. The overhead lights flickered on, and I began to look around at the space. It was a little dustier than I remembered, which made sense, and a little shabbier, but all in all, it wasn't a total mess. It just needed a bit of a scrub, some new paint, and a bit of love and attention. All of which could be easily administered.

"Okay," Gem called. "I think I found the heating." Something electrical began to whir from above us as Gem reappeared, wiping his hands on his jeans. "Hopefully it'll get warm in here before we both freeze our nuts off."

"Where do you want to start?" I asked as I looked around, not sure what we should do first. I'd offered to come and help Gem open the shop because I wanted to be there for him. It was a big step and the start of something new and exciting. I wanted him to know he had my support, even if I didn't really know what I was doing.

"First things first, I want to take pictures of everything so I've got a record of what it looked like when I moved in." Gem pulled his phone out of his pocket. "I know that's suspicious of me, but I've dealt with landlords before, and if commercial ones are anything like residential ones, they'll try to screw you over as much as possible."

That made sense, so I volunteered to take the upstairs and take pictures of anything that might later prove to be an issue, even if we were going to redecorate.

"What colour scheme were you thinking?" I asked when I came back down and found Gem leaning on the fitted counter, which was the only thing that had been left in the space apart from a couple of small, built-in shelves in the back room. He'd put his bag down next to him and pulled out a chunky, ring-bound notebook that seemed to be full of lists.

"I was thinking maybe a nice deep red for the outside," Gem said. "Or maybe green. There's quite a few blues on the street already, and although they're a bit more… toned down—I don't know how to describe them—I think I want to avoid that. I think it needs to be bold since it's such a small place, and it's easy to walk past."

"That makes sense." I nodded. "What about inside?"

"I was thinking fairly neutral since I'm going to be putting up a lot of shelves. Plus, I don't want it to feel smaller than it already is." He looked around and frowned. "I'll get some tester pots tomorrow, but I'll probably go for a pale grey or cream. Something similar to what's already up. It's boring, but it should do the trick."

"That sounds good," I said. "Just let me know when you've got the paint, and I'll come and give you a hand."

Gem's frown deepened. "Are you sure? I don't want to take up too much of your time. You're busy enough as it is."

"It's fine. I wouldn't have volunteered if I couldn't do it." Gem's expression suggested he didn't believe me. He was probably right not to because, busy or not, I'd be here either way. But it surprised me that he'd twigged that if I cared about someone I'd be there for them, even at my own inconvenience. I thought I was better at hiding it than that.

Gem overlooked my white lie and continued. "If you're sure, but it's not going to be at reasonable times. I'm still working at The Lost World for another month since I need the income."

"Did Jay mind you putting in your notice?"

Gem shook his head and grinned. "No, he actually hugged me and told me it was about fucking time. Also, I think he was pleased I'd listened to him and taken him up on his suggestion. I think that made him forget he's going to be without staff in a month."

"Hopefully that doesn't lessen his victory," I said.

"Nah, I'm sure he'll find someone else pretty quickly. And if he gets his act together, he can have them start before I finish, and I can walk them through everything."

"That would be good. Are you planning on hiring anyone?" I wasn't sure if Gem's plans included staffing. It was something we'd talked about, but Gem had initially maintained he didn't think he'd need anyone for the first year or so. Otherwise, he'd said, he'd just be adding to the cost, and there was no guarantee he'd make enough money to cover their salary as well as the business's running costs. I didn't know whether he'd changed his mind since.

"No," he said with a wave of his hand. "Not yet. I think they ended up in year three of the plan? Maybe year two?" He shrugged then fixed me with a pointed look. "By the way, I noticed you never answered my question about whether you're sure you wanted to help out."

"Oh, er, yes, I'm sure." I felt my face prickle, embarrassed at having been caught out. I wasn't used to people noticing when I'd casually steered the conversation away from questions about me. It made my throat tighten, and all at once I suddenly felt overcome.

I'd had a crush on Gem for months, and I continually tried to suppress it by endlessly telling myself Gem wasn't interested, and even if he was, I'd never act on it because I'd be too afraid of what might happen. I liked living in fantasy worlds where I had more control over what happened... or where I could at least pretend I wasn't so much of a coward.

Besides, Gem might be a nerd, but I was a *nerd's nerd*. That combined with my shyness and anxiety didn't make me optimal boyfriend material for most people.

I'd had a couple of relationships, and my longest running one had continued through university and a couple of years out the other side. But that had fizzled out when he'd moved to the US to work for a big animation studio and I hadn't wanted to go with him. It had been amicable in the end, even if it had broken both our hearts. We kept in touch, though—the odd message here or there, liking each other's pictures on Instagram, random comments, but it wasn't anything more than superficial.

Recently, I'd had nothing. And that hadn't bothered me until a couple of months ago when my siblings started pairing off. I was suddenly struck by the realisation that I might end up alone, and that I was too nervous to do anything about it. Dating apps terrified me, and I didn't get out enough to meet people. Eli kept offering to introduce me to people he knew, but I doubted he could find me love because I'd never been truly honest with him about who I was. It would be difficult for him to introduce me to someone without knowing my secrets.

But it was just as hard to introduce myself to potential partners. What was I supposed to say? *Hi, I'm Finn. I'm twenty-eight, incredibly nerdy, horribly shy and anxious, but if we ever get close to the bedroom, I really want to take control of you, tie you up, edge you, spoil you, and give you so many orgasms that you melt into a pile of goo?* Yes, that would go over incredibly well. I could picture it now.

"Finn?" Gem asked, snapping me out of my mental wanderings. "You okay? You disappeared on me there."

"Sorry. I was just, er, thinking." I swallowed and tried to smile. "Don't worry about the odd hours. That actually works quite well for me because I can record while you're at work and then help you here afterwards. It can be my hobby for a while. My mother is always telling me I need to take a break from screens. She'll be delighted."

And I can spend more time with you.

It was something I suddenly wanted to voice but couldn't bring myself to.

Gem was the only man I'd ever met who seemed to understand me. It was like he had a key to the labyrinth guarding my heart without me giving him one, and he seemed determined to find the castle, whether he realised it or not.

"Don't worry. I can find plenty for you to do," Gem teased.

"At least it will be warmer in here than the garden. Mimbles is always trying to get one of us interested in gardening with her, but it's just not for me. I like the results, but I'm not a fan of the cold and the mud in the winter or the sunburnt neck in the summer."

Gem laughed. "I mean, I can't guarantee warm, but I can guarantee there won't be mud. If there is, then we'll have done something horribly wrong."

My laughter joined his, and I couldn't stop myself from hiccupping. It was something I hated but always did when

I laughed properly. Gem stared at me, and I felt my face flush. "Sorry, I know the hiccup thing is weird."

"No," he said slowly. "It's not that. I…" He shook his head, dismissing whatever he was going to say. "How're your DIY skills?"

"Er, not horrible. Why?"

"We'll have to build a lot of furniture, and I don't want you drilling through your own hand."

I winced. "Have you—"

"Known someone that's done that? Yeah, I have. And it wasn't pretty. He didn't have the most common sense, though, so he probably shouldn't have been handling a drill in the first place."

I didn't want to think about that any further. It sounded horrible, and I'd never been good with gore or horror. I couldn't even watch medical or veterinary shows that showed surgical procedures. They always made me feel sick.

"Sorry," Gem said. "I probably shouldn't have said that. You look a little pale."

"It's fine, I'm just not good with medical stuff. I'm kind of a wimp."

Gem frowned. "It's not wimpy at all. It's a perfectly valid feeling! Don't you go putting yourself down in front of me again." He raised an eyebrow and grinned. "Or I'll have to cut off your cake supply."

"How rude," I said, imitating Eli's dramatic gasp. "And after everything I've volunteered to do for you but haven't actually done."

"I know. I'm a rotten bastard." I wanted to tell him he

wasn't, but the glint in his eye told me he was joking, and if I suddenly turned the conversation serious, I was afraid things would get awkward. There was a moment of silence between us, and my chest squeezed.

"So… what are your plans, then?" I asked, pointing at Gem's notepad. "Did you find a name you liked yet?" It was my customary tactic whenever I felt awkward—distract, distract, distract. But Gem seemed to be wising up to that, and I was afraid he wouldn't take the bait.

"No," he said finally. "Not yet." He looked at me with a gentle smile curling his lips. "You fancy getting some Chinese and talking it out? Maybe help me measure the place up? Work out where to put things?"

"I'd love that."

And that was how we found ourselves sitting on a cold, wooden floor eating Chinese food out of plastic tubs and throwing around progressively worse business names. It felt like the most perfect date neither of us knew we were on.

CHAPTER EIGHT

Gem

As I scrubbed a suspicious-looking stain on the upstairs wall for the third time in two days, I was starting to wonder whether it might just be easier to paint over the bastard. Or put some furniture in front of it. I didn't think people would be looking too closely at the walls, although just because I never did when I was browsing somewhere, didn't mean other people wouldn't.

I'd never been as obsessed with cleaning as I had been the past two days, and if she could see me, I was sure my mum would pitch a fit given all the nagging she'd had to do when I was a teenager to get me to even make my bed or open a window.

My muscles were burning from slogging bags of cleaning products to and from my car and from lugging lukewarm buckets of water around as I attempted to scrub the living daylights out of the place. I'd already spent a fortune in B&Q on sugar scrub for the walls, tester pots, and painting supplies, and I really wanted to get to that stage as soon as possible.

Since I didn't have the biggest budget in the world, I'd decided I'd be doing as much as possible myself, and so far, it seemed like the only things I'd need professional help with were hanging the sign outside the door—since there wasn't room for any branding on the window—and a website. I'd gone with Castle Games for the shop name, which had been the only surviving option from the list Finn and I had made. It was simple, but it would do, and I could use the rough outline of Lincoln Castle on my branding.

"You know what," I said to the spot on the wall, which had refused to budge. "You can bloody well stay there for all I care." I dropped the sponge into the bucket next to me and climbed to my feet, wincing as my muscles reminded me they weren't used to this much exertion.

I stomped down the stairs, bucket in hand, and headed for the back room to dump it into the tiny sink. The place was definitely looking better. My next task was to paint some tester squares on the wall and then start sanding down the front door and the windows so I could paint over them. Because the shop was old, the windows had wooden frames and grilles, and each individual piece of wood was going to need sanding and painting if I wanted it to be a different colour than farmhouse grey.

At least it wasn't raining, but I was pretty sure my fingers were going to freeze off if I spent a lot of time outside. The wind seemed to have come straight from the frozen depths of hell, and it had the ability to get inside all the layers I put on. I might have been Scottish and grown up with the cold, but that wind was pure evil. But if I wanted to have the shop open for Easter at the start of April, then I needed to get a crack on.

It didn't take me long to get the testers up on the wall, and I remembered to make a note of the name, in pencil, under each one because otherwise I'd be fucked in a day or two when I needed to pick one and couldn't remember which was which. Then I pulled on my gloves, coat, and hat, grabbed some sandpaper, stuffed my phone and earbuds into my pocket, and headed for the front door. When I got there, I was surprised to find Edward lurking on the street like a malevolent vampire.

"Hey," I said. "You okay?"

"Of course." He smiled brightly, which was always dangerous. "I've come to help."

"You? Help?" I asked, unable to stop myself from teasing him. Edward was a world-famous cosplayer, and I loved his stuff, but I'd always teased him about it because all he ever seemed to do was complain about either being bored or not wanting to work. Then again, I only saw him when he came to The Lost World, and that was his favourite tool for procrastination.

"I am very helpful!"

"What are you avoiding today?"

Edward laughed. "Making adjustments to the lining of Leo's wedding suit. It's very tedious, and I'm bored, but Jay said if I don't want to do my own work, I should come and help you with yours."

"You were being annoying, then?" I asked with a wry smile. "Was it about the capes?"

"Perhaps." He winked. "I don't know why Jacob doesn't want a cape. He'd look very dashing in one. So would Leo. I even offered to do them with fur trim so they'd look more regal, but that idea got shot down in flames before I'd even finished describing it." He sighed dramatically. "Honestly, it's very difficult having a best friend with such boring taste."

I knew better than to get embroiled in this discussion, so I pulled out a large piece of sandpaper so I could start working on the door. "I guess you'll just have to make a cape for yourself."

"You know, that's a rather marvellous idea! I've always wanted a cape," Edward said. "What are you doing today?"

"I've been cleaning," I said, pulling the door towards me and holding it in place with my foot so I could start on the edge closest to me. "And now I get the great joy of sanding the door, the window frame, and the grilles so I can paint them." I wasn't sure whether Edward would actually help or not, even if Jay had sent him to. My guess was that Jay thought Edward would take one look at the cleaning and DIY, decide his own work was much better, and go home without being a nuisance to anyone.

I watched Edward cast an eye over the size of the window, a little wrinkle appearing across his nose. Then he held out a gloved hand. "That's going to take you all night by yourself. Give me a spare piece, and I'll start on the window." He must have seen the surprise on my face because his smile widened. "I happen to be rather good at DIY. It comes with the territory, although my fibreglass skills aren't as good as Izzy's. Not that I'd admit it. Still, you should ask Jay who built all the bookcases in The Lost World, and if he tells you it was him, please know that he's lying through his teeth."

I laughed and ducked back inside to retrieve another piece of sandpaper. When I got back to the front of the shop, I saw that Edward had deposited his bag, walking stick, and hat inside the door, pulled his long, pale hair up into a neat bun, and was examining the window frame.

"Thank you," he said as I handed him the sandpaper. "I'll start with the grilles since they're liable to be fiddly as fuck and rather tedious."

"Less tedious than the suit?"

"Probably moreso, but this is new and therefore interesting. Plus, I have you to talk to, and that will keep me amused." The way he said it made a suspicious red light flash in my brain like I was about to be interrogated.

"Will it now?" I asked, returning to the door.

"Don't worry. I won't ask anything terribly challenging." I heard the smile in his voice over the scuff of sandpaper on wood. I chuckled and wondered if there was something I could say to divert Edward's attention before he even got started. "Jay said you're still going to be working at The Lost World while you're setting up here?"

"Yeah." I nodded. "I'm only there part-time, and I could do with the extra cash. Plus, it's not far to come up here afterwards."

"That makes sense. I've told Jay he needs to start looking for your replacement, but so far, he seems unenthusiastic about the prospect. I know he's very proud of you, especially because he thinks this was all his idea, but I think he's reluctant to let you go because you're so good at your job."

I smiled, Edward's words warming my heart. He was saying things I already knew, but it was nice to hear it from someone else. Especially someone who knew Jay so well. "Don't worry, I'll keep prompting him too. I'm sure there are loads of people who'd want the job."

"I told him he should hire Link. You know, that very sweet boy you foisted off on me at the party," Edward said. I glanced over at him, but he was focused on one of the corners. "He was rather like a puppy, and I think he'd be very trainable."

"He's not actually a dog though."

"I know, but it fits. I told him he should dump that ridiculous ex of yours, and I believe he did."

"That's because he's got a crush on you," I said. "Or you've put him under a spell."

"Sadly, there are no spells here, but the crush idea is adorable. The poor boy will be heartbroken when he finds out about Izzy." Edward sighed. "Although it is nice to know I still attract attention."

"I don't think you'll ever *not* attract attention."

"You flatter me, darling," Edward said. "What about you though? Any new man on the horizon?"

"Er, no." I shook my head, focusing on the door. This wasn't a subject I wanted to discuss because everything inside me felt strangely jumbled. I wasn't sure if it was just because I was sex deprived or if it was something else, but every time I'd seen Finn recently, a weird ache had pulled at my chest. At first, I'd thought it was heartburn, but since it hadn't gone away, I was getting the feeling it was tied to Finn.

It didn't help that I now had this ridiculous idea in my head that Finn was somehow the man I spent all my time jerking off to, despite having no evidence to that effect except some hiccupping laughter and the fact that Finn had a naturally gorgeous voice. They were dubious connections at best but ones my brain seemed desperate to make. I wasn't even sure where they were coming from. Finn was my friend, and nothing was going to happen between us.

Edward hummed suspiciously. "You don't sound sure."

"I am," I said. "I'm single."

"But you don't want to be." Edward said it as a statement, not a question.

"That's not really my choice."

"Why not?"

Fuck, I'd boxed myself in now. I either had to lie and hope I sounded convincing or tell Edward enough to get him to stop bugging me.

"You don't have to tell me, you know," Edward said. "I realise I'm being very nosy. But if you did want someone to talk to, I volunteer my services. I am an excellent listener, and I promise not to tell. I'm rather good at keeping secrets. Izzy and I hate-fucked in secret for years before I told anyone except Lewis, and he only knew because he caught us."

I moved the sandpaper to another patch of wood, contemplating Edward's words. "I just... I don't know how

I really feel about someone, and I don't know if they feel the same." I sighed. "I know I should just talk to them, but…"

"I take it this is someone you already know? Potentially very well?"

"Yeah." I wondered if I'd already given too much away. I didn't want to drop Finn in it without his permission.

"That does make it more difficult," Edward said, and I was surprised by the note of understanding in his voice. "It's always hard when you develop feelings, whatever those may be, for someone you know because rejection comes with the possibility of so much more pain. If it's someone you've only just met, it's different. It can hurt, but it's easier to shrug off. I don't blame you for being cautious."

"Thanks."

"But I will say that caution will only do you so much good. There comes a point where you have to make a decision and choose whether to risk your emotions or walk away. I know people will say you can just try to put your feelings to one side, but I believe eventually you reach a point where that becomes impossible. You risk making yourself miserable because you refuse to move forward. Does that make sense?"

"It does." Edward had hit the nail on the head, and the revelation was almost painful. Whatever I felt for Finn, my brain had been trying to suppress it out of fear. I cared about Finn, and he'd been there for me more times than I could count over the past nine months. I didn't want to ruin that because I was starting to feel something, especially because I didn't know if the feelings were genuine or just because I wanted to get laid. I felt horrible even admitting that to myself.

"I guess," Edward continued, "you just have to decide whether you've reached that point. And whether the risk is worth it."

CHAPTER NINE

Finn

"Are you okay to start with that wall?" Gem asked, nodding at the far side of the shop as he tipped thick paint into a tray. The shade was called Cornflower White, but right now it just looked like wet cement and seemed to have the same consistency as well.

"Sure," I said, picking up one of the paint rollers I'd just finished unwrapping and giving the roller a little spin. The whole of the downstairs floor was covered in dust sheets, and Gem had carefully taped up the skirting boards, door, and window frames with green masking tape that smelt like dried fish. I'd dug out a pair of very old jeans and an even older hoodie, which were both already covered in paint splatters from various rounds of redecorating at my parents' and siblings' houses.

"Cheers." Gem switched to filling another tray. "Hopefully it won't take too long with both of us. I was thinking if we can at least get one coat on the downstairs this evening, then we can do upstairs tomorrow, and then slap another coat on down here the day after. Or whenever we get time." He put the large tub of paint down and looked around the room. "It's definitely going to need two coats just to make sure it's got an even finish."

I nodded. "Agreed, but you're right. It shouldn't take us too long. Not unless you intend to start a paint fight." Gem shot me a wry smile and raised an eyebrow.

"Eli?"

"How did you guess?" I shook my head, smiling at the memory. "I was fourteen, and Eli was sixteen. It was the summer before Richard went to university, and I think it was just before he got his A-level results. I know he was very grumpy all the time, and Eli was antagonising him more than usual. Maybe because he was also waiting for exam results." I shrugged. "Anyway, Mum wanted to repaint the living room because it hadn't been done since they'd first moved in, and she'd decided we were all old enough not to draw on the walls or anything like that." In hindsight, Mum thinking Eli was mature had been a fatal mistake. He'd been a sixteen-year-old boy who didn't like his oldest brother. "I volunteered to help and so did Jules, Eli, and Lewis. Oscar was working a lot that summer, so he wasn't around much, and Richard was just... being Richard." Eli often called him Dick, and while I hesitated to agree, teenage Richard had certainly lived up to the name.

"Why do I get the feeling I know where this is going?"

"You probably do," I said. "It started well, and then Eli put some music on. It was just, like, rock music, the sort of stuff he still uses for his routines, but Richard didn't like it. He kept coming in and telling us to turn it down. Eli kept turning it up. Then Richard came in and started swearing at Eli, and he grabbed Eli's iPod to force him to turn it off. So Eli threw paint at him. Literally just grabbed the open paint tub and threw it at him. And Mum's living room has a feature wall that's bright teal…" I bit my lip, trying not to laugh. It hadn't been funny at the time. I'd been so anxious with all the yelling and the screaming—Richard hurling curses and death threats at Eli while Eli said he deserved it. I'd just wanted to curl into a ball in the corner.

"Fucking hell." Gem was staring at me. "Like all over him?"

"Well, he missed Richard's face. Eli isn't stupid. But yes, his whole body was covered in paint. It went everywhere. And then Richard made it worse by dropping Eli's iPod into a tray of paint." I sighed. "I'm not saying Eli should have started it. Absolutely not. But I do wish Richard hadn't retaliated. Lewis decided Richard had gone too far and put a paint tray under his feet. And it was just… a mess." I could still remember the way the paint had soaked into the dust sheets and left a pattern of teal footprints across the floor.

"Sounds like it," Gem said. "Your mum must have been pissed as fuck."

I nodded and picked up the nearest paint tray, heading over to the far side of the room so I could make a start. "Actually, it was my mum, Mimbles, who found us. And that was not fun. She was furious. She made us clean the whole thing up, then made Richard and Eli pay for new paint and for the carpet to be professionally cleaned. They also had to finish painting the room together, and neither of them were allowed to go out and celebrate getting their exam results." I dipped the roller into the paint, making sure it was evenly covered before I lifted it to the wall. "And that is why none of us were ever allowed near paint again without supervision."

Gem laughed. "Does this mean I'm your supervisor now?"

"Something like that. Although, I have to say I didn't get involved, so I don't know why I was banned. It was too… out of control for me," I said, choosing my words carefully. "And I didn't appreciate the shouting."

"I get that," Gem said. I glanced over my shoulder to see him starting on his own wall. "Your family is pretty chaotic anyway, and I've only seen all of you together once." Gem had met my family last December when Eli had taken part in a local drag competition. We'd all gone to support him, and everyone had gotten very drunk, which meant they were even louder than usual. It had been fun, though, and watching Eli win had been one of the highlights of my year.

"It's not usually too different. Only there's normally less alcohol and bad singing." I swept paint onto the wall, trying to focus on creating a smooth, even coat. Paint splatted onto my fingers, creating a speckled effect across my knuckles. "I sometimes feel like I need to apologise for how loud they are. I love them, but they can be a lot. Especially now that we're adding partners into the mix."

"Don't apologise," said Gem. "I like your family. And I'm glad I came with you. It was a cracking evening. And it was either that or put up with Jesse's bitching about something."

I frowned. Gem hadn't mentioned Jesse very often over the past few weeks, but I was concerned that he was more upset about the breakup than he was letting on. I just wasn't sure how to bring it up without seeming like I was being nosy or, even worse, fishing to see if Gem was ready to move on. "Do… do you miss him?"

"Fuck no! I mean, it was a shock seeing him with someone else, but I should have expected it. And thinking about it, we were never going to get anywhere. I'm pretty sure he was just using me so he didn't get lonely, and I just…" His voice dropped. "I liked that someone needed me."

My stomach twisted uncomfortably, and suddenly the words *I need you* were on the tip of my tongue, but I swallowed them back with force. Gem didn't need me, not in the way I needed him. I was being ridiculous.

Gem seemed to take my silence for pity because he quickly added. "It's fine. I'm over the bastard. Although, I'll admit I miss the sex." He laughed dryly, and my insides twisted again. "I mean, Jesse didn't have much in the way of personality outside of being demanding, but it did mean we fucked a lot. Maybe I should try to find some sort of fuck buddy, although I think that only works for really attractive people."

I felt my cheeks heating, and I desperately hoped Gem didn't notice and get the wrong idea. It wasn't that I was embarrassed Gem was talking about sex; it was that my brain had now conjured up all these delicious fantasies of

Gem in my bed. The suggestion that I could be his fuck buddy was right on the tip of my tongue, perilously close to tumbling off and out into the open. Even if I doubted I'd be what Gem wanted. But I'd give up a lot to make him happy, even my own desires.

"Sorry," Gem said, filling the silence I hadn't realised was there. "I didn't mean to make you uncomfortable."

"You didn't." I coughed, trying to clear my very dry throat. "It doesn't bother me. You're my best friend. You can talk to me about anything."

"Are you sure?"

"Of course."

"Okay," Gem said slowly as if he wasn't sure he believed me. I cursed myself and my inability to be anything less than a nervous, anxious mess around people.

There was another minute of silence. I dipped the roller into the tray again, trying to think of something to say. I thought I should probably try to change the subject, so I didn't say something ridiculous, but I didn't want Gem to think I was changing it because I was uncomfortable. My brain was churning, and I couldn't seem to grab hold of anything, and somehow I found myself asking the one question I shouldn't, "How long has it been?"

"Since I got laid?"

Shit. I shouldn't have asked, but I didn't have a choice now. "Yes."

"Since December," Gem said with a sigh. I made a small sound and tried to concentrate on the wall in front of me. But it was no use. My mind had decided it was going to focus on Gem's sex life to the detriment of all other activity. "What about you?"

Oh fuck. Fuckity fuckity fuck. That was a question I didn't want to answer. "A while," I said quietly. "Eli keeps offering to set me up with people, but I, er, I keep declining. And I just… well…"

"It's okay. You don't have to explain. I don't want to make you feel—"

"I'm not uncomfortable," I said. "I promise, I'm not. Sex has never made me anxious. It's the meeting someone part I find hard." That and the fact that what I looked like and what I wanted were very different things, and I still hadn't worked out how to explain that to someone I'd only just met. I could have settled for boring, mediocre hook-ups, but what was the point in that? If the choice was between jerking myself off and giving myself what I needed or spending the night with someone who could probably get me off but wouldn't give me what I wanted, I was always going to choose the former.

Perhaps I was a coward since I could easily have told someone what I wanted and seen what happened, but I didn't because I was afraid.

"Not a Grindr person?" Gem teased.

"No, definitely not. You?"

"I've tried, but I'm not exactly what most people want." I frowned and turned to Gem, allowing my eyes to roam over him. I didn't see why people would reject him at all, but then again, some of the men I knew were quite shallow. Even so, Gem was incredibly handsome, and just looking at him made my heart race.

"Why not? You're gorgeous!" I didn't know why I'd said it, but I couldn't take it back. Gem looked over at me, and it was too late to turn away and pretend I hadn't been staring. I froze like a deer in headlights. Gem put his roller down.

"I want to say you're lying," he said. "But you don't lie."

"No, I don't." I swallowed. I kept secrets, but that was different.

My grip on my roller was so tight I thought I might snap the handle in two. How had we ended up here? Having this conversation. It was like I'd fallen into some alternative dimension. Part of me wanted to run, to ask Gem to forget I'd even said anything, but another part of me—the darker, more controlling part—whispered in my ear that this was my chance. That I could have what I wanted if I only had the courage to reach out and take it.

I wanted everything with Gem, but maybe I'd be happy with just a little bit instead. A taste to keep me satisfied until I could figure out what the fuck I was doing. This was liable to end in tears, and I could hear the warning sirens screaming in my head.

Against my better judgment, I took a step towards him.

CHAPTER TEN

Gem

FINN MOVED TOWARDS ME, still clutching his paint roller in a white-knuckled grip. He looked half-terrified by his own actions, but there was a flame burning in his eyes I'd never seen before. A hunger that made my chest tighten and my dick throb. How the fuck we'd gotten here, I didn't know, but I wasn't about to question it. My feelings for Finn had grown more complicated over the past few days, and the idea of potentially getting my hands on him was something I wanted more and more with each passing second.

He was my friend. But could he be something more as well? There was only one way to answer that question.

I took a couple slow steps across the room, worried if I moved too fast I would spook him and he'd flee. I wasn't sure why I was treating Finn like a skittish colt, but maybe it was because this situation felt so unexpected, and I was half waiting for him to realise what was going on and tell me to forget it.

"So," I said as I reached him, "you think I'm gorgeous?" I was going for teasing, but my voice came out hoarse.

"Yes." Finn sounded more confident than he looked, a tiny smile curling the edge of his lips. It was his dangerous smile—the one I already knew I'd do anything for. "I really do." He suddenly seemed to realise he was still holding the roller and chuckled, lowering it to the floor before moving closer. Finn was taller than me, and there was something heady about looking up into his warm, hungry eyes. He fixed me with a look that made the bottom drop out of my stomach, and my cock filled so fast it made my head spin. This was not the Finn I thought I knew, but that wasn't a bad thing.

"You're not bad yourself," I said, trying and failing again at being teasing. I heard the catch in my voice, the one I always got when I was reaching desperate. But how the fuck had I gotten there so quickly?

Finn chuckled again as he reached out one hand to brush it against my jaw. A slow tingle spread across my skin, and I let out a shuddering breath.

"What do you want?" Finn asked. That was the million-pound question. What did I want? I didn't think I even knew.

"I… I don't know." I swallowed. Finn's hand was cool against my cheek. It was all I could focus on.

"Do you want this to stop? We can go back to painting and pretend this conversation didn't happen."

"Is there another option?"

"Yes," Finn said, his dangerous smile widening. "There are several. Would you like me to list them for you?"

I found myself nodding. This felt like the beginning of a fantasy—something I'd always dreamt about but hadn't experienced, at least outside of listening to endless amounts of narrated porn. I'd let guys boss me around before, but there was something different about the way they'd done it versus the casual power in Finn's voice. It was like others had tried to demand power but hadn't expected to get it, but Finn didn't have to demand because he knew all it would take was a single word and I'd drop to my knees in front of him.

Maybe I was reading too much into the situation. Maybe my brain was just desperately making connections because it needed something I'd never been able to give it before. It wasn't something I could think about now.

Finn's thumb caressed my cheek. "If we're going to do this, the first thing I'll say is that if I ask you a question, I want you to answer me. With words. I don't expect full sentences, but I do expect a coherent, verbalised answer. Okay?"

"Yes," I said with another nod. What the fuck was happening? Had my Finn been kidnapped and suddenly replaced? Or had this part of him been there all along, waiting in secret to be unleashed? I wondered how many people got to see this side of him and whether I should count myself lucky to be one of them.

"Thank you." He smiled at me and my heart leapt. "Your options are, we can kiss and then go back to painting. We can kiss and then go into the stockroom where you can have either a blow job or a hand job before we go back to painting. Or we can finish painting and then go back to your flat, but I won't do any more than the options you've already been offered. Not today. Or, as I said, we can forget this ever happened. It's up to you."

Yeah, there was no fucking way in hell we were going to forget this. I knew that doing this, whatever *this* was, would change things between us. But there was one thing I needed to know before I made my decision. Well, two things.

"Are you sure about this? I mean, do you actually want this? I don't want you to do anything you're not comfortable with," I said. "I know you, Finn. You can pretend all you like, but you do things for people when you're not actually interested in them for yourself. You're selfless, and that's amazing, but I don't want you to do this just because you think I need it or something."

Finn moved closer so I could see every detail of his face and feel his breath ghosting over my skin. His body brushed against mine, sending a jolt through me. "You're so thoughtful," he said quietly. "And I appreciate your concern, but trust me, I wouldn't have offered if I wasn't interested. I take consent from all sides seriously. And that includes myself. So, no, I'm not just doing this because I think you need it. I'm doing it because I know you need it, and so do I."

I shivered as his words sank into me. "Okay, then. I just wanted to know."

"I appreciate the concern." He drew his hand down to my chin, holding me in place. "Have you made your decision?"

"I think so," I said. "But do we have to come back to painting afterwards?"

"Yes." Finn chuckled. "You said you wanted to get the downstairs painted today, so we're going to. You just have to choose whether you want to do the painting now or later."

Either way was going to be fucking torture, but the way Finn was making it sound like I had a choice made my cock ache. I needed release. Maybe if I chose now, Finn would let me come again after we'd finished painting. Like an extra reward.

"By the way, if you do choose now, you won't get an extra orgasm afterwards," Finn said, apparently able to read my mind. "That isn't how this works."

"Spoilsport."

"Don't pout. It's not becoming, and I don't like brats."

I swallowed, trying to ignore the way he was hitting every single one of my buttons without trying. "Sorry," I muttered.

"Apology accepted." He leant down further so his lips brushed against my ear. "Now, make your choice, or you won't get anything."

"The second. The, er, the kissing and the stockroom. That one… please."

"Good. Thank you for choosing." Finn looked down at me, heat burning in his eyes. "I'm going to kiss you now." I opened my mouth to make a stupid joke, but the words vanished when Finn tilted his head and brushed his lips against mine. Sparks jumped across my skin like I'd been shocked as a wave of sensations flooded me. Finn's lips were soft but firm, controlling every aspect of the kiss. His tongue caressed the seam of my mouth, and I opened for him.

It was like I'd never been kissed before.

The intensity of the feelings should have terrified me, but all I wanted was more. Finn's hand was still on my jaw, holding me in place, while his other reached out to wrap around my waist and pull me incrementally closer until I was pressed against him. My fingers fisted in the front of the old hoodie he was wearing like I was trying to keep him there, in front of me, forever.

Finn released me slowly, and I choked back a whimper. I'd never had anyone make me feel so wrecked after one kiss, like I'd been momentarily disconnected from reality. I didn't think I'd be able to live without more of Finn's kisses. It was like I'd tasted something secret and forbidden, and the knowledge of it was something I'd never be able to forget.

"Would you like more?" Finn asked.

I wanted to tell him that was a ridiculous question because how could I not want more after that? But then an exasperated voice reminded me how important consent was to Finn, and I nodded. "Yes."

"Good." He slid his hand down to mine and interlaced our fingers in a way that felt ridiculously natural. My heart raced as he pulled me towards the empty stockroom then closed the door behind us. The room was full of random shit I'd acquired over the past week—mostly cleaning and decorating equipment. Finn released my hand and moved a few bits aside until there was enough space around us. That would teach me to keep everything tidier.

My aching cock pulsed at the realisation of what was about to happen. Finn smiled at me again, and my stomach tightened. He pulled me against him and our mouths met in another kiss. My hand slipped under his hoodie and t-shirt, desperately seeking skin, and Finn shivered when my fingers brushed against his waist.

"Your hands are cold," he murmured.

"Sorry, it's a curse."

"I'm sure I'll get used to it." He kissed me again while my stomach flipped. "Either that or I'll make you keep your hands to yourself. I'll take you apart without letting you touch me."

"Fuck."

"Do you like that idea?" he asked as his hands worked under my clothes. I bit back a moan as his fingers trailed along the waistband of my jeans.

"Yeah."

"What else do you like?"

"Er… I…" Fuck. Did I have to admit what I wanted? I didn't think Finn would judge me. We were friends after all, and he wasn't the type to do that. But once again we were crossing into unknown territory, and I wasn't sure if the map was marked 'Here there be dragons' or not.

Fuck it. We'd come this far. Might as well keep going. I could think about the consequences later.

"I like… I like the idea of, er, giving up control a little bit. Not, like, all the time, but I mean… Shit, I'm not explaining this well." I shook my head and snorted. "I like other people to be in charge when we fuck. It gets me out of my head a little."

"I understand," Finn said, running his thumb across my bottom lip. "I feel the same, except I prefer to be in control. It's a heady experience and one I take seriously."

"Do you ever not take anything seriously?"

"Sometimes." Finn smirked. "By the way, I wouldn't test me. It could get interesting for you. But only if you want it too. Like I said, I take consent seriously. It helps me know just how far I can push you. And if this is something you want to do again, we're going to sit down and talk about everything. We should be doing it now, but—"

"One blow job is not going to break things, I promise," I said.

"So you've made your decision, then?"

"I guess I have." I hadn't meant to, but apparently my subconscious had decided for me. "Er, I don't have any condoms, but if it helps, I got a test after the whole Jesse shitshow, and it came back negative. It just depends if you're up for that."

"I wouldn't have offered if I wasn't," he said. His voice was low and soft, and fucking God, it was a turn-on. He kissed me again, his tongue leisurely exploring my mouth. Then he sank to his knees in front of me. "If you were in my bed, I'd take my time with you, draw this out until you couldn't take any more. But I think today will have to be different because I'm not sure how long I can cope with kneeling on this floor." I chuckled weakly. "Also, we still have to finish painting, and if I did everything I wanted to you, you wouldn't have the energy left."

"You can't tease me like that," I said. Finn reached for my belt, unbuckling it, and popping open my jeans. I suddenly panicked that I'd put on crap, old underwear that morning, but then I remembered I'd thrown half of them out over Christmas because I'd had to concede there was such a thing as boxers with too many holes in them. "It's not fair."

"Life isn't fair. But don't worry, I'm still planning on doing that at some point. Just not today." He looked up at me with an intense gaze that had me rooted to the spot. "Trust me."

"I do."

Finn gently pushed my jeans down around my thighs, leaving my boxers in place. I glanced down and cursed internally as I realised I was wearing boxers patterned with fucking D20s. My sister had gotten them for me at Christmas as a sort of joke, even though we both knew I loved shit like that. Finn traced a finger over the hard line of my cock and looked up at me with a smile. "I like your underwear."

"Thanks," I said. "My sister got them for me."

"Sounds like something my sister would do." He stroked my cock leisurely, totally unfazed by the fact that he was torturing me. He'd said he wasn't going to draw this out, but if this was Finn moving fast, his moving slowly was going to kill me.

He leant forward and pressed a gentle kiss to the head of my dick, which was straining against the brightly patterned fabric. I whimpered, my hands balling into fists. I still wasn't sure what to do with them. Finn glanced up at me again. "You can put your hands on my head if you want. But you're not allowed to push or pull me farther onto your cock, do you understand? You'll get what I give you, not what you want."

My cock visibly pulsed, and I nodded. "Yes." The temptation to add *sir* to that sentence was unreal, but I wasn't sure if that was Finn's thing, and I didn't want to ruin this moment by suddenly discussing dynamics. It had taken us enough time to get to this point following Finn's wobbly steps towards me while he'd been clutching the pain roller. I didn't want to draw it out any further. My hands reached for Finn's hair as he pulled my boxers down to meet my jeans, letting my cock spring free. His short hair was soft in my hands, and it distracted me for a second... until I felt the wet heat of Finn's tongue brush across my slit.

"Shit!" The word came out louder than I intended, and Finn snorted. I wanted to say something witty, but then Finn wrapped his hand around my shaft and all my words faded. His grip was tight as he slowly started to pump my dick, but it wouldn't be enough to get me off. He was teasing me again.

Finn pressed another kiss to the head of my cock before wrapping his lips around it. His tongue flicked out again, caressing my slit and sending another bolt of pleasure through me before he slowly slid my cock deeper into his mouth. My fingers tightened in his hair as I cursed. Finn started to work my cock—sucking and licking and pumping my shaft with his hand while using the other to roll my balls between his fingers. It was nothing like the fast, careless blow jobs Jesse had inflicted on me. It had always felt like he was giving me head out of bored politeness instead of desire.

"Fuck, yes… just like that…" A garbled mess of words spilt from my lips as Finn bought me closer and closer to the edge. I watched every move he made, the sight making my chest clench and my cock swell. Finn glanced up at me, and the sight of his soft, hazel eyes full of heat and his slick lips stretched around my shaft were almost enough to make me come. Not that it was going to take much more.

Pulling off my cock with a slick pop, Finn's eyes met mine while his hand continued to jack me. "Tell me when you're close."

"I'm really not far," I panted. "You keep doing that and it's not going to be long."

Finn smirked like he was pleased with himself, and that did something completely new to my insides. Then he sucked my cock back down, and I knew I was done for. It barely took two pumps of his mouth before I was crying out a warning, and as Finn tightened his hand and his lips, I grunted and came down his throat, clutching his hair as he swallowed every drop of my load. He released my dick gently, his tongue swiping up the last few bits of cum clinging to the head of my dick. Then he sat back on his heels, letting my hands slide from his hair, and began to pull my boxers back up, a satisfied smile across his face.

"Did you enjoy that?" he asked as he tucked my cock away. The tone of his voice suggested he already knew the answer.

"Fucking hell," I said. It was all I could manage. Finn's

smile widened. He reached for my jeans, tugging them up and handing them to me.

"Good."

My hands found the waistband of my jeans, snapping into action even though the rest of my brain hadn't caught up. Finn rose gracefully to his feet, and my eyes drifted down to his groin. "What about you?" I asked. "Did you not want to get off? If you give me two minutes, I'll—"

"That's very sweet," Finn said, cutting me off. "But I'm fine. This wasn't about me. It was about you."

"But…" I was struggling to wrap my head around what he'd said. Surely he wanted something? Everyone wanted something.

Finn leant in close and kissed me gently. I could taste myself on his lips. "Another time," he said softly. "I like making people feel good, and I don't always need to get off to do that. Besides, we still have painting to do."

"Are you still gonna make me do that?"

"Yes. That was the deal." I felt him smiling against my mouth as I kissed him again.

"Are we… Do you want to do this again?" I asked.

"Yes, I do. If you do."

"Yeah." There was so much I suddenly wanted with him. Like this one experience had suddenly opened a door into a new realm of possibilities. I'd always had Finn firmly in the 'friend' box, but that was now broken. I just hoped that whatever happened between us, I would still have a friend at the end of it.

CHAPTER ELEVEN

Finn

IT TOOK eighteen hours for the implications of what Gem and I had done to sink in and for me to start freaking out about it. I'd been taking a break from recording and was sitting on my sofa, dipping cheese on toast into tomato soup and watching *The Way of the Househusband* when the full force of what we'd done dropped onto my head like a ton of bricks. I'd actually gasped, staring at the screen while my breaths came in rattled pants.

What had I done? What had I done? Shit, fuck, balls, what the fuck had I done?

I'd blown Gem in the back room of his shop but not before I'd casually dropped the whole soft Dom attitude on him. Well, not all of it, but at least enough for him to get a very good picture of what I was like in bed.

What the fuck had I been thinking? I clearly hadn't; that

was the issue. Otherwise I'd never have done anything like that.

But Gem had been talking about how much he missed sex, and my ridiculous brain had seen an opening. And when Gem had responded to everything I'd been doing, I had grabbed the idea with both hands and taken off into the distance before I could think better of it. Sometimes it felt like there were two parts of my brain: the shy, quiet part and the devious, horny, controlling part that reared its head at the most inopportune moments.

For some terrible reason, all I could compare it to was the Venom symbiote, but I wasn't going to examine that comparison too closely because I couldn't deal with the whole monster-fucking thing today. Not on top of every-thing else.

Grabbing my phone off the cushion next to me, I franti-cally messaged Chantelle. She was the only person I could talk to about this, and she'd be able to tell me if I was over-reacting. Although, in my mind, I wasn't sure whether I was reacting enough.

Message sent, I returned to my lunch, but my enthusiasm for my cheese on toast had waned, and now it just tasted like cardboard. I tried to focus on the anime, but nothing was registering, and it was all just a colourful blur. I kept glancing at my phone, waiting to see whether Chantelle had read my message or not. The temptation to call her was strong, but I didn't want to bother her if she was busy. In the grand scheme of things, my problem wasn't *that* important or even that bad, despite what my brain was trying to tell me. The world wasn't ending, and there was no horde of zombies trying to break down my front door. All that had happened was that I'd casually sucked my best friend's dick. No big deal.

Although the horde of zombies was starting to sound better by the minute. I'd happily take mindless, brain-munching—including a gruesome, painful death—if it meant I didn't have to think about what I'd done.

Chantelle called me ten minutes later when I was putting my crockery in the sink and debating breaking into my emergency stash of chocolate ice cream.

"You all right, babe?" she asked. "What's wrong? Did something happen?"

"Er, sort of," I said, suddenly feeling silly. Was I really going to bother Chantelle with this? "I'm sorry. This is probably ridiculous. Don't worry, I'm just in my head."

"Babe, what happened?" Her voice was soft and encouraging but with a firm edge I knew I couldn't refuse to answer. "Come on, tell me."

"So you know how I've been helping Gem with his new business? Well, last night I was up there helping with the painting, and, er, well we got onto the subject of dating and his ex-boyfriend—the one who ghosted him then showed up at his work with someone new."

"Ah, yeah, that wanker."

"Yes, that one," I said, walking through my flat to my bedroom and flopping down onto my bed. "Anyway, we started talking about sex, and I'm not even sure why I brought it up, but I asked how long it had been since he'd had sex, and then he asked me the same, and then I said he was gorgeous and…" My speech was getting faster and faster as everything started spilling out of me.

"Babe, babe," Chantelle said, cutting through my thoughts. "Slow down. Take a breath. What happened?"

I took a deep breath, exhaled slowly, and counted to five. "I gave Gem a blow job in the stockroom of his shop while also giving him a very good idea of the sort of man I am in bed." There was no need to sugar-coat things for Chantelle. With anyone else, I'd never have been so honest or open, but considering she'd helped me write scripts for my side hustle before and we'd had a long discussion over the use of *pussy* versus *cunt*, I didn't think there were many boundaries left for us to break.

There was a moment of silence, and I pulled the phone away from my ear to make sure it was still connected. "Are you still there?"

"Yeah, I am," Chantelle said. "I'm just trying to think of how to word my response."

"Do you think I fucked up? I mean, I think I might have. Quite badly, if I'm being honest."

"Finn, babe, I love you, but shut up," she said. "Okay, first of all, when did this happen?"

"Last night."

"And you didn't tell me until now? Rude! I thought you loved me." I chuckled, the tightness in my chest easing fractionally. "Second, why is this a bad thing? I thought you liked him. I know you wouldn't have done this unless you wanted to, so why are you freaking out? Talk it out with me."

"Well, we're friends. Nothing more. And I don't want to

ruin that. Gem is one of the only people I've ever met, apart from you, who really gets me, and I don't want to lose what we have."

"What makes you think you're going to?"

"Oh, please. In what world does this situation end well?" I asked, my voice dripping with cynicism. "We're friends but adding sex to that mix is not going to magically mean Gem falls in love with me and suddenly sees me the way I see him."

"Fine, stop, then," Chantelle said. "Go tell Gem you just want to be friends, and there'll be no dick sucking." I hesitated, and there was an awkward pause. Shit, I didn't want to do that, and Chantelle knew it. She was calling me out on my bullshit, and I either had to admit I didn't want this to end or concede defeat. "I didn't fucking think so," she added. "You want this with him. And I know that it's scary as fuck to go into this with no agreement on what it is, but you deserve to have some fucking fun, so treat it like that. Why does it have to be a relationship?"

"I guess it doesn't." There was a heavy, uncomfortable feeling in my stomach that was bothering me though. "But what happens when it inevitably goes wrong or something changes? It won't last forever. You and I both know that. At some point, he'll meet someone else, or he'll decide he wants to move on. What happens then?"

"If he meets someone else and chooses them over you, I'll fucking kill him," Chantelle muttered. "Look, babe, all you can do is go into this with your eyes wide open and hope that if it does go tits up, that you can still be friends at the end of it. Also, can you stop being so fucking dramatic?

Like, sure, it might not end well, but it might be the best fucking thing that's ever happened to you. So stop pouting, put on your big knickers, and try and be positive. 'Cos if you think it's all going to go up in flames, you might as well set fire to it now and be done with it."

I groaned, rolling onto my stomach and hugging a pillow. "Why do you always have to be right?"

"It comes with being a mum," she said. "Means I'm always right. It was a bonus thing I got when Kelsey was born. Kinda wish it had been a bottle of rosé though."

I laughed. "How is the little monster?"

"A little fucking monster, I'll tell you. She's five going on fifteen. I think I need to get her enrolled in something, burn off some of her energy, but…" She paused, and I knew where she was headed. Activities were expensive, especially in London, and Chantelle's budget wasn't the biggest in the world. "I'll think of something."

"Hey," I said. "I meant to ask you. Do you fancy doing some more editing for me? I'm too busy to do everything, and I'm drowning. Think you'd be up for it?" Chantelle had done some audiobook editing for me in the past when I'd been swamped, but I mostly tried to do it myself. With the way my diary was shaping up for the spring, I wasn't going to have time to do anything but work unless I got some help.

"Are you sure?"

"Yes, please. I'm not above begging," I joked. "I've overbooked myself, and with the other audio and helping Gem, I've got zero time for editing. Obviously, I'll pay you, and I can get you any software you need."

"Okay, yeah, that sounds great. Just let me know what you need. I can do it in the evenings when Kelsey's in bed and when she's at Ryan's. I've still got all the stuff from last time, so that'll be fine."

"You're a lifesaver," I said. "I'll send you a list. Also, I still owe Kelsey a Christmas present, so if you find something she wants to do, I'll pay for some lessons or something."

"You don't have to do that."

"Tough, I want to."

"God, you're better than her fucking dad."

"Someone has to be," I said wryly. "And you can't do everything."

"Can and will. Also, I found some cheap train tickets in a couple of weeks' time. Would that work for you?"

"Of course, just let me know the dates, and I'll be all yours." It would be wonderful to see Chantelle in person again. I'd missed her like crazy, and it made me realise I needed to take more time off to go and visit her. My time and budget were a lot more flexible than hers, and there were places in London I could stay without imposing on her. Lewis's boyfriend Jason owned a flat there with his brother, and he was always offering it to us if we needed it.

"Amazing. Can't wait," Chantelle said. "I know what you're doing by the way."

"What? I'm not doing anything."

"You're distracting me so you don't have to talk about Gem again."

"Maybe," I said with a smile, squeezing the pillow I was

holding a little tighter. "But I admitted you were right. Isn't that enough?"

"No. Tell me what you're going to do so I know how to respond next time you message me."

I chuckled. "You're not going to let me get away with anything, are you?"

"Fuck no. And if you hadn't wanted me to be your voice of fucking reason you wouldn't have messaged me. I'm like that little angel on your shoulder."

"Demon more like," I said. "Fine. I'm going to keep going with whatever this is. I'm too attached to the idea not to, and maybe it will all work out."

"Yay for positivity," said Chantelle, and I snorted at her obvious sarcasm. "Have you told him about Fantasy and Filth yet?"

"No! No. There are some things I'm just not ready to share with him, and that is one of them. If I hadn't been drunk at the time I'd discovered the whole thing in the first place, I wouldn't have told you. Not because I don't love you, but I'm really not sure you needed to know that I like telling people how to get off."

Chantelle laughed, and the sound warmed me from the inside out. "I'd have found out anyway. You know me. I'm too fucking nosy for my own good."

"That's true," I said as I rolled onto my back to stare at the ceiling. "But still, I'm not telling him. Not yet." Maybe not ever, not unless I had to. There were some things my friends didn't need to know, and the fact that I ran an audio porn channel and subscription site was one of them. If we ever got into a relationship, then it might be different, but even then, I had no idea how I'd bring it up. That was a conversation for another day and not something I needed to worry about if Gem and I were just sticking to the whole friends-who-fuck arrangement.

"I have thoughts about that," Chantelle said, "but I'm not saying anything."

"Good, I don't want to hear them," I teased. I'd probably had all the same thoughts she had, and I didn't need her to call me out on them.

"Have you recorded anything fun recently?"

"No, but I have some stuff coming up." I really needed to record the two scripts that were lurking in my documents because I'd basically run out of things to post. I'd been planning to do one today, but I wasn't sure if my head was in it.

"Is that Finn speak for 'I have things planned, but I haven't actually done them'?"

"Guilty as charged," I said with a soft chuckle.

"Do it today," Chantelle said. "It'll take your mind off the whole Gem thing. Or it'll get you super horny for next time. Either way it's a win."

"Thanks. I think." I sighed and puffed out my cheeks, knowing that I really needed to get back to work. My bed was comfy, though, and I was suddenly tempted to dig out my old Gameboy Colour and hole up in bed all afternoon playing vintage Pokémon games. "I should probably get back to work."

"So should I."

"I'll send you a list of projects and some dates. Is the same rate as last time okay?"

"That sounds great. Thanks." Chantelle paused, and I could almost hear her thinking. "Don't think too much about this Gem thing, 'kay? Just have fun. You need that."

"Okay. I'll try." We said goodbye, and I stared at the screen of my phone, wondering what to do since work didn't hold much appeal. Chantelle was right; I needed a distraction. Throwing myself off the bed, I grabbed a towel and bottle of lube and headed for my booth. Once inside I grabbed my headphones and pulled up one of the new scripts, which had a strong focus on orgasm control with a side of soft punishment.

I set the software up, adjusting the microphones—since I used two for recording audio porn—checked everything was working, took a deep breath, and tried to clear my mind.

As I opened my mouth, the image of Gem on his knees slid into my brain, meshing with the delicious sounds he'd made yesterday and my own fantasies. I took another breath, trying to focus on the script. But the image of Gem stubbornly refused to leave.

Fine. I wasn't going to deny myself. I smirked and let myself lean into the fantasy as I began to speak.

"Oh, baby, what have you been doing?"

CHAPTER TWELVE

Finn

"How the fuck did we get through so much paint already? I didn't think this place was that big?" Gem grumbled as he poured more grey slop into the paint tray. We were attempting to get the second coat on the downstairs today, but neither of us was in the mood for painting.

Gem was in a foul mood for reasons I couldn't quite discern, and I felt just as bad. I was still vacillating between the hook-up thing being a good or bad idea, even though we hadn't talked about it in the three days since it had happened. We probably should have, and maybe that was the reason we were both so grouchy. That and the fact it was freezing cold, blowing a gale, and pissing it down. I'd managed to get soaked to the skin just walking from my car to the shop. My poor umbrella had been useless in the wind, and my waterproof coat had been tested to its limit. I'd have been drier if I'd thrown myself into the sea.

"At least it doesn't need to be a thick coat," I said. "It's just to even out the colour."

"Huh, it's not like anyone's going to fucking see it. I doubt anyone will even come if I open this bloody place." Gem snapped the lid back onto the tub with more force than necessary. "Feels like I'm just pissing money away. Might as well just invest my loan in bloody pyramid schemes."

I snorted, remembering the time one of Richard's previous girlfriends had attempted to recruit me into her MLM scheme. I'd tried to say no, but she'd been incredibly forceful, and that had just increased my anxiety. I knew I was quiet, but I hated not being listened to. The only problem was that if someone I didn't know tried to force their opinion on me or refused to let me get a word in edge-ways, I tended to shut down because I couldn't cope with the situation. I still remembered the rising feeling of panic and the overwhelming urge to run.

But my family being, well, my family, hadn't been impressed with the situation and the whole thing had ended with Oscar pouring pasta salad over Richard's girl-friend's head.

It was one of those stories that had since become a family legend, and for some reason, that made me feel better about the whole thing.

"Please don't do that," I said, picking up the tray Gem had just filled. "I've already had one person try to recruit me into one of those schemes, and it didn't end well for them."

Gem snorted. "Pasta salad lady?"

"Pasta salad lady." I smiled, a feeling of warmth spreading across my chest as I watched Gem do the same. I loved the fact that I could make him smile, even on the days when he felt like shit. "That reminds me, I really must message Oscar. I haven't spoken to him for ages."

"Where is he right now?"

I thought for a second. Oscar was a travel writer who spent most of his life flitting from place to place and writing the most incredible stories about them. If I'd been the sort of person who wanted to travel, it would have made me wildly jealous, but since I was a home bird I was happy to look at his photos, read his articles, and listen to his stories about the places he'd been and the people he'd met. Since he'd started working for internationally renowned magazine *The Traveller* last summer, I'd bought two copies of every issue—one to read, and one to keep. "Singapore, I think. Then off to Sri Lanka."

"Sounds nice."

"Probably is," I said. I looked down at the tray of paint and out the window at the rain. This whole thing was sucking the life out of me and not—as Eli would say—in a fun way. The temptation to suggest we abandon this endeavour for something more fun was growing stronger by the second, and despite my moaning to Chantelle about whether or not this was a good idea, I couldn't deny that getting naked with Gem was far more interesting than painting a room while soaked to the skin. "What are your plans after this?"

Gem looked up at me from where he was fiddling with his paint roller. "Not much. Go home. Shower. Eat my weight in pasta. Maybe jerk off."

"Would you like company?"

Gem raised an eyebrow. "For which part?"

"The shower and the jerking off," I said. "Although I won't say no to pasta. We might need it."

"Are you propositioning me?" Gem asked teasingly, standing up and casting his eyes over me. I felt the heat in his gaze, and it made something possessive swirl in my stomach. I only ever wanted Gem to look at *me* like that, not anyone else. That heat was mine, that desire was mine, everything of his was *mine.* All I had to do was convince him to give it to me.

"Yes." My mouth twisted into a smirk. "I am. All you have to do is say yes or no."

Gem snorted. "I'm not going to say no."

"Good. But thank you for answering me," I said, watching as Gem's lips twitched and he swallowed. I wondered if he realised he did that when I praised him. It was a button I wanted to push further, just to see what happened. Gem looked around at the paint trays and then back at me. I knew what he was thinking because I felt the same: should we just abandon our plans here for the evening and come back tomorrow, or should we be good and get it done?

I was tempted to be firm and say we should stay, but then a trickle of icy water dripped from my hair and ran down the back of my neck.

"Let's put the paint back in the tub," I said. "It won't take long. We can come back tomorrow and finish it."

"Thank fuck." Gem reached for the paint tub and wrenched the lid off. "I thought for a second you were going to make me stay here and paint."

"No, not today."

"Is that because you're horny?"

"Maybe," I said. "Or maybe it's because you offered me a hot shower, and I've got cold water dripping down my neck. It's hard to tell."

Gem laughed as he scraped the paint back into the tub and then reached for my tray. "At least you're honest about it."

I stepped towards him, crouching down and running my finger along his jaw. "I'll always be honest with you."

That was a lie because I'd already withheld things from him. But this wasn't the time to admit them. I was already keeping so many secrets about who I was and how I felt, it was easier just to keep lying rather than start to unpick the web that surrounded me.

The moment Gem's front door closed behind us, I let out a breath and felt the tension start to leech from my muscles. This was what I'd needed ever since that first moment in the shop three days ago, and the wait had been an itch under my skin I just couldn't shake. The first time had been fun, and there'd been something delicious about the desperate urge to have Gem then and there, but I couldn't deny I preferred the comfort and privacy of a locked door where we couldn't be caught or disturbed.

Gem dropped the chain across the lock, then looked at me expectantly like he was waiting for me to tell him what to do. The possessive monster in my chest hummed with delight.

"We should shower first," I said, stepping close to him and drawing his mouth to mine because I couldn't go one more moment without kissing him. I knew this was dangerous, that I was treading a path that might lead to heartache, but any resistance was futile. His lips were cold against mine as was his cheek under my fingers. "You're cold."

"It's fine." Gem shrugged. "I'll warm up."

"Shower." The way I said it made it clear it wasn't a suggestion.

"Are you going to join me?" Gem asked as I released him and gave him a gentle push towards his bathroom.

"Perhaps. It will depend." Mostly on whether both of us would fit, but I wasn't going to say that. "But I will definitely watch."

There was a saunter in Gem's step as he headed towards the shower, and I couldn't resist walking up behind him and smacking his ass. Gem groaned, and I squeezed the firm muscle. "You're not moving fast enough," I said quietly, letting my breath ghost over his ear. "But your ass is lovely."

"Do you want to fuck me?" Gem twisted his head so he could kiss me. It gave me time to think of an answer. In truth, I did want to fuck him. I wanted to spread him out and break him down into atoms until there was nothing left but the pleasure I'd given him, but I also wanted to take this slowly, to learn everything that made Gem tick so I could better use it against him.

The only problem was that if this was just supposed to be a series of fun hook-ups, taking it slowly would be the opposite of what Gem expected, and while he might be open to that, it might also annoy him and ruin whatever this was. I knew I was overthinking, but that was what I did. I wouldn't be me if I didn't overthink the simplest question and turn it into an enormous mountain nobody could scale.

"I do," I said. "But I'm not going to. Not today." As predicted, Gem's face fell. "I know this is just for fun, but I want to take my time with you. I want you to be so desperate for me that when I finally decide to fuck you, it will be everything you've ever needed, everything you've ever wanted..." *And you'll be mine.*

The last words went unspoken, but Gem still gazed up at me with something that looked like understanding. It almost frightened me.

"Those are... those are bold claims," he said finally. I chuckled because it was cute to see Gem trying to pretend he wasn't affected by my words.

"They are, but they're also true." I brushed my lips against his, letting my tongue tease the seam of his mouth. Gem let out a muffled whine. "And we still haven't discussed everything. I'm not fucking you until we do."

"How about we do that in the shower?" Gem asked with a raised eyebrow and a devious smile. "I'll tell you what I like, and you can lay out some ground rules while we get clean. Two birds, one stone and all that."

I frowned. Usually I liked to have any form of conversation about limits, likes, and dislikes somewhere neutral because it meant both of us would have a clear head and there'd be less chance of getting distracted. I knew Gem and I weren't heading for anything like a lifestyle arrangement, but I knew I'd feel more comfortable progressing our sexual relationship if I had a better idea of what he was comfortable with. I'd always been the sort of person who liked knowing where the boundaries were before I got started. It made things simpler and reduced my anxiety knowing all the parameters.

"You okay?" Gem prompted, and I realised I'd gotten lost in my head.

"Yes, sorry. I was just… overthinking. It's a thing."

"It's not a bad thing," Gem said, reaching down to take my hand and squeeze it. "Come on. We can shower and talk, and I promise to keep my hands to myself. We can even have separate showers if you want, but I still want to watch you because I'm desperate to see you naked."

I chuckled and shook my head, but I let Gem lead me to his bathroom. "Okay, then."

Gem left me standing in the doorway of the small room while he stripped off his clothes, keeping his eyes locked on me while he did. I'd gotten hints of his body over the year and a good look at his cock when I'd blown him, but seeing him completely naked was a different experience. If I'd ever thought I'd be able to shed my feelings for Gem, that ship had sailed. He had broader shoulders than I'd expected, and his chest was dusted with dark hair that was tinged with red. I knew Gem didn't think he was attractive, but I didn't understand where that came from because, to me, he was beautiful.

"Wow," I said quietly. "You're gorgeous."

Gem rolled his eyes and scoffed. "I'm average."

I frowned. "No, you're not. I forbid you from saying that. You're not allowed to be mean to yourself."

"And if I am?" Gem raised an eyebrow, and I could see the challenge in his expression.

"Then we'll have to talk about that," I said. "Now, get in the shower."

"Are you coming too?"

I looked at the bath, which had a shower head attached to the tiled wall at the end. The bath wasn't tiny, and while it would be a squish, I could stand behind Gem. "In a minute. But first…" I walked over to the toilet, which had the lid closed, and sat down. It was as good a chair as any, and since it was right next to the shower, it would give me a good view of Gem through the glass screen. "Let's talk."

Gem climbed into the bath and turned the shower on, waiting until it was hot before he stepped under the spray. There was something about the way the water cascaded over his body that made my insides tighten. My cock throbbed, and the desire to rush through this conversation surged. Dammit, this was why I'd wanted us both to be dressed and sitting on the sofa or something.

"First," I said as I tried to assemble my thoughts, "what are we doing? Is this just sex?"

Gem bit his lip, and if it wasn't for the heat of the water,

I'd have assumed he was blushing. But I didn't know why. "That's fine with me," he said. "Still friends but with sex too."

I wanted to ask him if that was really what he wanted, but it didn't seem like the right time or place to ask. Depending on his answer, it could begin a far more complicated conversation than either of us anticipated. "Okay, that's fine." Or at least, it would have to be for now. "We can always re-evaluate if anything changes."

"Er, yeah. That works."

We left it unspoken what those changes might be. And I was fine with that. I didn't need to hear Gem say our arrangement was only going to last until his next relationship. He only wanted a fuck buddy, and I had to live with that.

"Good. So, tell me, what sort of things do you like?"

Gem reached for a bottle of body wash and poured some of the orange liquid into his hand. "I like… when you… The other day when you took control, I liked that. Like I said, it gets me out of my head. But only during sex. I couldn't do it outside of that."

"That's fine. That was my starting point anyway."

"Cool. Okay, so… God, this is kinda weird."

"Why?"

"I don't know. I'm not used to talking things out like this."

"Do you think it's unsexy? Unnecessary?" I asked as my eyebrows knitted together in a frown and I folded my arms across my chest.

"No, it's not that. Definitely not that." He chuckled and

reached down to grasp his cock between soapy fingers, and I watched as he stroked himself slowly to full hardness.

"You're not supposed to be doing that."

"Sorry." He let go reluctantly and sighed. "It's just I'm not used to someone caring enough to actually ask in advance."

My heart pounded, and it took all my effort not to reach into the shower and pull him into my arms so I could show him how much I cared. I hated how little Gem seemed to think of himself, and I wondered if he'd been so beaten down by life and the behaviour of his exes that he couldn't see how wonderful he was. It made the monster in my chest snarl with anger and jealousy because how could they have done this to him? Gem deserved so much more than their disregard.

"Don't be sorry," I said. "You should never be sorry for the way you feel. But thank you for telling me and for helping me understand."

"Sure. Although I feel like I'm kicking off some sort of fucking pity party."

"No, you're not." I waved my hand at him to continue, hoping to get us back on track. "Now, please continue telling me about all your deepest desires."

Gem laughed. "Okay, I like praise and dirty talk. I like being edged, even though I mostly do it to myself. I like getting fucked, but I also like fucking someone. I like being rimmed. I like being told what to do and being given the illusion of choice, but I also love giving someone pleasure, especially if they tell me what they want. I don't mind having my orgasms restricted, but I've only ever done that to myself, so I'm not sure how I'd feel about it with a partner. I like toys too. Mostly, like, dildos and plugs and cock rings. In terms of things I don't like… no bodily fluids except cum, no surprises, and I'm not great with pain. I'd prefer nothing more than gentle spanking, and I don't think I'd ever be into being punished. I just want this to be fun."

I listened to his list, making sure I filed away all the information for later. It all made sense and was perfectly fine with me, especially if we were just supposed to be doing this as friends for fun. "That's all fine," I said, giving him a smile. "If anything changes or something comes up that you're not sure about, then tell me. Since we're never going to do anything even vaguely non-consensual, a simple *no* is fine, and I'll always listen to you."

"That sounds good." Gem grinned at me through the glass, which was starting to steam up. He drew a smiley face in the steam, then wiped it clean. Something fluttered in my chest as I watched him—a warm feeling I hadn't felt in a long time. I stood and started to pull off my wet hoodie, dumping it on the floor before tugging my jeans over my thighs. Since they were soaked through, they were a nightmare to remove, and I ended up hopping on one foot while trying to pull them off the other leg. How fucking dignified of me.

Luckily, Gem seemed to think it was funny rather than embarrassing.

I stepped into the bath, feeling the warm water swirl around my feet. Gem reached out and pulled me against him under the spray, his skin hot and slick against mine. I reached out and wrapped my hand around his neck, drawing him to me. Gem's kiss was deliciously desperate. He ran his hands across my chest and around me until he was holding me against him. His tongue pressed into my mouth, and I moaned as he took what he needed. His cock was still hard, and it brushed against mine, causing both of us to groan.

"Can I touch you?" Gem asked, his mouth barely an inch away from mine.

"Yes. Touch me." I hadn't gotten off the last time we'd been together because I'd been too focused on bringing him pleasure. But now I wanted it all.

Gem reached down and wrapped a slick, soapy hand around our shafts, starting to jack them slowly as we exchanged more heated kisses. I was so tempted to take over, to take that control away from him, but the way he was stroking me made it impossible for me to do anything more than stand there and groan.

"Yes," I said. "Just like that. That's so good. Keep going, yes… just like that, fuck!" I gasped as Gem twisted his hand across the sensitive head of my cock. There was something about someone else's hand around my shaft that made everything feel different, but in a delicious, heightened way. "Mmm. Fuck yes. Gem, keep going. You can do it harder," I said, trying to keep my voice level and failing. Gem tightened his grip on my cock, and I let out a deep groan that seemed to echo off the tiles. "Fuck yes! Just like that. That's perfect. You're so fucking good at that. It feels amazing." My hand tightened on the back of his neck, keeping him there so I could kiss him over and over as he worked our cocks in his fist.

"F-Finn," Gem fumbled out. "I'm getting… Fuck, I'm close."

"Can you hold on for me?" I tilted his head back so I could gaze into his eyes, watching as pleasure, need, and the desire to obey me warred within them. "Just a little longer. Can you do that for me?" Gem's rhythm faltered, and I dropped my other hand to wrap it around both his fist and our dicks. Pleasure shot down my spine, and I felt my balls tighten. I knew I was close, but I needed a fraction more, and I intended to get what I needed. "Don't stop. I'm nearly there. Be good for me and wait."

"Please." The word was laced with desperation, and the sound made something purr in my chest. I loved hearing that word. "I can't…"

"Yes," I said firmly, "you can."

"I… I…"

I tightened my grip around his hand, squeezing our shafts as I made him pump them hard. Gem's eyes widened, and I smiled hungrily at him, knowing I was there. "Come for me," I whispered. "I'm right there with you. Come."

Gem cried out, his body tensing as his cock shot ribbons of cum across our fists. I felt his dick pulsing against mine, and watching his face as he came was everything I needed to push me over the edge with him. I rested my forehead against his as my chest heaved, hot water still running across my skin.

It took both of us a minute to move again. Gem slowly released our softening cocks, and I let go of his hand. He tilted his head up to kiss me softly, and something inside me tried to say that it felt like more than a *just-sex* kiss, but I refused to listen.

I knew wherever this was going, it probably wasn't going to end well because I wasn't the right man for him. But this was giving me everything I'd ever wanted, and it was easy to slip into the fantasy.

The only problem would be when reality started to bleed in.

CHAPTER THIRTEEN

Gem

SITTING on the battered old sofa in my living room, I scrolled through the digital catalogue for the distributor I was thinking of using and tried to focus on the task at hand. Now that the painting was complete and the opening date I'd chosen was looming in the distance, I really needed to figure out what the fuck I was going to stock. The business plan I'd written with Finn and Tristan had some broad parameters and example titles, but there was a big difference between that and what I wanted my finished product list to look like.

Some of it was going to depend on availability, and some would depend on my budget, but the rest was down to me and what I thought would sell well. And while I was tempted to pick the things I liked playing, along with a random selection of other stuff, I knew I had to approach this with more logic than that.

Jay, Edward, and I had already mined The Lost World's games night attendees for all the information we could, and that had given me a rough list to build on. After that, I'd spent several hours talking to my friend Lila over cocktails. She'd been part of my RPG campaign and was a good friend, although we didn't get to spend as much time together as we wanted because she was busy with her multiple jobs. She'd started by telling me this whole thing had been a long time coming, then given me some fabulous business advice, a long list of games she thought I should stock, and promised to be first through the door on opening day. All in all, it had been a fun evening.

After that, I'd spent endless hours trawling various board game subreddits and game-related websites to cross-reference and build on my initial list, which was tedious as fuck.

If I hadn't already been committed to this endeavour, spending hours taking a deep dive through the internet would have made me back out simply because there were so many people out there who seemed to spend their lives bitching about trivial shit like the fact that some art had changed or that there was some new lore for their favourite RPG that meant they couldn't be a sexist bastard anymore. The worst were the occasional neckbearded assholes kicking up a shit fit about the inclusion of women, people of colour, and LGBTQ people in their favourite games or local community.

They could all get fucked as far as I cared, and I made a mental note to get an enormous progress pride flag, like Jay had at The Lost World, and hang it up where everyone could see it. I wasn't having any fucking trolls in my shop. The idea of the customer being right didn't give them the right to be an asshole.

Since the catalogue looked good, I flicked to another page of the distributor's website—the one that talked about how to get registered as a retailer with them. I frowned at the screen and groaned. What the fuck did *minimum conditions for trade* mean? I had a brick- and-mortar store, and technically I'd have a webstore too when it was finished. Was that all they meant? I pulled up the account application form and made another noise, tempted to close the whole thing. But if I wanted to stock product, I needed to stop dithering and fill in the fucking form.

Part of me wondered why on earth I'd ever thought this was a good idea and why the fuck I'd listened to Jay and Finn when they'd encouraged me. Then I remembered Finn's smile and the way he'd said he was proud of me when we were writing the business plan, and my nerves eased. Damn you, fucking praise kink.

It was more than that though.

It was having people believe in me for once when I'd pretty much given up on myself. Finn's encouragement was the thing keeping me going when I felt like giving up. The small voice in my ear that whispered this was another thing I was going to fail at was still there, but it was getting smaller. I just hoped I could keep it at bay.

But at least when it got bad, I could get Finn to take my mind off it.

My cock throbbed at that idea, remembering the feel of his hand on mine as we'd jerked off in the shower a couple of days ago and the way he'd later let me sink to my knees and blow him while he sat on the sofa, his fingers tangling in my hair while filthy praise and soft moans filled my ears. His dick had felt so good in my mouth, and I knew I was going to need it again.

I still wasn't looking too closely at whatever this was with Finn because that would mean adding a whole new set of problems to my mental load. We'd decided this was just sex, but I wasn't convinced either of us believed that. I wanted to pretend we were just fucking. It was easier than working out what the fuck the new, complicated feelings I was starting to have for my best friend were. Easier to say this was just friendship and fucking than doing the hard, emotional work.

Once again, I was being a coward. But if it meant I got laid and neither of us got hurt, I'd take it. The problem would be when things started to get messy.

I ignored that train of thought and reached down to palm my dick through my jeans, groaning as the pressure made my cock stiffen. I looked at my laptop and the account form, then clicked to another tab. A short break wouldn't hurt, and I really needed to get off or I was never going to be able to concentrate.

Opening MyFans, I scrolled through Fantasy and Filth's account until I found one of my old favourites I knew would make me come quickly. I wasn't going for a leisurely jerk-off session here. I just needed something quick to take the edge off. I didn't have any headphones, so I kept the volume low because the last thing I needed was for old Mrs. McKinley next door to hear what I was listening to. I slid the laptop onto the cushion next to me and unbuttoned my jeans to pull out my cock as the rich voice of the narrator purred from the speaker.

"Oh, hello, baby. What are you doing? Did you want something?" There was a soft chuckle. "No, I'm supposed to be working. You know that. I promised you we could play later when I'm done." There was a little pause and another laugh. "Oh, I see. You want attention. Are you really so desperate for me that you can't wait? Is that right, baby? Are you a desperate, needy, slutty boy who needs to be played with?"

"Yes. Fuck yes." I groaned, spitting on my palm and reaching for my dick, pumping myself slowly as I listened. I'd never be the sort of person to demand attention, but the fantasy was sexy, and I loved the way the narrator spoke with a calm control that demanded respect. It made my cock ache in desperation.

"Come here, then," the narrator said. Then he tutted and let out a low, chastising sound. "No, baby, on your knees. Crawl to me. Beg for it. Tell me how much you want my cock, and if you're a very good boy, I'll give it to you." He groaned. "That's it. Fuck, you look so pretty on your knees for me. That's it, look up at me, don't look away. Aww, baby, you're so hard already for me. Are you that desperate?"

"Oh God. I fucking need it," I said as I reached my other hand down to shove my jeans out of the way so I could spread my legs. I rolled my balls between my fingers as the sound of the narrator slapping his cock against his hand slid into my ears.

"Open wide for me. That's it. No"—the man growled and a shiver of delight shot down my spine—"I didn't tell you to suck it, did I? I told you to open your mouth, but you wanted more because you're such a needy, desperate slut for me. And now I've got my hand in your hair, and I'm holding you here while you look up at me from your knees. Do you think you can be good for me? Yes?"

"Yes. I'll be good."

"Good. Now open your mouth. Wider, that's it. Good boy." I moaned at the sounds of slapping. "Do you like it when I slap my cock against your cheeks… your lips… your tongue. I know you want it, and I love seeing you look at me like this—when you know your place and know that you're mine. You'll take what I give you because you're so good for me. But I know you'll tell me if you want something different or if you don't like it because you're a good slut who tells me what he wants. Aren't you?"

All I could do was groan. Tightening my grip on my cock, I began to jerk myself faster before sliding my other hand between my legs to tease my hole. I really wished I had a fucking dildo in here or even some lube because I needed something inside me. I could get a finger in with spit, but it wasn't going to be enough.

I'd said this was just going to be a quick break, but now I wanted to drag it out. The two plans warred inside my head, but the desperate need to be filled won out. Hitting Pause on the audio, I kicked my jeans off, grabbed my laptop, and made a frantic dash to the bedroom. Throwing the laptop on my bed, I grabbed some lube and my favourite dildo and climbed onto the mattress.

When the audio started again, the sounds pouring out of my speakers made me moan with need.

"Suck it. That's it. Mmm, fuck, get it all the way down your throat. Show me how much you want it," the narrator said, his voice heavy with desire. His words were punctuated by low, possessive growls and deep groans of pleasure that made my whole body come alive. I wondered if Finn would ever make noises like that… If he did, I'd probably die.

I lubed up the dildo as the narrator talked about how it felt to have his cock sucked and how perfect I was on my knees for him. It oddly reminded me of the way Finn had spoken to me the other day, but I brushed the thought away.

"That's enough. Fuck, I said that's enough." His voice was rough, and he sounded as desperate as I felt. I groaned as I pumped my cock again, my slick fingers starting to work my ass open enough for my toy. "Get up here and give me a kiss. God, you look so fucking perfect like that. Mmm, do you need more? Does my little slut want more? Was having my cock in your mouth not enough?"

"No… I want… Fuck, I want you to fuck me," I said, suddenly wishing Finn was there so I could feel his cock inside me. He hadn't fucked me yet, only teased, and the longer he drew it out, the more I wanted it. I pulled my fingers out of my ass and grabbed the dildo, pressing it to my slick, stretched hole as the narrator groaned, murmuring praise as he grabbed lube and began to finger his partner open. I was so desperate for more, but I loved moving at the same speed as the audio because it allowed me to sink deeper and deeper into the scenario. Holding the dildo there, I waited, releasing my grip on my cock so I didn't shoot my load before I was ready. This quick jerk off to relax had turned into a full-on session, but I didn't care because it was everything I needed.

The narrator groaned, and I shuddered with pleasure. "That's it. You're being so good for me. Now, I'm going to put the tip of my cock right against your hole… Fuck, just like that. And then… Mmm…" With a moan, I pushed the dildo slowly into my hole, relishing the burn since I hadn't quite opened myself up enough. "Fuck, mmm. Fuck, baby, move your hips slowly for me. I want you to take it all." He growled, and I moaned, pressing it all the way in until I felt the silicone balls bumping against my ass.

"Fuck," I said, closing my eyes and listening to the other man's moans and soft words, unable to stop myself from imagining Finn above me, his cock deep inside me as he whispered filth in my ear. My dick pulsed, and I wrapped my hand tightly around the shaft, jerking myself as slowly as I could manage while starting to fuck myself with the dildo.

"Fuck, baby, you look so good on my dick. Such a good boy for me." The narrator moaned again. "I can't wait… mmm, to, fuck… fill you with my cum. Because I love filling you with my load. I want you to jerk your cock for me… Fuck, I want you to come for me… because when you do, your ass feels so good around my cock, and it always, shit, always gets me there too. And it's your job to make me feel good, baby. You wanted to distract me, so now you have to make me feel good. But I know you will, fuck, because you're such a good boy for me."

I groaned as red-hot pleasure burned down my spine, making my balls tighten. I thrust the dildo in and out of my ass as hard and fast as I could, angling it so I could hit that sweet spot inside me over and over again. My fingers tightened around my cock, and I knew I wasn't going to make it to the end. I was going to come, and there was nothing I could do to stop it—or at least, nothing I wanted to do.

"Fuck, baby, that's it… Make yourself come for me," the narrator purred. "Jerk yourself hard. I know you want to please me…"

The rest of his words were lost in my shout as I came hard, cum splattering my fist and the old jumper I was wearing as my ass tightened around the dildo, milking every drop of pleasure out of it.

I lay on the bed, staring up at the ceiling with wide eyes and a heaving chest as the audio continued to play. Hazily, I reached over to hit the Pause button on the recording, which still had another four or five minutes to play. Next time, I'd make it to the end… but only because the narrator sounded so amazing when he came.

I let out a long, shuddering breath as the last vestiges of pleasure drained away, leaving me with nothing but a deep, satisfied feeling and a wave of tiredness. Pulling out the dildo, I dropped it on the bed beside me and frowned. There was something niggling at the back of my mind, though I couldn't put my finger on what it was.

Dragging myself off the bed, I headed for the bathroom to wash my hand and the dildo and dump my cum-stained clothes into the washing basket. I gazed into the mirror above the sink, thinking about the conversation Finn and I had had there. It had been a weird as fuck place to have a discussion about boundaries, but I was glad we'd had it. It had been kind of hot listening to Finn ask what I wanted and watching his face as I'd told him. He'd tried to keep his expression neutral, but it had been hard to miss the way his lips had twitched or the heat burning in his eyes.

I needed the next time to happen soon because I really wanted to get to someone's bedroom and move from shower handjobs into something more intense.

The niggling thought made itself known again. Except this time, it had more of a shape.

There was something about the way the narrator said things like *just like that* and *be good* that had a familiar weight to them. Like I'd heard them recently but in a different situation. I frowned and headed back to my room to find some clean clothes. As I pulled on a hoodie, my brain slowly replayed the shower with Finn and the later blow job, mentally attempting to lay the vocals out alongside the narrator.

Maybe they were similar, but that didn't mean anything. There were only so many ways you could say dirty things, and if my cock was involved, I was pretty sure my brain wasn't really paying attention anyway.

Picking up my laptop, I walked back to the sofa so I could get back to the supplier account form. The time for distractions was over. I needed to get this done if I ever wanted to get any bloody stock. But then I realised the narrator had uploaded a new video—a Q&A—and all my other thoughts went out the window.

I hit the button for the video, figuring it would at least give my heart rate a little longer to return to normal, even if my brain was trying to find a connection that wasn't there.

"Hello, everyone," said the voice, sounding far more relaxed this time around. "Thanks for joining me for this month's Q&A. We haven't done one of these in a while, so thank you for submitting your questions. I'm sorry if I don't get a chance to answer all of them." There was something warm and familiar about his speaking voice outside of the audio porn, and I swallowed. "First question: are you really British, or do you just know how to do a good British accent?"

He chuckled softly, and I frowned, my brain starting to whirr.

"Yes, I am British. This is my actual accent and my actual voice. I hope that doesn't disappoint you. Next question: how did you get into producing erotic audio? Love your work so much." He paused for a second, and when he spoke again, I swore I could hear him smiling. "Thank you, that means a lot. I started producing this for fun after some encouragement from a friend. I made the mistake of showing them some other work I'd found on the internet one night, and they said I should give it a try. They're not the sort of person to take no for an answer, so here I am." He laughed again. "But I'm glad they encouraged me because this job gives me so much creative freedom, and I love recording all these fantasies for you. And knowing that there are a lot of people getting off to my work is quite powerful, so there's that."

I snorted. Yeah, I bet it was. Especially if you were the sort of man who liked being in control.

"Are you single?" was the next question, and I found myself holding my breath for reasons I couldn't put my finger on. It wasn't as if I was going to suddenly meet the man—the UK wasn't *that* small, and the universe wasn't that kind. Besides, liking a guy for the way he could get me off didn't mean I'd like his personality. He could be a wanker in reality. But a little voice in my head whispered *if it was Finn then maybe…*

I shook the thought away because this was starting to approach the realm of far-reaching conjecture. "Yes, I am," said the man. "I'd like to date, but it's hard to find someone because I'm so busy. There's someone I'm interested in, but I'm not sure they feel the same. But that's probably far too much information, so yes, I'm single."

Something tugged in my chest, but I didn't have time to think about it because the narrator was speaking again.

"What do you do for fun? Apart from making super sexy audios that make me ridiculously hard." He let out a soft breath. "That's always good to hear. I hope you're always a good boy. But for fun, well, I'm quite boring to be honest. I play a lot of board games and role-playing games —the Dungeons and Dragons kind, not the sexy kind—and I've just finished helping a friend test a game." My frown deepened, the numbers in my head starting to add up, a very clear picture starting to emerge. But I still wasn't sure if I was just imagining things and jumping to conclusions or whether my assumptions were correct. "Apart from that, I play a lot of video games. I'm replaying a lot of the *Final Fantasy* games at the moment because I have a lot of different old consoles, and I'm a nerd. Like a super nerd." He laughed again, and this time there was a soft little hiccupping sound at the end.

The pieces snapped into place, and I shot up off the sofa like I'd been struck by lightning.

CHAPTER FOURTEEN

Finn

I STARED at the pieces of the large bookcase laid out on the floor in front of me, complete with bags of screws and IKEA's finest pictorial instructions. There was absolutely no way we should be able to get this wrong. So why were we on attempt number three already?

"This is bollocks," muttered Gem darkly, picking up the instruction booklet and skimming through it. "My nephew could do this, and he's seven. Why the fuck can't we get this right?"

"Beats me," I said as I shook my head. I was sure I'd built these—or some variation of them—before, so it shouldn't have been that hard. Maybe it was because I kept getting distracted by Gem's face or the way his hands reached for the bits of wood, or the way he looked on all fours, bending over the laid-out pieces. I frowned and tried to snap myself out of it. This was not the time to be focusing on how handsome Gem was or how much I wanted to fuck him. This was the time for building furniture. And maybe if it went well, the other parts could come later.

"Okay, let's try this again." Gem peered at the paper and then looked at the various parts in front of him. "Those two end pieces, put them next to each other with that groove thing on the outside and the four holes at the top." I was sure this was how we'd had them the first time, but not the second, so at least we were already doing better than one of our attempts. "Then," Gem said, turning the manual around to show me, "we need those twelve screws. The big ones with the weird, hexagonal bit in the middle."

I looked at the various bags of screws that were littered around us. We'd opened several and strewn their contents across the shop floor before realising it would have been easier to keep everything in their separate little bags or put them in bowls—anything to keep them together. "Here," I said as I handed some to Gem. "I should have realised we'd already opened them."

"No worries." He took the proffered screws and began to twist them into the holes, spreading the instructions out between us so we could make sure we were filling the right ones. "You know, I'm sure there's a bad hole or screw joke in here somewhere."

I chuckled. "If I was Eli, or even Lewis, I'd have made it by now. Unfortunately, I'm not that funny off the top of my head."

"I think you're funny," Gem said. "Just different funny. Eli's like loud, dramatic, over the top funny. You're sharper.

Like he's a battering ram, and you're a dagger or something."

"I'd say more letter opener, but I appreciate the sentiment." I smiled at him, and Gem snorted. He said something under his breath I didn't catch. "Sorry?"

"Nothing," he said quickly. "Just bitching about these screws. I should have bought one of those electric screwdrivers."

My eyebrows knitted into a frown, but I didn't say anything. I didn't want to push Gem into admitting something he wasn't comfortable with, especially if it involved me.

"At least we seem to have put them in the right place this time," I said.

"Yeah, we've filled the correct holes. It just takes a good screw." He winked at me, and I groaned.

"That was bad. Like horrible, not even funny bad."

"Then why are you smiling?"

"Because it was so horrible I'm wondering why I even had to listen to it."

"You're gonna hurt my feelings, you know," Gem said with a wry smile.

"Are you that dramatic?"

"I might be."

"I'm related to Eli, and that man is the very definition of dramatic. He owns two of those ridiculous pageant tiaras for crying out loud. He wore both of them at Christmas and tried to get us to call him Your Majesty."

Gem laughed. "Did it work?"

"No. Lewis and Jules took the piss out of him until he

gave up," I said, chuckling at the memory. "But my point still stands. Unfortunately, you will never be as dramatic as my brother and, therefore, not dramatic at all."

"Bloody drag queens! Ruining my attempts at theatrics."

"It's what Eli does best." Although, to give him his due, even Eli knew he could be melodramatic, and half the time I thought he did it just for the fun of it and to piss off Richard. I looked down at the pieces in front of us, which were now fitted with screws. "Okay, what next?"

"Those bits, I think," Gem said, pointing at two shelf-type pieces and a thinner strip, which I assumed was some form of supporting foot. "With the dowels." He picked up some short, wooden dowels and rammed them into a couple of holes before starting to fit them to the boards. I frowned, looking at the instructions and then back at Gem.

"You're putting them in the wrong way round."

"No, I'm not."

"Yes," I said, "you are."

"How? They're meant to go in these slots." Gem pointed at the paper in front of us. "See?"

"Yes, but they're meant to go in the other way around." I jabbed at the diagram and a small box with two additional pictures, one which had a large X through it. "The wood grain needs to face the groove because that's the back of the bookcase." I reached out and plucked the shelf from Gem's hands and twisted it around before slotting it into place. "See?"

"I don't see," Gem grumbled.

"Trust me."

"Fine. But if it's wrong—"

"It's not wrong," I said with a raised eyebrow. Then I grinned. "Just do as you're told."

"God no! Where's the fun in that?" Gem's expression was teasing as he slotted the other shelf into place. Despite his protestations, he'd turned it to match the one I'd done.

"I'm beginning to understand why they say couples should never build furniture together, especially if it's from IKEA." The moment I said it, I wondered if I'd overstepped. I'd meant it in a fun, offhand way, but maybe Gem would see it differently. We weren't a couple, and I didn't want him to think that was how I saw us. I mean, *it was*, but that was only in the deepest, darkest corners of my heart where I hoarded that dream like a precious stone.

But Gem just threw his head back and laughed, the sound bouncing joyfully off the freshly painted walls. "Right? I mean we're on attempt three already. I think if we were married, we'd have just given up by now."

"To throw pieces at each other or fuck?"

"Definitely the second," Gem said. "I've never heard of the first. Another family legend?"

"Yes," I said. My family really did have a lot to answer for. "When Mimbles and my dad were first married, they apparently decided to try to build a dining room set together. It apparently ended with Mimbles jabbing him in the ribs with a chair leg and throwing a bag of screws at him. So not that bad really, but DIY really does bring out the worst in couples. And you know how stubborn my mother is. Dad was apparently just as bad."

"I believe that." He'd only met Mimbles and the rest of

my parents once, at Eli's competition, but it was enough to leave an impression. "My mum just did all the DIY in our house. She can pretty much do anything. Except plumbing —she refuses to do plumbing because apparently she tried once and ended up flooding the house. She always told us that her favourite Christmas present was the year my dad bought her a new drill, just after they first got married. Everyone thought he was a terrible husband, but she loved it. It's the one she still uses, even though it's practically ancient now."

"See? I think that's the way to do it." I looked at the instructions and reached for some round, plastic screw top things that would hold the base board and middle shelf in place. "You need one person to just build everything and the other to either leave them alone or only assist when two pairs of hands are really needed as long as they promise not to say anything."

"Does that mean I just need to leave you to get on with it?"

"No." I looked at Gem, who was smiling at me again. It was the same beautiful smile that always made my whole body light up like a Christmas tree. "If anything, I should let you build them, but we've already established—"

"I suck? And not in a good way."

I snorted. "Yes. That."

"I could suck in a good way," Gem said, waggling his eyebrows ridiculously. I could barely keep a straight face.

"Maybe later if you're good and help me with these." I gestured at the pile of cardboard boxes that contained numerous bookshelves and display units. "Or at least half of them."

"You're no fun." He'd said it teasingly, but I felt my face fall. I'd heard those words before but never in a good way. It was always in a *you're too quiet and shy to be fun* way, and it had always stung. Gem must have noticed because his expression changed, and he reached out across the half-constructed bookshelf to cup my face in his hand. "I'm sorry. I didn't mean to hurt you."

"It's fine."

"No, it's not." He ran his thumb along my cheek, and I leant into the touch. "I don't like seeing you upset, and I don't want to be the bastard that does that."

I attempted to shrug, but it was half-hearted at best. "You didn't mean it."

"Mean it or not, it still doesn't mean it wasn't a dick move." He tilted my head to look at me, his eyes roaming over my face. It was strange to be on the other end of the gesture because it was usually something I did to him. But this wasn't a heated, controlling tilt, this was softer. Like he wanted to look at my face to make sure I wasn't hiding from him. It was… sweet and almost overwhelming. "Have people said that to you before? The no fun thing."

"Yes," I said. There was no point in hiding it from him, and I wanted to be honest. Gem deserved that from me. "Mostly when I was at school and then at uni. I've never really been very sociable or much of a partier. There are always too many people, it's too noisy, and I can't… I don't know… Control the situation doesn't sound right, but it's how I feel. There are too many variables I don't have control over, and if I'm with people I don't know that well, then I don't feel safe. But it's hard to explain that to people you've just met, and at uni they just took it to mean I was weird and antisocial." I sighed. "Chantelle was nice about it though. She never made me go out with her unless I wanted to, and usually we'd just drink and chill together until she went out. Then when she came back, I'd make us toast, and we'd sit on the sofa." Usually we'd end up cuddled up together while she told me about her night. The only exceptions were the nights she went home with someone, but she was always good at remembering to text me to let me know where she was. She'd always send me a picture of the person too, just in case.

"I'm sorry," Gem said. "I was probably one of those wankers who'd have teased you. But it was because I was an insecure cunt who hid behind alcohol and being loud in an attempt to fake confidence. I grew up a lot after I left uni. So trust me when I say those people were assholes, and I'm sorry they made you feel that way."

"It's fine, but thank you."

He leant over and kissed me softly as if he could take all my troubles away with his mouth. It worked, though, and I felt myself relax.

"At least you had Chantelle. She sounds like an interesting person."

"She is," I said with a small smile. "You'd like her. She's coming to stay next week, and she's bringing Kelsey too. We should all hang out. That is if you want to? How do you feel about children?"

"I'd love that, and kids are great. My nephew is one of

my favourite people." Just the way Gem said it made it sound like the absolute truth, not just a polite pleasantry. My only problem would be getting Chantelle to keep her mouth shut, but I knew she'd do it if I asked, even if she didn't agree with my tactics. "Just let me know when and where."

"I will."

We lingered there for a moment, close together with Gem's hand on my cheek. I wished it could have lasted longer, but the reality of a looming opening date and piles of flat-pack furniture were too hard to ignore.

"Come on," I said eventually. "We should get these bookcases built."

"Yeah. We should."

Gem pulled away reluctantly, and the look on his face made me wonder just how far we'd stumbled away from *just friends* already.

CHAPTER FIFTEEN

Gem

FUCK THIS. Fuck that. Fuck all of this bloody bollocks. This was a wank idea from the start, and I never should have listened to Jay.

I stared at the mess of boxes, shelving parts and random shit littering the stockroom. The mess had even started to seep out into the main bulk of the shop, and it was starting to look like a never-ending sea of chaos. The fact that it was ten at night on a Friday wasn't improving my mood. I'd been at work all day and spent all evening here, and now I was exhausted.

"Where the fuck does it all come from?" I muttered darkly to myself as I grabbed the remains of a cardboard box and viciously ripped it apart so I could fold it down and shove it in the growing pile of recycling. Since the shop's bin was full, I was having to stick everything in my car and take it to the tip, which meant spending more of my precious free time doing random shit and less doing something productive. I'd hardly had any downtime since I'd started this fucking venture, and it was starting to catch up with me.

I needed food, sleep, and a good fuck or wank—I wasn't picky—and not necessarily in that order.

I also needed to tidy this shit up and finish getting the furniture built and in place so I could start getting stock in and arranging it. I had no idea whether any of the big box games, like Gloomhaven or Descent: Legends of the Dark would even fit on the shelves I'd gotten. I didn't think the depth would be a problem; it was more likely going to be the height of the shelves and the weight of the fucking things. I'd probably just have to have one out on display and a couple in the back in case they got sold. Not that there was a lot of room in the stockroom for excess.

Grabbing another box off the floor, I checked there was nothing important inside it before ripping it up and squashing it. It was oddly cathartic.

There was a knock at the front door, and I turned, trying to work out who the fuck would be here this late. I walked out of the stockroom, still carrying the remains of a box and saw, through the glass, Finn standing outside in the glow of the streetlamps. My heart soared, the clouds of my mood rolling back like the sun breaking through after a storm.

"Hey," I said as I pulled open the door. "I didn't think you were coming tonight."

Finn shrugged and stepped inside, holding up a plastic bag. The delicious scent of Chinese takeaway wafted out of it, making my stomach rumble and my mouth water. "I know, but you said you were coming here straight after work, and from your messages, it didn't sound like it was going well, so I figured I could at least bring you dinner."

I closed the door behind him, trying to work out what to say. Usually, I wasn't lost for words, but I was now. Who knew it would take a man just showing me basic kindness to sweep me off my feet? Or a man reading between the lines and realising I felt like shit. God, was this what my sister had been banging on about for years—about my bar for relationships being on the floor and men still tripping over it?

"Is this okay?" Finn asked, and I realised I hadn't said anything. I'd just been staring at him, still holding chunks of cardboard.

"Yeah," I said. "It's fucking amazing. Thanks."

Finn smiled, and my chest felt like it might explode. What was it about Finn's smile that could change everything? I'd never met anyone who made me feel so relieved and cared for with one simple expression. Like I was worth something to him.

"No worries." Finn walked over to the counter and put the bag down, quickly clearing some space. A pang of embarrassment shot through me because I should have been able to keep the place tidy.

"Sorry about the mess," I said as I dumped my shredded box onto the pile of recycling to go to the tip. Finn was rummaging in the bag and laying out various foil tubs and plastic containers alongside a plastic bag full of prawn crackers.

"It's not a problem. Honestly, it's to be expected with

everything going on." He rummaged in the bag and produced a handful of paper napkins, some plastic cutlery, a couple of pairs of disposable chopsticks, and two empty tubs. "I didn't think you'd have anything to eat with, so I asked if they had anything spare. Also, I asked for some extra tubs since I didn't think you'd have plates, and it's kind of awkward to just pass a tub of rice back and forth without spilling it everywhere."

"That was nice of them."

"I hope the food I got is okay," Finn said, popping open the lids. "I got some fried rice, beef chow mein, chicken in oyster sauce, and some prawn toast. I figured I'd just get what we'd had before."

"It's fucking perfect." I grinned at him and walked around the counter to the other side. I picked up one of the empty tubs and began helping myself to food, resisting the temptation to just stick my head into one of them. Looking around, I realised there was one small snag in our dinner plans—the shop still didn't have any fucking furniture that wasn't bookcases. "Are you all right with sitting on the floor again? I really need to get a stool or a couple of chairs to perch on."

"The floor is fine," Finn said, taking his tub of food, a spoon, and some chopsticks and settling himself cross-legged on the floor with his back against the counter.

I joined him, and for a few minutes there was no sound except us eating. The food was warm and delicious and everything I wanted, and the fact that Finn had brought it made it a hundred times better. If we hadn't just been friends, I would have called this a date.

"So, how was your day?" Finn asked.

I shrugged. "Could have been worse. Work was fine, just busy, and I'm back tomorrow too, which means I'm going to be knackered on Sunday, but at least I'm off. This two-job thing is killing me, and this one isn't even up and running."

Finn nodded. "Yes, but this one requires a lot of physical and mental energy because you're doing most of it yourself. Even when I'm here, you're still making the decisions because it's your business. Plus, you're dealing with people all day, and that's exhausting in itself. It would be different if your second job didn't require any face-to-face interaction or physical labour."

"I guess." For a second, I wondered if my hunch about Finn having a sexy second job might be true since the way he spoke made it sound like he was speaking from experience. But I pushed the thought away. Now wasn't the time, and I had no idea how I'd even bring it up. If I did, I'd want to play it off as a joking enquiry, and I didn't have the energy for that. "I'm just worried I've made the wrong decision, that this is going to be a fucking disaster, and I haven't even started yet." Finn's eyes narrowed, and his lips pursed like he was debating whether or not to give me a bollocking. I grinned. "Come on, you can't tell me you wouldn't be worried too?"

"I suppose," Finn said. "In fact, I know I would be. I felt the same when I started narrating—that it wasn't going to work out, and in six months, I'd be back to figuring out what to do with the rest of my life. But I knew I had to give it everything I had because if I went into it thinking I was going to fail, then I was dooming myself from the start. You can be worried, that's absolutely fine, but what you can't do is let that fear hold you back or dictate your actions. If you think you're going to fail, then you're going to fail. It's like starting a marathon with your laces tied together. You'll just fall over and stop instead of untying them and getting back up." He paused and shook his head. "That's a very bad analogy. I'm sorry. But do you get my point?"

"That I shouldn't take up running?"

Finn bumped my shoulder and grinned. "Don't be a dick."

"Fine, I get it. Basically, I shouldn't be such a pessimistic bastard and should give this a fair shot before I decide it's shit and pack it in."

"Yes, something like that." Finn looked at me with that firm expression that always sent heat coursing through my veins. "Promise me you'll try?"

"I promise." I meant it too. This wasn't some fake bullshit I was spewing to make him happy; this was a promise I intended to keep. Because I'd do anything for Finn, and that realisation wasn't as shocking as it should have been.

Finn nodded in a pleased way and shoved the rest of his chow mein into his mouth. It shouldn't have been as cute as it was. "What?" he asked around the mouthful of food.

"Nothing," I said with a wry chuckle. Finn frowned, but it just made his face look very round and squishy. "You look like a hamster when you do that. A very cute hamster."

Finn swallowed. "Thanks? I'm not sure whether being a hamster is a good thing or not."

"It is." I scraped my last bit of fried rice and oyster

chicken onto a spoon and debated whether to get a second helping. I half hoped Finn would let me take the leftovers home for lunch tomorrow because there was nothing as good as reheated takeaway the next day. Except cold pizza for breakfast. That was the king of all leftovers. "What are your plans now?"

"I came to help," Finn said.

"You don't have to. I know you came all this way, but…" I sighed and rubbed my face. "I'm just kinda done with today. Before you arrived, I was ripping up boxes."

"No worries." He pulled his bottom lip between his teeth like he was debating what to say.

"You could come back to mine," I said. "We don't have to do anything if you don't want."

"What if I want to?" Finn asked with a smirk that sent shivers across my skin. It was like he'd flicked a switch. Shy, quiet Finn was gone, and in his place was the sharp, sexy man who made me crumble with one look. "I did come all this way. It would be a shame not to make the most of it."

"It would," I said. My mouth was suddenly dry, and I licked my lips, wishing I had some water. "Do you want to go now?"

"In a minute. Much as I desperately want to fuck your brains out, I'm currently very full of Chinese food, and I don't think the two things would mix well."

I threw my head back and laughed, knocking it against the counter. "Yeah, we should probably wait a bit."

"We could fold some boxes while we wait," Finn suggested with a teasing smile.

"Fuck that shit. They can wait until morning."

"Okay then, no box folding." Finn relaxed beside me, resting his hand on my thigh. "By the way, do we need to stop and get anything?"

"No. I have plenty of lube."

"Good. I just wanted to check," he said. "Do you like jacking off with it? Or do you use it with toys?"

"Er, both." I felt my face flame, but I had no idea why the fuck I was suddenly embarrassed. Maybe it was just the casual way he'd asked.

"Interesting. I'd like to see them one day."

My cock throbbed inside my jeans, and I reached down to palm myself. I couldn't imagine anything hotter than letting Finn play with me.

Unless he wanted to tell me how to use them while he watched.

CHAPTER SIXTEEN

Finn

THE DOOR TO Gem's flat clicked shut behind us, and I couldn't resist pulling him into a kiss now that we were truly alone. We'd spent the past hour chilling at the shop, sitting on the floor and chatting quietly about everything and nothing until we felt the urge to move. This hadn't been my specific plan for the evening, but it felt like the natural progression. I loved how easy things felt with Gem —nothing felt forced or like an obligation.

We were here because we wanted to be.

Gem groaned against my lips as I slipped my hand under his jumper. His skin was hot against my fingers, and I suddenly found the layers of clothing between us annoying. I needed to see Gem naked again, and I needed to see him writhing in pleasure while I fucked him, moaning as I whispered filth into his ear. I would take away his stress with my body and my voice and make him think of nothing but me. Everything we'd done so far was a fantasy come to life, and it made the possessive monster in my chest purr with happiness when Gem responded to my words with broken pleas and desperate moans.

I'd used the same words on him as I used in my scripts since both scenarios were different extensions of me, and I loved being able to use them on a real partner instead of a nebulous listener I had no connection too. That didn't mean I didn't enjoy the power that came with my blog, but there was something heady about experiencing it in reality rather than just reading comments on a screen.

Even if I had started thinking about Gem more and more when I recorded my Fantasy and Filth scenes.

I cupped my hand around the back of Gem's neck, holding him in place. "I want you," I said. "I want to watch you strip down for me, then get on your knees and suck my cock because you look so perfect kneeling for me." Gem groaned against my mouth, his fingers fisting in the front of my t-shirt. I couldn't help chuckling at his desperation before pressing a slow, teasing kiss to his mouth. Just one. "Then I want you on your hands and knees for me, baby. I want to play with your hole and get you ready for me before I fuck you. I want to make you feel good, and that means you're going to come for me while I'm buried deep inside your tight, perfect ass. And if I want to use you, you're going to take it all." Gem moaned, louder this time. "How does that sound? Do you want that?"

"Yes," Gem said, his voice a harsh whisper laced with need. "Please, I want that. I want all of that."

"Good." I tilted my head back so I could look over his

face. "You're so handsome… so perfect for me… I'm going to…" I trailed off, the words *make you mine* lingering on my tongue. Would they be too heavy? If I said them, would they ruin the moment and destroy what we had? Even if I didn't mean them in *that* way and it was only something I said in the heat of the moment, it could still change everything. Gem was looking at me with wide eyes, waiting for me to finish my sentence. I chose the safe option. "I'm going to make you feel so good."

"Please. I need you."

Gem's words ignited a fire inside me, and I felt heat and desire burning in my eyes. The way he responded to my touch, to my words… it made me shiver. This man was everything to me, and if he asked, I'd give him anything he wanted. And that was more dangerous than I could possibly have imagined.

I kissed him fiercely, nipping his lip and swallowing his moan before I pushed him away. "Your bedroom. Now. Get out some lube and put it beside the bed, then I want to watch you strip for me. If at any point you're not comfortable with something, you are to say so immediately. Fantasy is different from reality, and I never want you to do anything you don't want to, even if you agreed to it in principle. Do you understand?"

"Yes."

"Are you still okay without condoms? I know we haven't been using them since we both had previous negative results, but this is another step, and I just want to be completely sure."

"Yeah, I'm fine without them." Gem nodded and swallowed, looking at me as if he wanted to say something else. Whatever it was, he changed his mind. Instead, he grabbed my hand and pulled me towards his room.

I watched as he did as he was told, digging out a bottle of lube before turning to me and slowly removing his clothes, his eyes never leaving mine. I was tempted to take over, to strip him down piece by piece and then shower him with kisses, but tonight, I was feeling horny and possessive, and I wanted to pretend he belonged to me.

As Gem unbuttoned his jeans, I reached for my own hoodie and t-shirt. Gem grinned, trying to watch me as he finished stripping off, and I snorted as he almost tripped over his own feet. "Careful," I said. "Don't hurt yourself. We can't have any fun if I have to cart you to hospital."

"I'm not going to break anything," Gem said with a wave of his hand. "I might just bruise something."

"Well, I don't want you doing that either." I moved closer to him, lifting his jaw with my finger. "You are... just... Please don't hurt yourself. I'll still be here when you've finished getting undressed."

Gem frowned, and I wondered if he'd realised what I'd said hadn't been what I'd meant. But how could I tell him he was precious to me? That he was too beautiful to see bruised.

I stepped back and finished removing my clothes while Gem did the same. I slid my hand down my chest and reached for my cock, giving it a few leisurely pumps. Gem licked his lips. I smirked and beckoned him towards me with one finger. "Is this what you want? Do you want to suck my cock?" Gem groaned and nodded, dropping to his knees in front of me and reaching for my shaft. I put my hand on his head, frowning at him as I held him just out of reach—not hard or with any real force but enough to make him stop.

"I didn't hear an answer. I said, is this what you want? Do you want to suck my cock? I told you that you always need to answer me properly, so answer me, or I'll stop." I stroked my finger down his cheek, loving the way Gem looked up at me with awe and desire. He was so fucking perfect for me. "Do you need me that much, baby? Do you need to feel my cock filling your mouth, giving you what nobody else can?"

"Yes," Gem said. "Please, I need it, Finn. I want to suck you, want to make you feel so good… want you, fuck, I want you to fuck me and fill me with your load. Please… I need you."

"You're so good for me." I caressed his head, pulling his mouth gently towards my cock. "And you look so perfect on your knees for me. Open wide. That's it… Fuck!" I groaned as Gem wrapped his lips around the head of my dick and sucked. "Oh fuck! Yes, just like that. Take it deeper, nice and slow… Take it as deep as you can."

Gem moaned around me, the vibrations thrumming through my shaft and sending ripples of pleasure through my body. I gripped his hair slightly tighter than I'd intended, and Gem groaned again, his hand reaching for his own cock. Interesting. I was tempted to tell him not to touch himself, but as long as he didn't come, I didn't mind him edging himself a little. It would make it so much more fun when he was fucking himself on my cock and begging for release.

I pulled Gem deeper onto my cock until I felt the head bump against the back of his throat. Gem gagged but didn't pull back. Instead, he swallowed around my cock and made me groan. I tightened my grip on his hair and Gem moaned around me, starting to work my dick with a desperate eagerness I'd not seen before.

"Oh fuck, baby. That's… fuck, that's fucking perfect. Just… just like that. You look so good like this," I said, barely able to keep my composure as I let out a low, rumbling growl. "It feels so amazing. That's it… show me how much you want it… Fuck!"

Gem's mouth tightened around my shaft, groaning around me, and I heard the tell-tale slap of skin as he jerked himself off hard and fast. That was not going to work.

I gripped his hair and tilted his head up towards me, and wow… he looked perfect like that. His mouth was slick and red, stretched around my cock, and his eyes were wide and slightly wet where they'd watered from choking on my dick. Desperate need was written across his expression, and he was so beautiful that I wanted to remember this moment forever.

There was something about moments like this—where the other person was so beautifully vulnerable—that made my heart clench. Gem was giving me everything I'd ever wanted, and it was making me fall for him in ways I hadn't expected. I'd never dreamt we'd click on such a deep, sexual level, but we were perfect partners, and it heightened every experience into something exquisite.

"Look at me," I said, keeping my voice calm but knowing there was an edge to it that wasn't to be disobeyed. "You're doing such a good job, baby, but you're not allowed to come. You have to wait until I'm buried deep in your ass for that and only when I tell you to let go. Do you understand?"

Gem nodded, and there was a muffled affirmative sound from around my cock. I chuckled and released his head, pulling him off my cock with a slick pop then groaning as I noticed just how wet and swollen his mouth was. "Yes," Gem said. "I understand."

"Good," I whispered, leaning down to capture his mouth in a deep kiss. I wanted to draw this out, but my patience was starting to wear thin. "Get on the bed on all fours. It's my turn now."

Gem opened his mouth as if to argue but then thought better of it. Instead, he pressed a cheeky kiss to the head of my cock before climbing to his feet and onto the bed. He positioned himself in the middle of the mattress, lowering his arms and raising his ass until he was presenting it to me like a delicious feast. He looked so fucking tempting I could have eaten him alive.

I let out another low rumble, walking over and gently smacking one ass cheek then the other before retrieving the lube and a pillow to kneel on. "Move down a little so I can kneel on the floor," I said. "Otherwise this is going to be uncomfortable." Gem chuckled and then shuffled up the bed. I understood why most porn seemed to use king or super-king-sized beds; it just made it easier for both people to fit. Somewhere deep in my mind I made a mental note to look at replacing my bed one day soon. Just in case.

I dropped the pillow on the floor because I was not going to kill my knees on Gem's shitty carpet, sank down at the end of the bed, and gazed hungrily at Gem's ass. It was round and peachy and covered in dark, curly hair. I couldn't wait to taste it. Sliding my hand up his thigh, I slowly caressed his ass. Gem pressed back into my hand, and I grinned before leaning forward to press a kiss to his cheek. Then I reached out with my other hand to pull his cheeks apart to reveal his dark, tight pucker.

"Look at you," I murmured. "Such a perfect hole… so pretty… just waiting for me so patiently."

"P-please," Gem said. "Finn, please. I need you."

"I know. You're being so good." I squeezed his ass cheek and then leant forward to flick my tongue over his hole. Gem cursed and moaned, which was just what I'd wanted. Slowly, I began to take him apart with my tongue, licking and teasing the sensitive skin until he was a whimpering mess. The sounds dripping from his lips were like a perfect symphony, and it made my cock throb knowing that I was bringing him so much pleasure. I might have been in charge, but the thing I wanted more than anything was to make Gem soar. Yes, I'd love an orgasm at the end of this, but that wasn't my main goal. My main goal was to make Gem come so hard he forgot all his stress and all his worries so he had a moment of freedom from his real life, one that was filled with nothing but bliss.

"Mmm, you taste so good, baby," I said. "I can't wait to

be inside you. You're so good for me... my perfect, beautiful boy."

Gem groaned, murmuring soft curses over and over. "Yes, please... I need it. Fuck me. Please, Finn, fuck me." I opened the bottle of lube and poured some onto my fingers before slowly pressing one into his waiting hole. Gem gasped. "More... fuck! Yes, fuck, I want more."

"Patience." I pressed a kiss to his cheek as I worked my finger into him. "You'll take what I give you when I give it to you."

"Yes... but... ahh, fuck!"

I smirked to myself as I added another finger and started to stretch his hole. Gem groaned, and between his legs I could see his hard cock dripping precum onto the sheets. I let out a low, rumbling moan. "Mmm, baby, you feel so good. I can't wait to get my cock inside you. I know you're going to feel amazing, and I can see how much you want it." I reached between his cock to jerk him slowly, and Gem cried out in pleasure at the touch of my hand, thrusting his hips desperately as if that would get me to give him more. "So needy for me. Don't worry, I won't make you wait long." I pressed a third finger into his waiting hole. "I just want to make sure you're all ready for me because I don't want to hurt you. I want you to be able to take it all."

"Fuck... oh fuck, please."

"You sound so pretty when you beg," I said, kissing his ass again as I slowly let go of his cock and slipped my fingers from his hole. I poured some more lube onto my fingers and slicked up my cock, which was hard and aching. I was desperate to pound Gem hard until I came, taking what I needed from him, and I suspected he'd like me using him. But I also wanted to draw this out so I could hear him beg again because those sounds were wonderfully sweet, and I craved them.

"Fuck me, please Finn. Just… fucking get it in me!" As I stood, I saw Gem's fingers fisting the sheets, his knuckles almost white. The sight sent another wave of possessive pleasure rolling through me.

I gripped his hips and tapped the swollen head of my cock against his hole. Gem pushed back against me, and I didn't need any more encouragement. I pressed my cock into him slowly, watching as he took all of me inside him. "That's it… slowly… don't rush. I want you to take it all. Mmm… fuck you look so good taking my cock." I leant down and kissed his spine, right between his shoulders. His skin had the faint taste of salt.

I filled Gem with my cock, giving him a moment to adjust and myself a moment to breathe. It had been a long time since I'd felt anything this good, and while I tended to have pretty good control over myself, there was a definite chance I'd come before I was ready, and I didn't want that to happen. I had plans, plans that involved feeling Gem fall apart around me.

My hand tightened on his hip as I began to move, sliding my dick in and out of his perfect, tight ass. Gem groaned and started to rock his hips, fucking himself on my cock, and I growled. "That's it… mmm, yes… God, fuck… that feels so good," I said, leaning down and trailing kisses across his shoulder. "Just like that. You're so perfect, and you feel so fucking good. Your ass is just… mmm!"

"Yes," Gem moaned, the sound broken and beautiful and so *needy*. It was everything. "More."

"More?"

"Yes! Fucking give it to me." I was tempted to tease, but all I wanted was to bring him pleasure. And if that was what Gem wanted, that was what Gem would get. I pulled him onto my cock and started to fuck him hard and fast, tilting his hips and listening to him cry out as I hit his sweet spot with every thrust.

Another possessive growl slipped from my lips, mixing with Gem's desperate moans. "Fuck, yes… I want… Jerk your cock for me," I said, starting to struggle for words. "I want you to come for me… want to feel you come."

Gem didn't need to be told again, and soon I heard him jacking his cock as fast as I fucked him. I was already getting close, and I knew I needed Gem to come before I could give in to the building wave of pleasure deep inside me. "Yes… fuck, baby. That's it. Come for me. I want to feel it… Come for me. Give me what I want."

"Finn!" Gem cried out and his ass tightened around me, milking my cock as he came. I barely managed another couple of thrusts before he pulled me over the edge, and I came with a deep groan as my cock emptied inside him.

My heart was racing, and I felt sweat beading on my forehead as I pressed another line of soft kisses across Gem's shoulders. I slowly pulled out, releasing his hip and running my hand over his ass. A bead of cum trickled from his hole and I groaned, ridiculously tempted to lean down and lick it up.

Gem flopped onto the bed with a groan and then rolled onto his back, staring at the ceiling with wide eyes and a loose smile. "Jesus," he muttered eventually as I stretched out next to him. "I think I'm fucking dead."

"I hope not," I said. I reached out and interlaced our fingers together. It was probably one of those gestures that was too intimate and blurred the lines between us even further, but I couldn't bring myself to care. "I take it that was okay, then?"

"Okay? Fucking hell, if that's only *okay*, then the sex I've had for my entire life has been dog shit." I chuckled, feeling a flush blooming on my cheeks. I hoped Gem would just mistake it for exertion. "Seriously, that was fucking amazing. Like… wow."

"It wasn't too much? The dirty talk and everything?"

"Nope. It was perfect… like genuinely." He looked over at me and grinned. "It's like you saw inside my head and pulled out all my dirty fantasies."

"Well, I did ask you what you liked."

"Yeah, but there's asking and then there's… *that*," Gem said. He squeezed my hand. "It was… Yeah."

"I can live with that."

He chuckled, then pulled me towards him for a kiss.

CHAPTER SEVENTEEN

Finn

"Oh my God, look at you!" Chantelle screamed as she embraced me in an enormous hug, squeezing all the air from my lungs. "I've missed you so much."

"I've missed you too," I said as she released me, and my internal organs resumed their normal arrangement. I hadn't expected any less from her when I collected her and Kelsey at Grantham station on Saturday morning, even if a few people were now staring at us. Usually, I'd have been embarrassed by their looks, but my happiness at seeing one of my best friends overrode anything else I might feel.

Chantelle had stepped back and was now giving me a once-over while holding Kelsey's hand. Kelsey was looking up at me with a shrewd expression, one I was sure I'd seen on her mother. She was the spitting image of Chantelle with long dark hair that fell in soft curls over her shoulders and large dark eyes. She was wearing a dark blue dress patterned with brightly coloured dinosaurs over very pink leggings and a puffy yellow coat over the top. At least we wouldn't lose her if we went out for the day.

"Hi, Kelsey. How're you?" I asked, giving her a little wave.

"I'm okay," she said, still giving me a wary look. We'd chatted via video several times, but I knew it would be different seeing me in person. I wasn't a face on a screen anymore, and I was considerably taller in real life. It made me realise how long it had been since I'd last been down to London for a visit. "What's that on your shirt?"

I looked down, trying to remember what t-shirt I'd put on earlier. I had a coat and a hoodie on over the top, but I realised you could still see part of the design peeking out. I unzipped my coat and hoodie to show her the picture, which was of the droid BB-8 from the Star Wars sequel trilogy. I had varying opinions about the films, but BB-8 was adorable, and when I'd seen the t-shirt on sale, I hadn't been able to resist.

"It's BB-8 from Star Wars."

She frowned and then sighed, and I'd never felt more judged in my entire life. "Why do all boys like Star Wars? It's very silly."

I fought the urge to laugh while Chantelle's expression rotated between mild horror and hilarity. "It is kind of silly," I said. "Dinosaurs are better."

"They are." She nodded. "You should get more t-shirts with dinosaurs. Pink ones."

"I should." I looked between her and Chantelle. "Shall

we go back to mine? And then, I was thinking we could have some snacks and plan what we want to do next?"

"That sounds great," Chantelle said, then she looked at Kelsey and frowned. "Shit. Car seat. I knew I was forgetting something."

"Don't worry. I've got one." I waved my hand. "I picked one up yesterday after I double-checked what she'd need. That's why I asked you how tall she was." It hadn't been hard to nip into Halfords and grab a seat, and they'd even shown me how to fit it into the back of my car. I hadn't thought about it at first, and it was only after I'd mentioned taking Kelsey out for the day to Gem that he'd suggested it.

Chantelle was giving me a look, and I knew what it meant—that I shouldn't have spent the money—but she didn't want to say anything in front of Kelsey. "I know," I said as we headed back to where I'd parked. "But public transport here is rubbish, and it wasn't expensive. Plus, I can keep it for next time you come and visit."

"Fine," Chantelle said. "But I owe you."

"You can buy me a stick of rock later." I laughed. "Or some candy floss."

It took us a bit of time to get Kelsey strapped in, especially because she objected at first, but her dislike was soon forgotten as we drove and she chatted nonstop about everything she saw out the car window.

"I was thinking," I said quietly, "we could go up to Skegness to the seal sanctuary. They've got seals, penguins, a tropical house, meerkats, and there's a pets corner too. Plus, it's right by the beach, and we can walk along to the pier. It's only about an hour away."

"That sounds amazing," Chantelle said. "Kels will love that."

"Cool. We can go in a bit. Maybe food first? I've got some bits for sandwiches and things. Gem gave me some pointers because I have no idea what kids eat." Even with my eyes on the road, I felt Chantelle's gaze boring into me as we drove. "What?"

"Nothing."

"Chantelle."

"What? I'm saying nothing." I heard the glee in her voice, and I grimaced. "Am I gonna get to meet him?"

"You might." She smacked my thigh.

"Mummy, don't hit people," Kelsey said promptly from the back seat. "It's mean."

"I'm sorry, baby."

"Are you going to say sorry to me?" I asked quietly, trying not to smile.

"No. You deserved it," Chantelle said. "I want to meet him."

"Fine! You're so demanding." I let myself smile. "Good thing he's coming with us. That is if you don't mind."

"Oh my God, I will murder you," Chantelle hissed. I burst out laughing.

It was going to be a good day.

Gem arrived just as I'd finished making a mountain of sandwiches, and Chantelle gave me a knowing smile as we ate while Kelsey peppered Gem with questions ranging from whether seals could fart to whether penguins liked the chocolate biscuits named after them or not. Gem answered all the queries with a surprising amount of good humour and wasn't bothered about sitting in the back next to Kelsey as we drove to Skegness. I was still partly surprised he'd wanted to come with us, but when I'd tentatively suggested the idea the other night— after we'd cleaned up and been stretched out on his bed, and Gem had insisted I stay, and I'd caved without question—he'd said he'd love to. And I wasn't going to turn down spending more time with him.

The drive gave Chantelle and me a chance to catch up, but I kept getting distracted when I heard Gem telling Kelsey Scottish folk stories and answering her questions about fairies. He was so good with her, and it made some-thing inside me twist and squirm.

"You like him," Chantelle said, noticing I wasn't paying attention to her.

"What?"

"You *like* him."

"No, I…" I lowered my voice. "This isn't the time or place."

"Fine, but I'm getting an answer out of you," Chantelle said. She would, and by the end of the day, I knew I'd have told her everything. Not that there was much she didn't already know.

Considering it was a cold, blustery Saturday in March, Skegness was busier than I'd anticipated, but I managed to find somewhere to park, and the four of us headed to the Natureland Seal Sanctuary. I hadn't been in years, but I remembered coming with Mimbles and Mum a couple of times when I'd been growing up. Kelsey had decided Gem was much more interesting than me or her mum, so she'd taken his hand, and the two of them had walked off towards the sanctuary, leaving Chantelle and me to follow.

As soon as we got inside, Kelsey let out a gasp and headed straight for the main pool where several large seals were gliding leisurely through the water or stretched out on rocks. They were very cute with their fat, speckled bodies and puppylike faces as they bobbed in the water, but the sweetest thing was watching Kelsey as she peered into the pool with a look of awe on her face.

There was something about the wonder of children that was utterly adorable.

It suddenly made me wonder if I'd ever have kids of my own. I had the sneaking suspicion that having biological children in the UK was quite difficult for LGBTQ parents, especially if you were a same sex couple, but I'd be very happy to adopt. And just thinking that made me realise I'd probably already made a decision about what I wanted for my future without consciously thinking about it. It was terrifying and freeing all at the same time.

I watched as a member of staff walked past and stopped to answer Kelsey's questions as she pointed at one of the seals. The man knelt down and began talking to her, and from beside me, Chantelle let out a soft laugh.

"I wonder if he knows he's never going to escape now. She'll keep him there for hours."

"At least she hasn't asked to take one home yet," I said, remembering the time that Lewis had very seriously asked Mimbles if he could have a seal pup for a pet and then tried to negotiate for a penguin when she'd said no.

"Easy answer to that one. Seals can't go on the train. They haven't got a ticket and there's no water."

"Penguin?"

"Hasn't got a ticket either, Finn. Gotta have a ticket or a pass to get on the train."

"That's very true," I said. "You could buy them a ticket?"

"Nah. Gotta book at least a week in advance for the big train, and we're going home tomorrow." She grinned at me. "Sometimes you have to have prepared lies for these questions. Not big ones but, like, little ones that get you out of trouble. Like last year when Kelsey kept asking why Father Christmas was everywhere instead of at the North Pole with the elves. So I said that some of them are actors, like you, who help him out and pretend to be Father Christmas when he's busy, but they still tell him *everything*, so she has to be good." She snorted and shook her head. "I think she's now convinced there's, like, a fucking Santa spy network, but she still thinks he's real, so that's something."

I laughed. "I like that one." As we watched, the keeper said something to Kelsey and then to Gem, who shook his head and pointed at us before getting up and leaving. I wondered what had just happened, but I had a sneaking suspicion we were about to be involved in something.

"Mummy," Kelsey shouted, running up to Chantelle and practically bursting with excitement. "The man who looks after the seals said if we come back here later, he'll feed them lots of fish, and we can watch, and he'll tell us all their names! So we have to go look at everything else now so we can come back."

"At three," Gem said, strolling up behind her with a smile on his face. "They feed them at three."

I looked at my watch. "That gives us about an hour and a half."

"Let's go," Kelsey said, grabbing my hand and then reaching for Gem's. "Come on." She began pulling us towards the pool and the path that led around to the left with a surprising amount of force for someone so small. Then she turned around to make sure Chantelle was following us. "Come on, Mummy, don't be so slow."

"I'm coming. You're just going too fast."

Kelsey sighed in that way all small children did when they thought adults were being ridiculous. Then she looked up at me and Gem. "Finn?"

"Yes, Kelsey," I said with a growing sense of trepidation.

"Is Gem your boyfriend?"

I stared at her, trying to find words while my face flamed. I was probably the colour of a fire engine, and it was definitely going to be noticeable to everyone within a hundred miles. "Er... my boyfriend?"

"Yeah. The man who knows about seals asked if Gem was my dad, but he's not. He's just your friend, so that makes him your *boy*friend? Karim at school, his daddy has a boyfriend called Rahul, and he makes Karim doughnuts on Sundays. Does Gem make you doughnuts?"

I looked helplessly at Gem, who gave me a smile, and that familiar warmth inside my chest blossomed. I knew I had to say *no*, even if the answer I really wanted to give was *yes*.

"No," Gem said. "Finn is just my best friend. Do you

have a best friend, Kelsey? Someone at school you like playing with?"

"Yes! Her name is Nadiya, and she has an ice cream truck we play with, and when we go to her house for tea, her mum makes us yummy chicken."

"An ice cream truck?" Gem asked with the most gorgeous level of enthusiasm.

"It's a Disney Princess one," Chantelle added from beside me. "Isn't it, bub? And her mum makes you curry, doesn't she?"

"Yeah!" Kelsey began chatting away about Nadiya and her other friends from school, happily diverted from the subject of Gem and me.

We continued walking, and Gem steered Kelsey over to look at the family of meerkats. I watched the pair of them, my heart aching so much I thought it might burst. I wanted all this to be real and to be mine, not just a fantasy I was living for a weekend. I'd known going into my arrangement with Gem that I'd struggle to separate the sex from my feelings, but now it was virtually impossible.

I saw the crash coming, and I knew it was going to hurt. But I couldn't stop myself from speeding into the welcome embrace of something I'd longed for my entire life.

CHAPTER EIGHTEEN

Gem

LEADING Kelsey around Natureland turned out to be the most fun I'd had in weeks, excluding the nights I'd had with Finn. Kelsey was funny and sweet and at the age where all she wanted to do was ask questions. She patiently listened while I read some of the information to her about what we were looking at before launching into a thousand questions from "Do these meerkats have names? Like Aleksandr from the TV?"—thanks Compare the Market for that one—to "Why is the sea blue?" and "Why don't I have a tail?" It reminded me of spending time with my nephew, who was nearly eight now but had asked similar things in the past.

I knew some people found kids annoying because of it, but it always just made me laugh. There was something adorable about the way kids just said whatever popped into their heads. Kelsey had already asked me why I was wearing such an old person jacket, but then told me it was okay because I was pretty old anyway.

Chantelle had been slightly horrified and tried to remind Kelsey that she had to say nice things to people. Kelsey's response had been to tell me she liked my beard because it was orange, which I'd taken as a compliment. I hadn't intended to grow any kind of beard or stubble, but my desire to shave had nosedived over the past few weeks due to exhaustion. I'd shave it later when the shop opened. For now, I was just going to embrace the ginger beard.

"Are you okay?" Finn asked me as we stood by the main seal pool watching the keeper feed them. Kelsey stood near the pool wall with Chantelle, watching with rapt fascination. "Sorry Kelsey kidnapped you."

"It's fine," I said. "She's cute. And it gave you a chance to chat with Chantelle."

"Thanks." Finn smiled at me, and my fucking heart melted. God fucking dammit, there was no way I was getting out of whatever we were doing alive. I'd told myself I didn't want another relationship and that getting involved with Finn was just meant to be fun, but now I was starting to see how much of a lie that was. "You're really good with her."

"She makes me think of my nephew. He's got the same kind of energy."

"That's sweet," Finn said. "Do you… Would you… ever want kids? I know it's not for everyone, and I know a lot of queer people who think it's quite… heteronormative? Plus, kids are expensive, and parenting is hard, so—"

He was rambling now like he always did when he was nervous, and it was adorable. Without thinking, I reached out and let my hand brush against his. "Maybe. I mean, if I was in the right relationship. Could be fun." I grinned. "I mean that in a kinda *this is an Indiana-Jones-style adventure complete with a ton of booby traps and people screaming*, but y'know, could be interesting."

Finn chuckled. "That's one way to put it."

"What about you?" I had no idea why I was suddenly so fucking nervous about Finn's answer. It wasn't like we were planning on having kids together. But now that I'd asked, my whole body was tighter than a stubborn shoelace knot.

"I think so too. I know it's hard, and Chantelle has never been afraid to tell me about the realities of parenting, but it hasn't put me off yet. I think I'm just more aware of how tough it really is and in awe of the fact that she does it by herself," Finn said. The knot in my chest loosened, and it felt like a door had opened somewhere, but it was somewhere I hadn't reached yet.

"Kelsey's dad's not around?"

"He is." Finn's face pinched. "And she still sees him, but I wouldn't really call him a parent. He's more interested in his new girlfriends and knocking them up than parenting the children he's already got." He shook his head. "Sorry, that was very rude of me. I just… have opinions."

"It's fine," I said. "I won't tell."

"I mean, Chantelle already knows how I feel because she feels the same. It just sucks for Kelsey because I think she already knows her dad is losing interest in her, and she's only five."

"That's bollocks." Guys like that pissed me the fuck off, and a lance of anger pierced my heart. I'd only known Kelsey for a few hours, but I already knew she was a fucking sweetheart who deserved the world. And Chantelle was a fucking goddess for everything she did. "Men suck."

"They do." Finn nodded. "And not in a good way."

"What are you two talking about?" Chantelle asked, and I realised feeding time had finished.

"Nothing much," Finn said. "Just wondering what to do next. Shall we walk down the beach a little? Maybe see if we can get some fish and chips? It would be a bit early for dinner, but…"

"That sounds amazing," Chantelle said. She looked at Kelsey who had started to eye up the gift shop and the display of stuffed animals. "She's starting to get tired, so we don't have to stay out long, but she loves the sea."

"Mummy…" Kelsey called, and I knew exactly what was coming next. Chantelle sighed but smiled.

"I'm not getting out of here without getting her a toy, am I?"

"Probably not," said Finn.

"I'll get it," I said. "As a thanks for letting me tag along today. It's been fun."

"Y'know, I feel like I should be thanking you for looking after her."

"It's fine. I don't mind." I turned and walked towards the little gift shop, fully expecting to find Kelsey knee-deep in a display of toy seals. As I walked away, I heard Chantelle mutter, "I like this one, Finn. You need to keep him."

. . .

We didn't spend long on the beach because there was an evil wind blowing off the sea that froze everything it touched. Kelsey was starting to fade, and one bout of tears was enough to convince us it was time to go back to Finn's.

Kelsey fell asleep as soon as the car started, and Finn promised Chantelle and me that he'd get us fish and chips from a place near his house since we hadn't wanted to disturb Kelsey. Chantelle hopped into the back seat, telling us she was tired too and would probably doze, so I sat in the front next to Finn, and we chatted quietly all the way home.

I was exhausted but in a different way than usual. Less of a soul-sucking, what the fuck am I doing sort of exhaustion and more the fun day out, running around kind. I still had to drive back to Lincoln tonight, and even though it was only a thirty-minute drive, the thought made me wince. Maybe I'd just ask Finn if I could crash on his sofa instead.

When we got back to Finn's, Chantelle planted Kelsey on the sofa under a blanket with *Encanto* on the TV. She was still clutching her new seal toy and staring happily at the lush, musical fantasy. I hadn't seen it for ages, and I kept trying to watch bits of it out of the corner of my eye as we put together a quick list for the chippy. I already knew I was going to have "We Don't Talk About Bruno" stuck in my head for days.

"I'll go," said Finn, scooping up the list and patting the back pocket of his jeans to make sure his wallet was there.

"Are you sure?" I asked. I was suddenly nervous about being left with Chantelle, even though we'd been chatting amicably throughout the day, because I had the growing feeling I was going to be ambushed.

"I'm sure. I won't be long." Finn headed for the door. "Help yourselves to drinks."

The door shut behind him, leaving Chantelle and me alone in the kitchen while the musical stylings of Lin-Manuel Miranda filled the silence.

"So," I said, searching for something to say. I wasn't sure why I was so worried, but maybe it was because she was Finn's best friend. She knew him inside out, and I doubted they had any secrets from each other. If Finn hadn't told her we were fucking, I was sure she'd have guessed. "Did you want a drink? Cup of tea maybe? Or a glass of wine? I know Finn bought a bottle of rosé."

"He's a sweetie," she said with a smile. "I know he hates it, so he only bought it for me. I can't drink a whole bottle though. Well, I shouldn't, not with Kelsey here. My tolerance is shot these days. Only takes a couple of glasses and I'll be asleep." She laughed.

"I'll have one with you. Can't let it go to waste," I said as I opened the fridge and pulled out the very nice bottle of wine Finn had bought. Then I tried to remember where he kept the glasses.

"I tell you eighteen-year-old me would think I was boring as… something." Chantelle glanced at the living room where Kelsey was still mesmerised and lowered her voice. "I'm trying to swear less. Her dad does it all the time, and she's started repeating it at school. So we're cutting down on bad words."

"My nephew's the same," I said, opening various cupboards until I found what I wanted. "My sister had to explain to him that just because she and his dad said some things that didn't mean he could too. I don't know how well it worked since I got told off for swearing when I went up for Christmas." I poured two large glasses of wine and handed one to Chantelle. She thanked me and took a slow sip.

"Oh, that's nice. Finn always did have good taste."

I sipped my own glass. Chantelle was right; the wine was good—sweet and fruity and incredibly drinkable. I could see us getting through the bottle very quickly if we weren't careful.

"How long have you two been together, then?" Chantelle asked, giving me a wry smile over the rim of her glass. I nearly fucking choked.

"What?"

"Come on. I'm not a total idiot. It's obvious you two are waaay into each other."

"Er… I mean…" My brain ran through my entire list of swear words and then some. Finally, I just asked a question. "Really? That obvious?"

"Of course. I mean, maybe not to everyone, but it is to me. I've known Finn for years, though, so maybe not everyone would notice. Why? Did you think you were being subtle?"

"Kind of."

Chantelle hummed at me like she didn't believe a word of what I was saying. I decided just to tell her the truth. "We're not dating, though… We're just friends."

"With added extras?" She grinned and sipped her wine. "Don't worry. I already knew that."

"I thought so."

"Don't be mad at Finn. I guessed."

"I'm not… I wouldn't." I couldn't ever be mad at Finn for telling her, even if she hadn't guessed. It was nice for him to have someone to talk to about whatever this was. I didn't even know what it *was* anymore. It was getting messier by the day, and my growing feelings weren't help-ing. I'd been so sure I could keep them separate, but that had been a lie. Today had shown me what my life could be like if Finn and I were together, and the picture had etched itself onto my heart, one painful stroke at a time. I was starting to want things I'd told myself it was pointless to dream about—love, a home, and a family.

"Oh my God," Chantelle said, interrupting my thoughts and sounding practically giddy. "You *like* Finn. Like proper like him." She grabbed my arm, beaming at me from ear to ear. "You do, right? Like not just as friends!"

"Maybe," I said, trying to stop the warning sirens in my brain from screaming mayday. I'd only just started to admit it to myself, so I had no fucking clue how to admit it to someone else. Chantelle raised her eyebrows and gave me a pointed look. "I don't know. I'm still trying to figure it all out. And I have no idea if he feels the same."

"If you really can't tell, then you don't know Finn at all. Do you really think he'd start something with you if he thought you were just a friend? I've known him for ten years, and he's never been one for casual shi—stuff." Chantelle frowned and sipped her wine. "I'm not going to say more because this is something you two have got to figure out for yourselves. Even if I want to knock your freakin' heads together. Just… think about what you're doing, okay? And if you hurt him, then there's nowhere you can hide from me."

I chuckled, but it was a weak one. "I don't doubt it." I opened my mouth to ask her a question about Finn and whether she really thought he felt the same, but the door clattered open, and the man in question appeared clutching a large plastic bag. His hair was ruffled from the wind and his cheeks flushed from the cold, but he looked so fucking gorgeous I thought my heart had fucking stopped.

"Oh, good, I see you found the wine," he said as he shut the door. "How is it?"

"It's perfect," Chantelle said, pouring herself another glass and topping mine up.

"Good. I wasn't sure what to get, so I got some recommendations from Oscar. He's good with rosé." He put the bag—which had already started filling the room with the smell of fish and chips—on the side and got some plates out. "Shall we finish watching the film with Kelsey or eat in here?"

"We'll eat in here," Chantelle said, transferring things to the small dining table wedged into the corner. "I don't want her getting ketchup on your sofa."

"Okay, we can do that." Finn bustled around the kitchen, dishing things up while Chantelle went to fetch

Kelsey. I heard her promise she could finish the film after she'd eaten. Meanwhile, I watched Finn with the growing feeling in my heart that I was never going to be able to walk away from him.

Not without one or both of us getting hurt.

CHAPTER NINETEEN

Gem

I spent Sunday moping around The Lost World, wishing I wasn't at work. I could have called Jay and told him something had come up, but that felt shitty considering everything he'd done for me. Plus, I didn't really have a reason beyond wanting to spend time with Finn.

He'd insisted I stay the night because by the time we'd finished the fish and chips and watched *Encanto* with Kelsey, I'd had another glass of wine. Once Kelsey had crashed and Finn and Chantelle had had a whispered argument, that Finn lost, about who would take which room—Finn trying to insist they take his bed and Chantelle saying they'd be perfectly fine on the sofa bed in his office—the idea of driving home had really lost its appeal. Maybe Finn had been able to see it on my face, or maybe he'd wanted me there, but when he'd offered, I immediately said yes.

The three of us had stayed up late with Chantelle and

Finn sharing old stories but never making me feel like a third wheel. I could see what Chantelle meant when she said she and Finn would have made the best and worst couple in the world, and a huge chunk of me was pleased it had never worked out between them.

When Chantelle had gone to bed, Finn had pulled me into his room, and we'd ended up snuggled up together in the middle of his bed. It had been one of the warm, soft relationship moments I hadn't experienced in a long time, and I'd wanted to cling to it for as long as possible. Finn had drifted off quickly, but I'd lain there for hours holding him close to me and watching him sleep.

We'd been woken up at seven by Kelsey knocking on the door and asking very sweetly if she could come in. Finn had thrown me a pair of his jogging bottoms, which had just about fit, before saying yes, and Kelsey had ended up sitting between us explaining that Chantelle was still sleeping. It had been cute she'd let her mum sleep, even if it had been at our expense, so we'd sat there reading books on Finn's tablet while Kelsey clutched her seal toy and snuggled into me. Apparently my years of role-play games had equipped me with a good variety of voices for stories, and eventually I'd ended up regaling Kelsey with overdramatised and highly censored versions of various games we'd played.

Her favourite had been a recreation of the time our characters had faced off against two evil sorcerers who'd been kidnapping people and had to fight them in a magical house. I'd given the story a magical, fairy-tale feel, and Kelsey had been enraptured as I talked about two of our female characters saving the day with their magic and freeing all the people. I'd even worked in a kiss between the heroines, one of whom was actually a princess.

Kelsey had been thrilled, and when Chantelle emerged from the other room, Kelsey had jumped out of bed to tell her a slightly warped version of the story. It had been adorable, and by that point, my desire to go to work was at an all-time low. But I'd still heaved myself out of bed and helped Finn make breakfast. They were off for lunch with his family, who had insisted on seeing Chantelle again, and I almost wished I could go with them, even if I was ninety-nine percent convinced his family would come to the same conclusion Chantelle had about our relationship.

I hadn't been able to get it off my mind as I'd driven to Lincoln, making a quick stop at my flat for some clean clothes.

Did Finn and I really act like we were already in a relationship? And what did that mean for our friendship?

"Earth to Gem! Come in Gem." I looked up to see Jay waving his hand in front of my face, the smile on his lips not completely hiding the worry in his eyes. "There you are. You okay?"

"Yeah, sorry." I shook my head and looked around the shop, glad it was quiet and I hadn't just been ignoring a customer. Luckily for me, it had been pissing it down all day, and not many people wanted to venture outside. "Just, er, thinking about something."

"The game shop?" Jay asked, putting a stack of books on the counter. Several of them had slips of paper sticking out the top, and I guessed Jay was making a start on the weekend's online orders. "Anything I can help with?"

"No, it's not that. For once." I could have lied and made up some bullshit reason to cover my moping, but I was too distracted to even consider it. Jay frowned.

"Everything okay at home? With your family?"

"They're fine. At least I think so." Although that did remind me I needed to message them and check in. It had been a while. "No, it's… Well…" I sighed. "Can I be honest with you?"

"Sure."

"Can it be under a cone of silence?"

"Of course," Jay said, looking more worried than ever.

I rubbed my hand through my scruffy stubble, trying to decide where to start. "I think I'm falling in love with Finn," I said. "And I have no fucking clue what to do about it."

Jay stared at me, his smile turning sarcastic. "Was this supposed to be a surprise?"

"It's a surprise to me! How does everyone else already know?"

"Everyone?"

"Well, Finn's friend Chantelle. She thinks it's really bleeding obvious."

"I kinda have to agree," Jay said. "But I'm on the outside looking in, and I know you at least a little. Sometimes I think it's harder when you're the one it's happening to. You don't really get the external perspective, and there's more internal stuff to work through."

"Yeah, I guess." That didn't make me feel any better. If anything, it made me think I should have noticed by now.

"Also, you were with Jesse last year, and even though he was a…" Jay reached around for a word. "A person…"

"You can say dickhead," I said dryly.

Jay snorted. "Okay, a dickhead, you're a pretty committed person, so it's not a surprise you didn't really notice it until recently, even if it was there before." Jay shifted some of the books around, and I noticed him playing with his lip ring, which was what he often did when he was thinking. "What changed?"

We started having sex.

Was that it though? I wasn't sure it was. The sex had helped, but I think it had started before that. I just couldn't put my finger on when. The past couple of months had all blurred together, and separating everything out would be like sorting grains of sand.

"I don't know," I said. "It's all… soupy." I sighed and rubbed my stubble again. It really needed tidying up if I was going to keep it, otherwise I was going to look like some sort of wild man. "Maybe it's because he's always been there. I know we haven't known each other for long, but if I need anything, Finn is always there. And when I started talking about the shop, Finn just supported me and helped make it real. He didn't think anything of giving up all his free time to help me. He just did it." I smiled as various memories from the past few weeks floated into view like some overdramatic film montage. "Like last week, he came up and brought me a takeaway because he knew I'd be there late. And he helped me with all the painting and building shit, even though it's very obvious I shouldn't be allowed anywhere near IKEA instructions."

"You and me both," Jay said with a soft laugh. "Edward built most of mine."

"He told me."

"He tells everyone. He's never going to let me forget it."

"I don't think Finn's that bad," I said. "He'd probably just tell everyone he gave me a hand, even though he was the one who built most of them. Probably would have helped if I'd looked at the instructions properly from the start."

"I'm just clumsy. I don't think Edward trusted me not to nail or screw myself to them." He pursed his lips. "I mean, I only dropped a few bits on my toe. It wasn't that bad. It wasn't like I broke anything."

"The way Edward tells it, you were two seconds away from destroying everything, including yourself."

Jay scoffed. "He would." He looked at me studiously. "You know, when you talk about Finn, you sound happy. Unstressed. And I don't think it matters how long you've known someone. There's no mandatory waiting period. Feelings change. It happens all the time. Look at... look at Edward and Izzy. They were convinced they hated each other for years, now they're sickeningly in love."

"Yeah, but they were fucking in secret for most of that," I said. That story had always made me laugh because I'd never understood how someone could be so unaware of their own feelings. Now, I was starting to realise how easy it was.

"True, but they still thought they were enemies," Jay

said. "My point is, it's okay if your feelings for Finn have changed and you're starting to want something different. You're allowed to want that, and you deserve to be happy. You and Finn are good together, and I can't imagine him feeling differently about you. I've seen you together." Jay grinned at me slyly. "Besides, how often does being fuck buddies with your best friend lead to zero feelings developing?"

I stared at him, my mouth hanging open in shock. "How did you know?"

"That you're doing the dirty?" Jay shrugged. "Lucky guess. Well, that, and it's really obvious. I mean, you're practically moping around here like some lovesick teenager, and when he stopped by last week, the looks you were giving him were a combination of sickening puppy love and wanting to jump him in the middle of the shop."

"When did you get so good at reading people?" I asked. "You've always been shit at it before."

"Have not!"

"Yeah, you have. Edward said you had no clue about him and Izzy until he told you, and you thought he was making Jason up until you met him."

"Yeah, but come on," Jay protested. "How the fuck was I supposed to know he was telling the truth. He's Jason Lu. I had a crush on him for years and then suddenly he's dating Edward's PA? How does that sound remotely realistic?"

Jay had a point there, and I hadn't really believed it either when he'd first told me Lewis's boyfriend was the sexy as fuck demon prince from *Celestials*, but I wasn't going to tell him that. There was something I was missing because there was no way Jay had figured it out on his own. I loved him, but observant he was not. Then I realised what the missing piece was.

"Edward told you, didn't he?"

Jay sighed and rolled his eyes. "Fine, he did. He came up to me when you and Finn were talking last week and said—and I quote—'If those two aren't fucking, I'll eat my hat' and then he mentioned something about me giving him twenty quid if he was right."

"I guess you owe him twenty quid, then," I said, trying not to be annoyed that I'd been so obvious with Finn or that Edward had figured it out so easily. "Just, er, don't tell Finn you know. And don't let Edward tell him either. He'd be really upset if you knew. He's private for a reason."

"I promise. And I won't even tell Edward he was right, and not just because I don't want to give him money."

"Cheers. I appreciate it." I also didn't want Finn knowing that everyone knew until I'd had a chance to talk to him, whenever that might be. It probably needed to be sooner rather than later, but I didn't know how to even start that conversation. Telling him I loved him right off the bat wasn't going to work, and telling him while we were fucking felt like it would cheapen the moment. I didn't want Finn to think I was falling for him because of the sex, even if that was amazing as fuck. I wanted him to know I was falling for him because he was so goddamn amazing I couldn't imagine myself with anyone else.

I had the words. I just had to figure out how to use them.

CHAPTER TWENTY

Finn

"So, you remember how I said I was going to be positive about this whole thing? Well, that can get fucked. My fucking roof has leaked! So, yeah… I don't suppose you've got any whiskey? Or some spare towels?"

I listened to the voice message Gem had left me, horror and anger flooding through me. Fuck, fuck, and double fuck. This wasn't supposed to happen, but nothing like this was ever supposed to happen. I tilted myself back in my chair, staring at the roof of my sound booth with my mouth open in a silent scream.

Then I attempted to compose myself and checked when Gem had left the message—three hours ago while I'd been knee-deep in the murder mystery I'd been recording.

Hitting the Call button, I anxiously waited to see if Gem would answer, but no luck.

"Come on," I muttered as I scrolled through my phone,

hoping I had a contact number for Jay. I didn't. For a moment, I debated calling Lewis and Eli, both of whom lived in Lincoln. But then I remembered Eli was in Manchester for a few days with his drag tour, so he was out, and while Lewis would be amazingly helpful, he'd also get overly involved. He was my last resort, the person I'd call when I needed to summon the cavalry.

I tried Gem again but got nothing. This was all just wank, and I hated the fact that I was at least thirty minutes away, probably more considering the time of day. Still, late help was hopefully better than no help, so I saved all my recordings, made a couple of quick notes for when I came back, and locked my laptop. It didn't take me long to collect what I needed—phone, wallet, keys—and grab my coat to head out. The drive seemed to take forever with every second stretching out into a minute and every minute into an hour.

If this were a film, or even a novel, I'd have sped there not caring if I got caught. But despite the fact I knew at least one of the speed cameras enroute was out of order and that Lincolnshire didn't have that many speeding vans, I didn't want to chance it. That was how accidents happened, and I'd be no use to Gem if my car was on the side of the road. Besides, it wasn't as if anyone's life was in danger. This was a hideous inconvenience at most, and I knew that, by law, Gem's landlord would have to fix it. He also had insurance, but claiming against it before the business had even opened was not going to look good.

Eventually, I managed to find myself at the top of Lincoln, squeezing my car into a parking space. I was going to have to see if Gem could get me a parking permit—even if Lincoln's car parks weren't particularly expensive compared to some—because the amount of money I'd given the council over the past month would probably pay for the upkeep of the entire county's road network.

Perhaps that was a little overdramatic. I did tend to get irritable when stressed, and I always focused on the little things, like parking, to stop my brain from panicking over the major issue at hand. It didn't always work.

When I reached Castle Games, with its newly painted red exterior, I saw Gem hovering in the street, phone in hand. He looked like he was in the middle of a very tense phone call.

"I understand that," he was saying, looking about ready to tear his hair out. "But I need you to get someone out today. Tomorrow at the latest. This is my livelihood, and I can't open a shop that has a leaking roof. I can't even get stock in at the moment." He caught sight of me, and I waved awkwardly. "I really don't think you're listening to me. Can you please just call the landlord and let him know? If not, I'm going to start calling people myself and send you the bill."

Gem hung up, the heavy weight of the situation settling on his shoulders. "Hey," he said. "You didn't have to come."

"Yes, I did." I walked up to him and pulled him into a tight hug, not caring that we were in the middle of the street. "What happened?"

"I don't know." Gem sighed and stepped back, running a hand through his hair. "I haven't been in for a couple of days because we were out for the day and then I was at work, so I thought I'd come in this morning and get a load of stuff sorted because the stock is supposed to start arriving at the end of the week, and…" He sighed again, a bone-deep, weary sound that seemed to come from the very depths of his soul.

"You said the roof had leaked?" I asked gently. Gem nodded.

"Yeah. It's a fucking mess. Come see." He beckoned me to follow him, and we climbed the stone steps into the shop. My nose wrinkled as the unmistakable smell of damp hit me. Gem chuckled darkly when he saw me. "Yeah, the smell was the first thing I noticed."

"How is it so strong? It's only been a couple of days at most."

"I don't know. I think there's a problem with the roof. Or maybe the guttering? It's hard to tell." He waved me into the stockroom where buckets sat on the floor along the back wall, water dripping into them with audible *plinks*. The wall itself was stained brown, watermarks trailing down it like great tentacles of despair. There were a couple of towels piled onto the floor, already sodden from where Gem had attempted to mop up the water that had collected there. It was a good thing there hadn't been stock here, or it would have been ruined.

"Shit," I said.

"Yep, and it's just as bad upstairs. It's all come rushing down that back wall," Gem said. He walked out into the shop, and I followed him. The main room hadn't suffered any effects, apart from the damp smell, but as soon as I climbed the stairs, I saw what Gem meant about it being just as bad. While water hadn't collected on the floor, it had run down the back wall behind the bookcases. Gem had managed to unscrew some of them from the wall and pull them away, but I could see the water on the paintwork, and the thin, chipboard backs of the bookcases were soaked through. They'd probably dry out in time, but they were going to warp, and it would be difficult to stop them from moulding.

In the long run, it wouldn't be the leaking roof that was the problem, it would be everything else.

"Bugger."

"That was my thought," Gem said. "I rang the letting agency, and apparently, my landlord is currently unavailable, but because this is an external building issue, it's something he's responsible for. I double-checked the lease just in case. I think they'll probably let me get someone out to look at it, but they have to get his permission. If he's like any of the flat landlords I've had in the past, he'll probably just send his mate to look at it sometime next week and then say there's nothing he can do or that he'll be back to fix it sometime in the next six months."

I frowned. "But you're supposed to open next week."

"And that's the problem, isn't it?" Gem put his hand on the back of one of the nearby bookcases, and his face wrinkled. "I can push it back, but in my enthusiasm, I'd already started planning an opening and advertising it. I guess I'll just have to count that in the money-down-the-drain column."

"It won't be that bad," I said desperately trying to stay

positive, even though that ship was sinking fast. I knew Gem's landlord would have to do the repairs in a reasonable time frame, but I was also pretty sure there was no legally defined period for reasonable. I saw the hope draining from Gem with every passing second, and a feeling of helplessness threatened to overwhelm me. There was nothing I could do to help beyond tidying, drying, and repainting. I couldn't magically fix this with a few muttered words and the wave of a wand.

The temptation to call Lewis was strong, mostly because his organisational skills were second to none, and he could be utterly terrifying when annoyed. I'd had a front row seat when Lewis had bought his house while Jason was filming in Canada, and the way he'd dealt with his solicitor's incompetence and the estate agent's general, blasé attitude would have had most people running for the hills.

I didn't know any lawyers per se, but Eli did have a law degree and seemed fairly well versed in property law, although that had been more out of necessity than desire given his letting agency's approach to maintenance. Still, he might know something that could help, or he could possibly direct me to someone who could. Maybe Tristan knew someone given that he was a mortgage and financial adviser for very upmarket estate agents.

"I'm sure we can find a solution," I continued. "Or I'll know someone who can. My family may be loud and interfering, but they're good in a crisis."

"It's fine," Gem said. "Don't worry about it."

"It's too late for that." I chuckled softly. "Worry is my middle name."

"I thought it was Alexander?"

"Well, that too." I smiled, hoping Gem would do the same. He did, but it was stilted. It was clear he was just trying to put on a brave face for me if not for himself. "It's going to be okay. I promise."

"Yeah. Maybe." Gem didn't look convinced, but before I could say anything else his phone started to ring. The sound made me jump. Gem pulled his phone out of the pocket of his jeans, walking across the room as he answered it.

"Hello? Speaking... Oh, hey. Thanks for calling me back," he said, a pensive expression on his face as he peered out the window and into the street below. There was tightness across his shoulders, and he absentmindedly flexed his fingers as he spoke, the stress bleeding out of him. I couldn't help with the shop beyond offering manual labour when needed—although, perhaps I could bring baked goods since those always made things better—but maybe there was another way I could help Gem relieve stress. I just wondered whether he'd accept it.

Gem finished his call and turned back to me, and I realised with a start that I'd zoned out, too busy focusing on potential evening plans.

"Well? What did they say?" I asked. "I assume that was the letting agents?"

"Yeah," Gem said. "They managed to get hold of the landlord. He's in Florida for the month." Gem rolled his eyes. "But he's happy for me to get quotes from a couple of builders for the repairs, and he'll pay, but he wants full details of what the problem is and what's needed. I think he wants someone from the agent's to come and look at it or something. I don't know. I wasn't really listening at that point because I was thinking about finding someone who can get out here and get me a quote." He glanced at his phone and swore. "Guess my job for tonight will be making a list for tomorrow."

I looked at my watch and realised it was nearly five. "Why don't you come back to mine? We can have dinner, research some options, and I'll help you de-stress."

Gem grinned at me, and it was the first genuine smile I'd seen from him since I'd arrived. The fact that it was paired with a raised eyebrow and a side of cheek made desire flare in my chest. "De-stress? And just how were you planning on doing that?"

"First," I said, stepping towards him and prising his phone from his fingers. "You're going to put that down. You can't do anything more tonight. Second, I'm going to get you a glass of wine while I make food, then I might run you a bath while I pick my siblings' brains for builders—they can make themselves useful for once—and then…" I leant in closer and lowered my voice, letting my breath ghost over Gem's ear. "I'm going to fuck you until you can't even remember your own name."

CHAPTER TWENTY-ONE

Gem

FINDING myself in a hot bath surrounded by a mountain of bubbles with a glass of wine and a good book was not the outcome I'd expected when I'd walked into the shop and seen the mess. I'd been pretty sure my evening would consist of swearing, mopping the floors, more swearing, pizza, and an entire bottle of Jameson.

When I'd left the message for Finn I'd just been venting. I hadn't expected him to show up. But just like that, he'd arrived like my knight in shining armour. I didn't know why I'd doubted him.

I flipped the page of the book I'd borrowed and reached for the glass of red wine perched on the tall, wooden unit next to the bath and took a long sip. The water washed gently over my stomach, its heat sinking into my muscles and unknotting the stress.

"Knock, knock," came Finn's voice from the other side

of the door, accompanied by two gentle taps. "Can I come in?"

"Sure." I glanced at the page to check where I was, then closed the book and slid it onto the unit, careful not to dislodge too many bottles. The door cracked, and Finn appeared, looking less worried than he had before.

"How're you doing?"

"Better," I said. "I mean, I know it's still going to be a shitshow, but it's a shitshow I can deal with tomorrow."

Finn chuckled. "Good. I made you a list of builders to ring—a couple from Checkatrade and a couple Lewis and Jules recommended. Someone Jules works with, his cousin runs a construction company, and if we tell him we know Stefan, he'll come and help as soon as possible. Friend of a friend thing."

"Thanks." There was a swirling mix of emotions churning in my chest composed mostly of a heavy dose of guilt. "You didn't have to do that though."

"I know, but I wanted to." Finn looked away from me, focusing his eyes on the teal tiles along the edge of the bath. "You're my friend, and I care about you… a lot. I don't want to see you struggle. There's not much I can do beyond helping from the sidelines, so please, let me do this for you."

"Okay," I said because there was no way I could argue with him. There was something about the way he'd said what he said that made me stop and think, a note of emotion I couldn't name but could feel in the very depths of my soul. It made a note of hope sound somewhere inside me. "Then I won't be a dick about it."

"Good. I'd hate it if you did that." Finn turned towards me and smiled. Heat pulsed through me. He was so fucking handsome. I really wished he could see what I did.

"What are you doing now?"

"Not sure. Why?"

"Want to join me?" I shot Finn a ridiculous wink, and he laughed.

"I'm not sure we'll both fit."

"True, but where's the fun in that," I said. "Come on, get naked."

Finn rolled his eyes but conceded before I could nag him any further. "Fine, but if we make a mess, you can clear it up."

"Of course." I watched as Finn pulled off the hoodie and t-shirt he'd been wearing, my cock stirring as I watched his lean body come into view. Damn, he was sexy. "I'm surprised you agreed so quickly," I added as he shrugged his jeans off, leaving him in brightly patterned socks and black boxers.

"Me too. I'm, er, not usually spontaneous," he said as he removed the last of his clothes. I let out a little growl of delight. His cock was starting to fill, and I couldn't wait to get my hands on him to show him just how much I appreciated everything he'd done for me today. I drained my wine in a swift gulp and slid the glass back onto the unit before sitting up as much as possible. The bath wasn't huge, and it would definitely be a squish, but Finn would be naked and right there for me to touch, and that was all I wanted.

Finn frowned, clearly thinking through the potential arrangement of limbs. Then he stepped into the far end of the tub, his eyes widening as he did. "Jesus Christ, how hot did you make it?"

"It's not that bad," I said. "It's temperate."

"I'm surprised you haven't boiled," Finn said, putting the other foot in and lowering himself into the water. "How do you still have skin?"

"Don't be rude." I flicked some bubbles at him. Finn batted them away with a wry smile. His legs were drawn up to his chest, which meant I couldn't get to his dick. "Put your legs on mine," I said, pointing roughly. "You can stretch them out a bit that way."

"I don't think that's going to work." He still tried it, though, moving his legs slowly so he didn't send water everywhere. It sort of worked until I realised the tap was going to be digging into his spine. And I still couldn't reach his dick without being really obvious.

"What if you spin around? Put your back against my chest? You should fit between my legs."

"You know," Finn said as he moved, "I'm very sure I could make a joke there."

"You could."

"I'm not going to though." The water splashed over me, and although my legs were pinned to the sides of the bath, Finn just about slotted between my thighs. He rested his back against my chest, tilting his head back to rest it against my shoulder. It was a bit awkward, because he was taller than me, but it worked. I pressed a kiss to his temple, and he let out a soft, happy sigh. Somewhere in the back of my mind, a small voice pointed out that this wasn't something *friends* did, even friends who fucked. This was firmly a *rela-*

tionship thing.

I squashed the small voice. Not because I didn't believe what it was saying, but because I didn't care. I'd talk to Finn at some point about how I felt, but right now I just wanted to enjoy it.

"No?"

"No, because I'm a gentleman."

"You are?" I asked, unable to resist teasing him. I pressed a kiss to his neck and felt him relax against me.

"Yes." Finn tapped my leg playfully. "I am a nerd and a gentleman."

"I think I'm more of the roguish type. Here to seduce the gentleman." I reached around and gently ran my finger down Finn's chest.

"Oh? I thought I was supposed to be helping you de-stress," Finn said. "I had plans."

"This is helping." I kissed his neck again, and Finn let out a soft moan. "This is what I want."

"Okay… then touch me. Make me feel good." He twisted his head, his lips finding mine for a slow, deep kiss. Water splashed onto the floor as Finn rotated himself so we were face to face, and my hand slipped between us to run down Finn's body to his hardening cock. Finn groaned into my mouth as my fingers tightened around his shaft, pumping it slowly. The desire to get him off fast and watch him paint my chest with his cum warred with my desire to draw it out, drag him into the bedroom, and lose hours.

"Yes," Finn murmured. "That feels so good. I love it when you touch my cock."

I moaned as his tongue slid into my mouth, soft and

claiming. As we broke apart, I could see the globes of his ass over his shoulder, highlighted by the remains of the bubbles. It was such a perfect ass.

"Can I ask you something?"

"Anything." Finn levered himself up slightly so we weren't quite nose to nose, but my hand never left his dick.

"Can I fuck you?" I asked, silently praying his answer would be yes. "I want to spread you out and show you how amazing you are and how much you mean to me. I want to bring you the same pleasure you bring me, even though I know I'll never come close. I want you to tell me everything you want, and I want to do it for you. I want you to tell me how to fuck you."

"Yes," Finn said as he leant down to kiss me. "I want that too."

He pushed himself up and climbed out of the bath, water rushing off his skin and the remaining droplets glistening in the bathroom's soft lighting. He grabbed a towel and began to dry himself off, and I couldn't resist watching him.

"Are you coming?" he asked, giving me a devious smile.

"I suppose. I was just looking at you. You're so fucking sexy." I levered myself out of the water, taking the towel Finn handed me before leaning over to kiss him.

And I didn't stop kissing him.

One gentle peck turned into something sweet and deep, and then somehow, I was being backed up against the door with Finn's fingers in my hair and his dick grinding against mine. Eventually we made it to the bedroom, even if the steps between the bathroom and the bed were a hazy mess of fingers and tongues.

Finn climbed onto the bed, stretching out and making me stare. He looked so casually confident wearing a wry smile and with desire burning in his eyes, and I didn't know how I was still standing. He beckoned me with one finger, and I went willingly, slotting between his legs and covering his body with mine as we went back to making out. Finn groaned into my mouth, his hands roaming over as much of my body as he could reach.

"Before you fuck me," he said, "I want you to suck my cock and eat my ass. Get me wet and desperate for you."

"Your wish is my command."

I began to kiss down his body, worshipping every inch of him. Finn growled, his fingers fisting in my hair when I sucked his nipples into my mouth and pulled them between my teeth. The sound went straight to my cock, and I ground against the bed, desperate for a little friction.

"Stop that," Finn said. "You're supposed to be focused on me, not you. If you can't behave, I won't let you fuck me." I groaned at his words—because oh my fucking God could he be any sexier—and resisted rolling my hips again, even if it felt like fucking torture. "Good boy." Finn stroked my hair, and I leant into his touch, craving his praise. "Now keep going. I want your mouth on my cock."

He released me, and I slid farther down the bed. I pressed kisses across his hips and then onto the shiny, silken head of his cock. Finn had the perfect dick, and I loved having it in my mouth. It was no hardship to kiss down his shaft and tease his balls with my tongue before swallowing his cock down as far as I could. I knew Finn loved me taking as much as I could, even if it made me choke and gag, and doing that made pleasure shoot through me. Pleasing him, worshipping him… it sent me to a relaxed, happy place that I'd only ever experienced in fantasies.

Finn whispered filthy praise to me as I sucked him, his words punctuated with low moans and growls that sent me higher and higher. The sounds were achingly familiar, but I wasn't sure if it was because I already knew them as Finn's or whether I'd heard them somewhere else before. My brain was too preoccupied to figure it out.

"That's it… Fuck, baby, you've got a hot mouth," Finn said. "But you need to stop now. I want you to eat my ass." I didn't want to stop though. I was having too much fun, and I didn't want to lose the weight of Finn's cock on my tongue. But Finn wasn't giving me a choice. His fingers fisted in my hair, and he gently pulled me off his cock with a rumbling growl. "I said that's enough. Were you not listening to me?"

"I was," I said, hoping my cheeky charm would get me somewhere. But Finn's eyes were molten heat that seared into my soul, and I couldn't ignore the glint of disappointment at the edge of them. "But I… I love sucking your cock. I didn't want to stop."

Finn's smile was sharp enough to cut. "My poor boy. Are you that desperate?"

"A little." I suddenly wondered whether he'd be up for calling me a slut… just for him obviously, but sometimes it was something I craved.

"Are you sure you still want to fuck me?"

"Yes. Please."

"Then I want you to put your mouth to good use on my hole." There was no room for argument in his tone. "Use this too." He passed me a bottle of lube, which he'd procured from somewhere, and his smile softened. "I can't wait to feel you inside me."

I took the lube and watched Finn lift and spread his legs, exposing his ass to me. I swallowed. "Can I, er, can I request something?"

"Of course. What is it?"

"Can you… will you… sometimes, when we fuck, will you… would you call me a slut?" I felt my face heating, feeling more vulnerable than I had in a long time.

"Yes, baby. I can do that. Thank you for telling me," he said. "And if you ever don't like how I use it, or you want me to stop, please just say so."

"Okay."

"Good. Now, please open me up before I take matters into my own hands," Finn said. "And I promise that will not involve you at all."

The teasing threat was enough to make me sink down and run my tongue along his taint and across his hole. Another shiver of pleasure raced across my skin at the noise Finn made. I used one hand to gently pull his ass cheeks apart as I began to do as I'd been told, licking, sucking, kissing, and teasing the sensitive, puckered skin until Finn was a writhing mess. I loved the earthy taste of him on my tongue, and the desperate stream of growls, groans, and praise that filled my ears. My other hand found the bottle of lube, and I poured some onto my fingers, slowly pressing one into his hole alongside my tongue.

"Fuck! Oh fuck, that's it. Yes! Get me ready for you," Finn said. "I can't wait to take your cock."

I moaned and pushed another finger into his ass, pumping them in and out slowly. Finn gasped as I brushed the pads of my fingers across his prostate. Pressing a kiss to his taint, I started teasing the spot until I couldn't stand it anymore. I needed to be inside Finn so I could watch his face. I wanted to see the pleasure I brought him and watch him come on my cock, knowing I was making him feel good.

Pulling my fingers out, I slathered more lube onto my cock and repositioned myself so I could kneel between his thighs. Finn looked up at me with slick lips and a desperate expression that left me with no doubt that he was still the one in charge. Slowly, I jerked my cock, tapping it gently on his slick hole, waiting to be told I could fuck him.

"Such a good slut for me," Finn said, beckoning me down for a kiss and sliding his tongue into my mouth. "Waiting to be told what to do. You're always so good for me, and you always know how to make me feel amazing." His fingers caressed my jaw, adding a new dimension of tenderness to the kiss. "I want you to fuck me. I want you to start off slowly… tease me… and then I want you to give it to me hard. I want you to make me come on your cock." He smirked at me, and I knew what was coming. "But you're not allowed to come until I tell you to. And you're not allowed to come before me. Do you understand? Can you do that for me?"

"Yeah." I nodded. "I'll try."

"You won't try," he said. "You'll do as you're told. Because you're a good slut, and you want to make me feel good."

I groaned and nodded, knowing I'd do exactly as he said. Finn knew how to push all my buttons, and it was an incredible feeling. Lining up my cock, I slowly pressed inside him, watching Finn's face as I did. His ass felt incredible around my cock, and I knew I was going to have to concentrate to make sure I didn't blow my load in the next two minutes. I didn't think Finn would be disappointed in me if I did, but I wasn't going to give myself a chance to find out. Instead, I focused on fucking him slowly, sliding all the way in and out, and lifting his hips and wrapping his legs around my thighs so I could tease his prostate with the head of my cock with each stroke.

Finn groaned, his fingers fisting the sheets as pleasure rolled through him. And just knowing I was doing that to him made me dizzy.

"Harder," Finn said. "I want it harder now. Give it to me." I did as I was told, pulling him onto my cock and fucking him with everything I had. Heat shot down my spine, and I bit my lip as I tried to stave off my impending orgasm. "That's it... Fuck, just like that, baby. God, that feels so good!" Finn reached for his shaft and began to jerk himself hard and fast as if he knew I didn't have much control left in me. "Give it to me... I want it... Make me come. I know you can... Fuck!" Finn growled, his body tensing as his hand flew over his cock as he shot creamy ribbons of cum across his skin. His ass tightened around my cock as I fucked him, and it felt like he was trying to pull my orgasm out of me. I was so close, and I knew I wouldn't be able to hold on much longer.

"Come for me," Finn said softly. "You've been so good. I want you to come. Give me your load."

That was all I needed, and I cried out as I buried my release deep inside his hole, my fingers clutching his thighs. "Fuck," I said as soon as it felt like I could breathe again. "That was…"

"Yes, it was."

I chuckled and gently pulled out, lowering Finn's legs. Then I leant down and kissed him slowly. "Thank you. That was amazing."

"You're welcome." He kissed me again, and when I lay down beside him, he wrapped his arms around me, keeping the troubles of the day a distant memory.

CHAPTER TWENTY-TWO

Gem

WHEN I WOKE UP, tucked beside Finn, it was still pitch-black outside. A quick glance at my phone told me it was only half three. I groaned and rolled over, hoping I'd drift off again, but now that I was awake, I really needed to piss, and by the time I made it to the bathroom, I knew I wouldn't be getting back to sleep any time soon. The floating, relaxed, post-sex sensation was gone, and my brain was firing on all cylinders, thinking through everything that needed doing and wondering how early was too early to call the builders.

Grabbing my t-shirt and boxers off the bathroom floor, where I'd abandoned them last night, I dressed and made my way into the kitchen. I flicked on one of the lamps, hoping that grabbing some water and chilling on the sofa in the living room for a bit would help my brain switch off again. Finn's tablet sat on the little coffee table by the sofa surrounded by a stack of papers. I shifted everything to the left slightly so I could grab a coaster from under the tablet. Underneath it was Finn's planner—an old-fashioned Filofax in a deep red, faux-leather binder. It was totally Finn, and the sight of it had a sleepy smile crossing my lips.

The organiser was open to this week, and I saw a list of builders and their numbers neatly printed under yesterday's date. It made my chest tighten for reasons I couldn't explain. Maybe it was because Finn had done this for me without question. It was tangible proof he cared about me and that I meant more to him than something casual he would discard when things got difficult.

I put the glass of water down and settled myself on the sofa. Glancing at the diary again, I wondered if Finn would mind if I took a photo of the list. I knew I shouldn't really be looking at it, even though it was right there. It was private, and Finn hadn't given me permission to look. Not that I expected it to be full of secrets, but still, personal boundaries were a thing. Then again, looking at one page wasn't going to hurt, especially if it was already open and I was just taking a picture of the information already there. And I didn't have to tell Finn. Or I could tell him later when he was awake.

It was better to beg forgiveness than ask permission.

Leaning over the table, I positioned my phone over the date so I could make sure I captured everything. Out of the corner of my eye, I spotted some small letters printed under Friday that caught my attention: Upload F&F Bonus 3. I frowned, trying to work out what was different about it. I scanned the week, looking at how Finn described the rest of his work. The language was similar but there was something about it that nagged at my brain.

"It's nothing," I said. "Don't be nosy."

I hoped by saying it out loud I'd be dissuaded, but my brain refused to let it go. I sat back on the sofa, pulling up Twitter in the hope I could distract myself with some mindless scrolling. Instead, I ended up on Audible, looking through both of Finn's narrator profiles to see if I could find anything with a similar title. I knew he used one name for the cosy mysteries and crime novels he did and another—which was just a minor variation—for romance novels. There was nothing with that title pattern though, and nothing that even suggested bonus content. Unless he was doing it privately for someone, although he'd never mentioned doing anything like that.

Shaking my head, I tried to focus on something else. This was absolutely none of my fucking business, and I had no idea why I was suddenly so obsessed. Maybe it was because somewhere deep inside my brain, I was still clinging to the idea that Finn was the narrator of Fantasy and Filth, even though I'd dismissed the idea so many times it wasn't even funny anymore.

Yeah, they had the same laugh. But so do a ton of other people. I'd heard someone make a little hiccup laugh in The Lost World last week when I'd been stocking shelves. I'd looked around to see who it was and found a couple of young women comparing various new fantasy releases. It wasn't exactly an uncommon sound. And, yes, the narrator had said he was playing through all of *Final Fantasy*, which was something Finn had also been doing, but those games were fun to play.

I couldn't keep trying to make connections because I wanted them to be the same person, but there was something sexy as fuck about the idea.

The reality would be different, though, and I had no idea how I'd even bring it up. How the hell would that even work? I couldn't just start a conversation with "Surprise! I know about your secret, and I've been subscribing to your MyFans for nine months and love getting off to your work." Yeah, that was never going to happen.

Finn might have been more confident and kinky in bed than I'd ever imagined, but he wouldn't be the only man who was different in his day-to-day life. It was always the quiet ones who got you, and Finn was the quietest man I knew. Which was why it made sense for him to be a phenomenally kinky bastard who knew how to push every single one of my buttons without even trying.

I sighed. I was going around in circles, and I wasn't getting anywhere.

Except…

Shit.

I reached out and flicked back a couple of weeks. There was a little note for "Bonus 2" under the Friday several weeks ago. With shaking fingers, I tapped through Chrome to find my MyFans account and the Fantasy and Filth page.

"This is ridiculous," I muttered. But it didn't stop me. I swallowed, staring at the screen. There was a post from the same date labelled "Very Late Valentine's Bonus: Part Two." And when I scrolled further back, I found part one, which had been posted on a date that matched the pattern.

It wasn't *proof* proof, but it was as close as I could get without some major snooping and a violation of Finn's privacy. I'd crossed a lot of lines to get to this point, and my pounding heart was evidence of that. But it did mean I was right—potentially at least—and my emotions swelled. Finn was the narrator, the man I'd been unrealistically crushing on for months. And he was also the man I was falling for.

For once, life didn't seem to want to punish me.

Except, I realised it was. In two ways. First, it had given me this knowledge knowing I either had to keep it a secret or tell Finn I was his biggest fan and most devoted subscriber. And second, it had made me realise that Finn was keeping secrets from me and a pretty big fucking secret at that. I wasn't angry because I didn't have any fucking right to be, but I was… upset. But I didn't know if I had any right to be that either. It wasn't as if Finn and I were in a relationship, and it wasn't as if he had to tell me when I hadn't made any commitment to him.

We were friends, though, and I'd thought we were close. Then again there was close and there was *close*, and this fell into the second category. I wondered if he'd actually told anyone else. I got the feeling Chantelle knew from things Finn had said on previous recordings, and after meeting her, I wouldn't be surprised if she'd pushed Finn to go for it. But I didn't think anyone else knew and certainly not his family.

Then again, if I recorded sexy as fuck audio porn that people got off to on a regular basis, I wouldn't tell my family either. I didn't think I'd tell *anyone*, so I understood Finn's reasoning. I just needed to find a way to tell him I knew and that I was okay with it. More than okay with it. I mean, I'd happily recreate every single one of his scenarios if he'd let me. I wondered if he'd be up for that. I also didn't want him to think that if, by some fucking miracle, we got together that he'd have to stop. I knew some guys would be dicks about it, but I loved the idea of him recording the scenarios, especially if he was thinking about me while he was doing it. Plus, it was just words, and at the end of the day, I'd be the one he was coming home to.

"Fucking hell!" I scrubbed my face, trying to work out what to do next. But four in the morning wasn't the time to figure that out, and it wasn't like I could do anything at this exact second. I wasn't going to wake Finn up just to demand an answer or explanation—no matter how much he liked me, pulling some shit like that was never going to endear me to him.

Swinging my feet off the sofa, I walked back to his room. Finn was curled on his side, his head barely visible above the duvet. Just knowing he was there stripped my worldly worries away, and I smiled as I pulled off my clothes and climbed in beside him, pressing against his back and pulling him into my arms. Finn let out a little snuffly sound and a sigh, and I realised that whatever happened, I never wanted to let him go.

CHAPTER TWENTY-THREE

Finn

"WHAT THE FUCK are they doing up there?" I asked, glancing at the ceiling of the storeroom as something heavy clattered above us. It sounded as if someone was about to come crashing through.

"Fuck if I know," Gem said, giving the ceiling an evil glare as we scooped the last of the sodden towels off the floor and tossed them into an enormous, rainbow IKEA bag. "Apparently there was a problem with some of the slates? And something had rotted? Something the landlord should have fucking noticed if he wasn't so busy swanning around on my rent."

"At least he agreed to pay for it and didn't quibble the quote."

"Yeah, but that's only because the guy he suggested wanted to charge double." Gem winced at another loud bang. "And your brother and Tristan both gave me some helpful wording to put in an email to the letting agency."

"That always helps," I said. I was glad Eli had offered advice without prompting when I'd first mentioned the issue in the family group chat because it meant I hadn't had to convince Gem to ask him. Not that I thought Gem wouldn't, but he was stressed, and I worried it might be an issue of pride or feeling like he was overstepping. Either way, it was all made easier when Eli just offered off the bat. "How long will it take?"

"Should be done by the end of the week. Depends if they can get everything they need." Gem looked around at the mess that was the stockroom and shook his head. All the shelves had been pulled away from the walls, and there were a couple of large dehumidifiers whirring away, attempting to dry the room out as fast as possible. Gem had pushed the stock delivery back by a week to give it time to dry out because he didn't want to store the boxes in a damp room—mostly because he was worried if they sat there, they'd start to mould. I didn't think everything would stick around for as long as he seemed to think it would, but I didn't say that.

Gem had been very on edge over the last few days, and at first, I'd put it down to the situation with the shop —as was only natural—but now I was concerned something else was going on. I just wasn't sure whether to mention it because I didn't want to make things worse. If Gem wanted to bring it up, he'd bring it up, and all I could do was be a good friend and support him as best I could.

And maybe dream up a few decadent ways to take his mind off everything.

"Fingers crossed," I said as I moved the bags towards the door so Gem could take the towels home and wash them. "And at least you didn't have to wait too long to find someone. I know when Mimbles and Mum had their roof redone, they had to wait six months to get booked in."

"I guess, but this is more of a patch job than anything. Hopefully it'll last."

"I'm sure it will." Gem frowned but didn't say anything. I pursed my lips, both concerned and annoyed by his attitude. I knew it was tough, but I did wish he'd be a smidge more positive. It wasn't as if the whole thing had caved in, and nothing had been lost. Still, I got the feeling it was just another stone on the pile Gem was carrying, and the weight was starting to get to him. He'd put so much pressure on himself to do well, and despite his promise to me that he'd do his best and give it one hundred percent, I thought the roof might have been a bit too much. Especially because it was only ten days until the shop's grand opening, and nothing was ready. We were virtually back to square one in some places.

"What's next?" I asked, looking around the room. "Clean the walls? Repaint?"

"Yeah, we need to clean everything. In here doesn't necessarily need repainting if the stains come out. The shelves are going over them anyway. It's not like anyone else is ever going to see in here. They might not even see anything at this rate."

Gem walked away to grab some sponges, and I felt

anger rising from deep in my chest. I wasn't an angry person usually, and it took a lot to piss me off, but right now I felt like a volcano that was moments away from exploding. And not even taking some deep breaths was helping.

"You okay?" Gem asked when he returned holding an open package of yellow dish sponges.

"No," I said, the word coming out sharp and snappish. "I'm not okay. In fact, I'm quite angry right now." Gem opened his mouth, and I held up a hand to stop him from talking. "No, I'm not finished. Look, I know you're stressed right now and that everything has gone tits up, but that does not give you the right to be so miserable. You promised me you were going to try your best, and now you're acting as if the world has ended when all that's happened is that you had a slightly leaky roof." I took another deep breath. Gem was looking at me with a stunned expression like he'd never expected such an outburst from me. Neither had I, if I was honest, but I had to make him see sense.

"I know it's a pain in the ass, and it's set you back and is costing you time, energy, and money, but I am asking you to please try to see the positives or at least don't mire yourself so deeply in the negatives. I'm not saying you can't be upset that this happened, that would be dismissive of me, but I am saying you need to stop acting as if the apocalypse is nigh, and that you're doing this on your own. I will be here every day if you need me, and I will do anything I can to help, but I will not sit by and watch you wallow in self-pity. You are better than this, and you know it."

Gem stared at me, his mouth slightly open. I glared at him as if daring him to argue. I watched him weigh up the decision and tried to extinguish the anger burning in my chest by taking a deep, slow breath. I had said my piece and continuing to be angry was not going to achieve anything.

We both needed a break.

"I'm sorry," Gem said. "I know I'm being a wanker. I didn't mean to take it out on you."

"Apology accepted."

"I've never seen you angry before."

"I don't enjoy the sensation," I said as faint, muffled shouting came from above us. "Although that noise isn't helping." A new idea flickered to life in my brain, one that would hopefully make both of us feel better and give us some space from the pressure of the situation at hand. Reaching out, I plucked the package of sponges from Gem's fingers. "Come on. We're taking a break."

"But—"

"No buts. We're both stressed right now, and it's not doing either of us any good. We need a change of scenery. We can come back later when the builders have gone and do some tidying then." I put the sponges into the bucket of cleaning supplies and went to retrieve my coat. "Come on. Let's go."

"Okay," Gem said, still sounding suspicious. "Where are we going?"

"Out." I almost said on a date, but I stopped myself. "We'll go and get some food, and then we can either see what's on at the Odeon or we can go to the board game café on Cornhill. I'm not sure if you have to book, though, but we can check the website while we eat."

Gem nodded and then grinned at me as he reached for his tweed jacket. "I thought you weren't spontaneous?"

"Sometimes the situation calls for it," I said as I tried to ignore the way my face was burning. Gem was right, usually I pre-planned everything, but right now we both needed to get out. So mild spontaneity it was. After all, it wasn't as if lunch and the cinema were revolutionary ideas.

"It really fucking does." Gem patted his pockets. "Let's get out of here before I fucking explode."

We headed for the front of the shop, locking the door behind us as we stepped out into the bright, spring sunshine. There was still a chilly breeze, but feeling the sun warm my face as we walked down Steep Hill made my stress start to melt away. "Where do you want to get lunch?"

"Do you fancy Wagamama?" Gem asked. "I'm kinda craving Katsu curry."

"Sounds perfect." I grinned at him. And then my heart nearly stopped as Gem slipped his fingers into mine, squeezing my hand lightly as he continued walking. Like nothing was different at all. I swallowed, trying not to trip over my own feet as my heart raced. We hadn't talked about anything changing, even though we'd originally promised we would, but this didn't feel like a change. It felt like more of a natural progression.

Wagamama was packed, but the waitress managed to squeeze us into a small table looking out over the Brayford. There were numerous swans and ducks floating across the body of water, along with a couple of rowing teams from the University of Lincoln, which was situated just across the pool.

"You know," I said once we'd ordered, "I wouldn't even want to row on that water. It's got to be freezing, and it's always full of…"

"Shit?" Gem supplied with a grin. "Me either. Although I bet eighteen-year-old me would have jumped into it if I was drunk and you dared me."

I rolled my eyes but couldn't stop myself from smiling. "You wouldn't be the first. And I'd have had no sympathy if you ended up with some horrible disease and hypothermia."

"None at all?"

"Well, maybe a little."

"I'll take that," Gem said. He looked so much more relaxed already, and it made me ridiculously happy to see him back to his bright, charming self. I never wanted to see him stressed or unhappy. It affected me in a way I'd never experienced before, and I didn't enjoy the sensation. "Not that I'd have deserved it."

"It sounds like you were an *interesting* teenager."

"You can say enormous twat," Gem said as he sipped his Coke. "It would be the truth."

I laughed. "That has to come with some stories though."

"It does but not many I'm proud of. I'm still surprised I actually passed my degree half the time. Although that might have something to do with the almighty bollocking I got from my mum when I finished my second year with a barely scraped two two." He shook his head. "I'm surprised she let me back in the house that summer to be honest. She and my dad didn't go to university, and she considered it a great opportunity that I was wasting." He shrugged. "She had a fair point. And I realised I had a fair bit of growing up to do… after I'd stopped sulking."

"I'd say I can't imagine you sulking but…" I shot Gem a teasing grin, and he snorted.

"I get it. I'm a dickhead," he said.

"You're not." I reached across the table and squeezed his hand. "I'm just teasing."

"I know." He smiled. "You're cute when you tease me."

I wanted to say something, but I had no words, and when I finally thought of something, our food arrived. I snapped my chopsticks apart and began to eat the glazed pork belly and greens that topped my bowl of ramen. "So, what do you want to do after this?"

"Not sure," Gem said. "Want to go see a film since the Odeon is right there?"

I nodded. An afternoon on a comfy seat watching something fun sounded like a perfect distraction. "Sounds good. Any preference on what we see? There's that new action film out, *Red Shadow Rising*."

"Isn't that the one with Jason's brother?" Gem asked. I nodded. Jason happened to be the brother of one of the world's biggest film stars, Henry Lu, who'd recently taken up the mantel of Hollywood's latest action hero darling. It always made me laugh because in these films, Henry always played suave, charming men with oceans of cool who drove fast cars, beat the bad guy, and got the girl without putting a hair out of place, while in reality Henry exuded continuous golden-retriever energy. I'd met him a couple of times through Jason, and he was wonderfully sweet if a little over the top.

"Does it weird you out knowing that if Jason and Lewis get married, you'll have a Hollywood superstar for a brother-in-law?"

"A little," I said. "But they'd actually have to get married first."

"You don't think they will?"

I frowned. "No, I think they will but not for a while. They seem very happy as they are, and with Richard getting married, I don't think Lewis will want to interfere with that." Lewis could be ridiculously outgoing when he wanted, but he was also an overthinker and a homebody, and I wasn't sure how he'd feel about being the centre of attention for the day. Especially because it would probably end up being a large wedding.

"Makes sense. And the film sounds good. Kinda stupid and easy to watch," Gem said. He pulled out his phone. "I'll get us some tickets."

There was a showing with tickets left in half an hour, so when we'd finished our lunch we pottered across the street to the cinema where Gem bought us a tub of popcorn to share. And as we found our seats and settled in to watch, Gem leant over and kissed me gently. "Thanks for this. It's just what I needed."

My cheek burned as the lights dimmed, and I realised I could pretend this wasn't a date as much as I wanted, but that wouldn't stop it from being a lie.

CHAPTER TWENTY-FOUR

Gem

I KNEW I'd been a grumpy bastard for a couple of days, but it wasn't for the reason Finn thought. The roof repairs and rapidly approaching opening might have been stressful, but there wasn't much I could do about them except keep going and throw as much time and energy at them as I could. They weren't the problem.

The thing that was eating me up inside was the knowledge of Finn's side hustle and the dawning realisation that I had to tell him I knew soon before I blurted his secret out at the worst moment possible. Like when he was inside me or had my cock halfway down his throat. I needed him to know that I knew and that I didn't have a problem with it—that I had the very opposite of a problem with it, whatever the fuck that was.

The fact that we'd practically been on a date two days ago had solidified the fact in my mind because I was starting to have very real feelings for Finn. But every time I thought about bringing it up, I found myself at a total loss for words. I still had no idea how the fuck I'd even start the conversation.

"Gem? You okay?" Finn's words cut through my thoughts, and I realised I was staring off into space while holding a paintbrush that was dripping onto the sheet under my feet. We'd been trying to repaint the upstairs back wall, but my brain had decided to wander off.

"Yeah, just thinking," I said.

"Everything okay?"

"Yeah." I looked at the wall and my paintbrush, wondering whether I should lie. "Do you think the wall is dry enough to do this?"

"I think so." Finn frowned, putting his hand out to touch it. "But we can leave the dehumidifiers on for another few days. You've got them until the weekend, right?"

I nodded. "They're picking them up Friday. Cutting it a bit close, but it'll be fine." The shop was opening at nine thirty on Saturday morning come hell or high water, even if it meant I'd be there all night stocking shelves, tidying, and generally trying to make it look presentable. If I needed to exist purely on Iron-Bru, Monster, and Red Bull for a day or two, I'd survive. I was following Jay's lead and closing on Monday, so I could crash then. "Besides," I added, "this is going behind a load of shelves. Nobody is going to look too closely."

"Are you moving things, then?" Finn asked as he looked at the mess of bookshelves and units abandoned in the middle of the room.

"I think so, just to make sure the worst bits are covered up." I put the paintbrush down in the tray. "And I'll get some of those mini moisture absorber pots to slide in around the shelves, just in case." There was a bang from above us and an angry cry followed by some muffled arguing. I grinned. I was used to the noise Stefan and co made by now, and it was going to be odd when they finished up this afternoon. There hadn't been any nasty surprises in the roof—like the whole thing needing to be replaced—but Stefan had been muttering darkly about old buildings and landlords last night. At least mine hadn't put up any resistance to paying, but I got the feeling Stefan had left a note on the quote along the lines of "We do x, y, and z now, or you pay for a whole new roof in the next year."

I really ought to learn something about building maintenance, just for my own benefit and so I had some fucking clue what people were talking about when they mentioned joists or insulation or tiling.

"That works," said Finn, wincing at another hammering sound. "When do you want to move everything?"

"As soon as it's all dry." I shrugged. "It'll probably be Thursday or Friday."

Finn's face pinched, and I could see his anxiety rearing its ugly head. I got the feeling Finn liked things to be done with plenty of time to spare, and this was not going to be one of those times. "Oh… that's a little—"

"Late? Yeah, I know. I'll be fine."

"Are you sure?"

"No, but I'm doing my best not to panic," I said, hoping that if I said it out loud it would squash some of the fear rising inside me. "I promised I'd be positive. This is what I've got."

"Okay." Finn nodded. "I, er, I'll try to help as much as I can, but…"

He trailed off, and I smiled. "It's okay. I know you have your own job to do. You can't do mine as well."

"I'm sorry," he said. "I'm just starting to fall a little behind, and it's absolutely not your fault at all. It's just I've slightly overbooked myself, and I also have—"

"A side hustle too?" Finn stared at me as the words fell out of my mouth. "Shit. I didn't mean to say that. This wasn't how I wanted this conversation to go."

"Side hustle?" Finn's voice had gone very quiet but with a noticeable tremble of panic. "Conversation?"

"Yeah." I sighed and ran my hands over my hair as I tried to work out what the fuck to say. "I know about your… side project. Your audio blog on MyFans." All the colour drained out of Finn's face until he looked like an anaemic vampire. "At least, I'm pretty sure it's you, and by the look on your face, I'm guessing I'm right?"

"H-how? How did you find me? I'm so careful." There was an audible note of panic in his voice now, and I could practically hear his heart pounding. A wave of cold fear washed over me. "I've never told anyone… I don't. I always…"

"Hey, it's okay," I said, reaching out for him. Finn recoiled and took a step back, his face contorted in terror. My heart sank. This was an utter shitshow and everything I'd wanted to avoid. "Nobody else knows. It's just me. And I didn't set out to find something on you for nefarious purposes or some shit like that. I, er, I've actually had a subscription for a while." I put my hands up, trying desperately to defuse the tension. But I'd never been good in situations like this. "I didn't know it was you. I just thought it was really fucking sexy. But then we started hanging out more and having sex, and I heard your Q&A, and I saw a note in your diary, and it fit with something you'd posted… It was just tiny puzzle pieces really. That, and the fact that I *really* wanted it to be you because… I… because…"

The last words wouldn't come. They were stuck in my mouth like they'd attached themselves with Gorilla Glue. Finn was still staring at me with horror like I'd morphed into some sort of gribbly eldritch being before his very eyes.

"How long?"

"Not long, I promise," I said. "I had an inkling for a couple of months, but I thought that was just me being desperate. But only in the last week or so. When I, er, when I came back to yours after the roof leaked."

"Oh." It was such a small, defeated sound, and it wrenched my heart in two with the force of an exploding star. "I'm sorry."

"What? Why are you apologising?" I stepped towards him again and this time Finn stayed still, but when I reached out to touch him, he was stiff, frozen in place by fear. "You have nothing to apologise for."

"I do. I didn't mean to keep it a secret, but nobody was ever supposed to know."

"Why not?"

"Because they weren't," Finn snapped. "It was private. For me. And I know what most people think about any form of sex work. I'm un-datable enough as it is without throwing that into the mix."

"What the fuck do you mean by that? You're fucking amazing, Finn. Why the fuck would you think that?"

"Just look at me." Finn gestured to himself, and I frowned.

"I am looking at you," I said. "You're fucking gorgeous."

Finn rolled his eyes. "You only think that because we're fucking. You'd never have even noticed me if I hadn't offered."

"That's not true." But it wasn't a point I could prove. I couldn't pull my memories out of my head and show them to him. All I could do was put my thoughts into words and hope he believed me, but at this point I wasn't sure he did. Finn's fear had taken over, and it was an emotion that was hard to argue with.

"Right, of course you would have." I'd never heard Finn sound so angry and upset, but I could see the desperation in his eyes. I didn't know if he wanted me to leave or stay, and I didn't think he knew what he wanted either. "Look at me, Gem. I'm a nerd's nerd. I'm tall and lanky and quiet and so shy I can't even talk to most people. I like anime and old video games, and that's fine. I'm not ashamed of that. But you can't look at me and tell me I'm some walking wet dream because I own a fucking mirror, and I know you'd be lying."

"So? I love all that stuff. I love you, you bloody idiot." Silence.

Finn's mouth opened, then closed again. Mine stayed

hanging open like some weird fucking fish. Of all the moments for those words to come out, now had to be one of the worst. And I'd called him a bloody idiot on top of it. If there was a bloody idiot here, it was definitely me.

"You don't mean that," Finn said, taking another step back towards the stairs. "You don't. You don't love me. You can't."

"I can, and I do."

"No… Why?"

"Do you want me to list the reasons? Because I will. Or do you not want me to be in love with you?" I forced myself to say the second part out loud, even if it nearly broke me. I'd never thought Finn would reject me like this. Nothing that had happened in the past few months had made me think it was a possibility.

"No… I… I want that. But I can't let you love me. Because I'm not right for you, and I'm so scared you'll wake up one day and wonder what the hell you've done with your life. You say you love me, and you say that you don't mind about the audio, but that's now. One day, you'll feel different, and I can't take that pain. Because I… I…" Finn looked like he was about to vomit. He clapped his hand to his mouth. Then he turned and ran for the stairs, his feet thudding on the wood.

It took me a second to work out what he was doing. As soon as I did, I followed him, thundering down the stairs like I was leading a full battle charge. "Finn, wait!"

He was already at the door. "I'm sorry," he said. He looked so dejected, and all I wanted was a way to make him stop. To stay here, with me, so we could talk this shit out.

But Finn was overwhelmed and drowning in emotion, and I couldn't do anything but let him walk out the door.

It closed with a bang, leaving me staring out into the street and wishing I could have made him stay.

All I could do was hope he'd come back to me or that I could find a way to reach him.

CHAPTER TWENTY-FIVE

Finn

MY SELF-PITYING wallowing on the sofa later that evening was interrupted by the front door banging open. I was given less than two seconds to process everything before I heard Eli cry, "Where is my beautiful baby brother? What mortal has injured his soul thusly? I shall smite them!"

"Calm down, dickhead," Jules added. "You're not fucking Shakespeare."

"This is true," Eli said. I turned my head inside my blanket pile to see Eli, Jules, Lewis, and Oscar standing in my kitchen, and the sight of them made everything a million times worse. How had they found out I was a mess? And how much did they know about what had happened? Fear and shame and anxiety spun in my chest like they were on the world's most dramatic spin cycle. I wanted them here, but I didn't, and it was for the same reason: because they were my family.

The fact that Oscar, who I hadn't seen since Christmas, was there intensified everything. He was the one who'd always looked out for me, even when I hadn't needed it, and I hated the idea that he'd come home for a break and had to deal with my mess. Or even worse, disturbed his life and time off just to come and look after me.

It was the straw that broke the camel's back, and from deep within my blanket fortress I started to wail. Which was completely the wrong move. The four of them saw me as if their vision was dependent on movement—or possibly distress—and they all piled into the living room and onto the sofa, engulfing me in a crushing pile of bodies. Jules grabbed me so tightly in her arms I wasn't sure whether I could breathe while Lewis slid off the cushions and onto the floor, making soothing noises and telling me to breathe. Eli was muttering something about death and destruction while Oscar reached through a gap in the blanket to find my hand, stroking the back with his thumb.

It was overwhelming and adorable all at once, and they all just sat there while I sobbed. I knew crying was healthy, but I couldn't help but feel embarrassed. This was a situation of my own making, and yet here I was crying as if I'd been the one who'd been wronged. I'd known from the start that things with Gem were going to end badly, but I'd still insisted on pursuing whatever we'd been doing.

"It's okay," I heard Lewis say softly, his hand reaching out to squeeze my knee. "Whatever it is, we can fix it."

"We can," Oscar said. "I promise."

"Do you think Mimbles and Paul would let us bury a body under their vegetable garden?" Eli asked. There was a soft thump and an indignant yelp, so I guessed someone had hit him. "What? I'm just saying. It's always worth asking! Unless you know someone with pigs."

"You're not helping," Jules said.

"Neither are you. Let the poor man go. I doubt he can breathe with your biceps wrapped around his neck." I let out a weak, snotty chuckle as Jules released me, and Eli gasped triumphantly. "He lives!"

"I'm fine," I said, emerging from my blanket cocoon so I could look at them all properly. "You didn't need to come."

"Yes, we did. Don't be silly," Lewis said.

"And you don't have to say you're fine either," said Oscar as he reached out to brush hair off my face. "You don't have to lie to us."

"I'm not…" They all glared at me. "Fine, but this is a mess of my own making, so it's probably what I deserve."

"Bollocks," Eli said. He sat on the other side of Oscar but was leaning across him as far as possible. "Nobody deserves to be sad."

"Exactly," added Jules. "You wanna tell us what happened?"

"Not really."

"Okay, let me rephrase," said Eli. "Please tell us what happened. Or we'll have to get it out of you in other ways."

"Like?"

"I don't know. Tickle you or something." He shrugged and grinned. "Come on. We promise never to judge you. We love you, and if we can forgive Lewis for dating a smoking hot celebrity in secret"—Lewis made an indignant sound which Eli ignored—"or Richard for being straight, then we can forgive anything."

"This is about Gem, right?" Lewis asked, looking up at me with a soft expression, his pink hair falling into his eyes. "He messaged me and asked me to check in on you, but he didn't say why. You two were dating?"

"You had a boyfriend? And didn't tell us?" Eli gasped.

"You didn't tell us about your boyfriend either," Jules pointed out. Eli waved a hand dismissively.

"That was different. Tristan is Dick's best friend, and I knew it would cause trouble. And the fact that he punched me in the face is proof of that."

I chuckled as I remembered that Sunday. It would be seared into the family memory forever. "I think that was even better than the pasta salad incident."

"I'm almost sad I missed it," Oscar said. "At least Lewis sent me the video."

"Yeah, don't tell Mum you saw it," Lewis said. "She wanted me to delete it."

"Where is it now?" Jules asked.

"On my Dropbox." Lewis shrugged, wobbling slightly where he was crouched. "Just in case I ever need it."

"All's fair in love and war," Eli said. "But we're getting off topic." I sighed, realising they weren't going to stay distracted forever. "Come on. Tell us everything. Did you get dumped?"

"No, not really."

"Good, because if so, I would have wanted to do illegal, exploratory brain surgery on Gem to find out what the fuck was wrong with him," Eli said. "You're perfect."

"I'm really not," I said. Oscar squeezed my hand tighter, and I knew I had to tell them everything, no matter how embarrassing it was. Mostly because I knew if I didn't, at least one of them would be able to tell I was leaving something out. They could all smell a plot hole at two hundred feet, and they all knew me well enough to know when I was lying. "Just promise me you won't judge me and that you won't tell anyone else."

"Promise," Oscar said with an encouraging smile.

"And no murdering Gem. This isn't his fault."

"If you're sure," Eli said.

"I am." I took a deep breath. "I guess this started in January. Or maybe before that. I'm not sure. I've had a crush on Gem since we met, but in January, he got dumped by the guy he was seeing—well, ghosted really—and then his ex turned up at The Lost World's birthday party with his new fling. Anyway, I guess I thought I might have a chance, and then, when I was helping Gem with the whole new shop thing, we started… we started hooking up."

"Oh?" Lewis had a wry smile on his face.

"Yes," I said, ignoring the undertone in his voice that suggested trouble. "We're… compatible."

"Sounds sexy," Eli said. I ignored him but couldn't help smiling when Lewis shot him a withering look and Oscar kicked him in the shin.

"Anyway," I continued. "Everything was fine, but—"

"You caught feelings?" Oscar asked. "Or you couldn't ignore the feelings you had and then you told Gem, and he was a dick about it?"

"No, it wasn't that. Well, I did—do—have feelings for him. And I think… I know now that Gem feels the same…"

"What's the problem, then?" Jules asked, her brow furrowing in confusion. "If you both like each other and the sex was good—I'm assuming it was—what went wrong?"

"It's not him at all. It's me." I sighed. "He found… He…" I felt my skin heating like I was face to face with the sun. I'd never been so embarrassed in all my life. There had to be some way for me to get around this without telling my siblings what was really going on.

"Oooh, secret sex tape? Collection of naughty things under your bed? Tentacle porn? Oooh, furry porn?" Eli asked, a gleeful smile on his face. "It has to be something salacious. It's *always* the quiet ones."

"Don't be a bellend," Lewis said and smacked Eli's leg. "Whatever Finn does or doesn't like has absolutely nothing to do with you. And as long as it's all safe and consensual, then there's nothing wrong with any of it."

"I know that." Eli huffed. "I'm not an idiot."

"Then stop acting like one," Jules said.

"I'm not!"

"Yeah, you were."

Eli said nothing but stuck his tongue out. Oscar groaned, and I chuckled weakly. "Look, I'll tell you, but it doesn't go any further. Ever. Do you promise?" I held out my little finger, and they all shook it solemnly with their own. We'd been pinky swearing since we were kids, and I'd never expected to do it as adults. Beside me, Oscar was starting to look nervous.

"Is it something we should be worried about? You're starting to scare me."

"No, it's not. I, er… Fuck… For the last three years, I've been recording audio porn as a side job, and I have a fansite, which none of you are ever allowed to go looking for. Anyway, Gem found out about it and told me he knew, and I freaked the fuck out, even though he told me it wasn't a big deal and that he actually liked it and thought it was cool, and I think he said something about membership, but I wasn't really listening at that point, and…"

"Finn. Breathe," Lewis said, patting my knee. I inhaled. Then looked around. They were all staring at me with a range of expressions on their faces. Lewis was grinning and didn't seem surprised, Jules looked oddly impressed, Oscar's brain seemed to have melted like his impression of me had utterly inverted, and Eli was staring at me slack-jawed, his eyebrows so high they looked like they might disappear into his hairline.

"So, yes… the reason things fell apart is because I panicked and ran away."

"Had you ever planned on telling him?" Jules asked. Her voice was surprisingly calm.

"Maybe? I don't know. I'd never gotten that far in my plans. Chantelle was encouraging me to tell him, because she's always known about my… side hustle, but I wasn't sure."

"Well, he knows now. And you said he doesn't mind, so what's the problem?"

"I… I don't know," I said. "I just… I was so afraid he wouldn't want me anymore and that I'd lose not only one of my best friends but the man I'm in love with. I'm not the sort of person who gets many chances, and I didn't want to ruin it, and even though he thinks its fine, what if he decides it's not? What if he hates it? And hates me for doing it?"

"You said he had a membership," Lewis said. "Or at least implied it. I don't think he's going to have a problem with it. In fact, he probably thinks it's *really* sexy, and you can do all sorts of filthy things to each other. Although, I'm guessing you've been doing that already, so you can keep doing all sorts of deliciously filthy things together." He winked, and I chuckled.

Oscar sighed. "This family doesn't really do boundaries, do we?"

"Oh, come on. We'd be boring if we did. Besides, it's not like Finn's giving us the details," Lewis said, rolling his eyes. "And it's kinda cool our baby brother is a sexual entrepreneur."

"Please don't say it like that," I said.

"I still think it's cool though," Lewis said. "And I think you need to talk to Gem."

"Agreed," Jules said. Oscar nodded. The four of us turned to Eli, who was still staring. Silent for once in his life.

"Holy shit," whispered Lewis. "I think you broke Eli."

"I'm not broken," Eli said, his voice deathly quiet and slightly high-pitched like he was trying to keep himself from exploding and making everything worse. I appreciated his restraint. "I'm just processing that our beloved baby brother, who we've all snuggled since we met him and who is an adorable, soft, cinnamon bun of a human being is apparently some sort of verbal incubus. I mean…"

"Aww, he's just jealous he's not the most interesting one anymore," Jules said with a laugh.

"Am not!"

"No, Eli is definitely the most interesting," I said quickly. "Especially because this secret is never to leave this room."

"We promise," Oscar said. "Right?"

The others nodded, and Eli sighed dramatically. "Like I said, it's always the quiet ones."

CHAPTER TWENTY-SIX

Finn

THE HARSH SOUND of the buzzer outside Gem's flat rang in my ears as I bounced on the spot, wishing the past twenty-four hours had never happened. I knew I'd reacted poorly, and I also knew that was the understatement of the century, but I was an adult, and that meant I had to own up to my mistakes.

"Hello?" Gem's voice, thick with static, sounded from the intercom.

"Hey, it's me. It's Finn. Can we talk?" I crossed all my fingers inside the pockets of my coat. Gem said nothing, but another buzzer sounded, and the door to the building unlocked. I took that as a good sign.

When I reached his front door, Gem was waiting for me. His face was set in a hard expression, and another wave of regret washed over me. I knew I shouldn't have said what I said, but all I could do was hope I'd be able to undo everything. And if Gem didn't forgive me, then that was something I'd have to live with. It would hurt every day for the rest of my life to know I'd thrown away the best thing in my life out of fear, but that wasn't an excuse. Even if I wanted it to be one.

"Hey," I said again, taking one hand out of my pocket and giving him an awkward wave. "Thanks for opening the door."

"It's fine. Do you want to come in?" He stepped back and ushered me into his flat. As I stepped through the door, memories of all the previous times I'd been there flooded my brain—from the very first time I'd come back here after a gaming session to the time we'd ended up in the shower. They all made me realise just how precious Gem was to me and how close I was to losing the man I cared for more than anything else. "Go on," Gem said, waving me towards the living room. "Don't stand on ceremony."

I toed off my ratty old trainers and shuffled down the little corridor into the sitting room, perching myself on the end of the sofa. As soon as Gem appeared, I blurted out, "I'm sorry." Gem raised an eyebrow and sat down at the other end, crossing his legs and looking at me with a clear indication to continue. I twisted my hands together in my lap, trying to remember the mental script I'd written and rehearsed on the drive. "I'm sorry for everything I said the other day. I was an asshole and incredibly rude to you, and I'm sorry."

"I didn't mean to corner you," Gem said. "And I wasn't trying to catch you out."

"I know." I sighed and bounced my knee. "I panicked

and just stopped thinking. It's not an excuse, but it's what happened. I just… I never expected anyone to find out about it, and when you said you knew I was so afraid that would be the end of everything. I think I stopped really listening after that. I just kept thinking about how it was going to end, and I was going to lose you, and then when that didn't happen, my brain decided it needed to happen anyway. That it was easier to cut my losses and run rather than risk everything. I know that's stupid."

"No, it's not." Gem gave me a small smile, and a weak ray of relief appeared among the stormy sky of my fear. "I was worried about telling you. I kinda thought something like this might happen. But I wish you would have listened to me."

"I wish I had too," I said. Then I stretched my hand out across the sofa, waiting to see if he'd take it. Gem's fingers slipped into mine, warm and calloused, and I'd never felt a greater sense of relief. I knew we were going to be okay, even if we had a little way to go. "So… you, er, you follow me?"

"Yeah, I've been subscribing for, like, a year now?" There was a red tint at his hairline, and he suddenly seemed very interested in a spot on the wall behind my head. I chuckled. "I found a clip on PornHub, and your profile said you had a subscription site, so that was that really."

"I want to ask you about your favourite piece, but I think that might lead to us getting sidetracked," I said. There were a lot of other questions I wanted to ask and things I needed to say before we got to the making up part.

I squeezed Gem's hand. "Are you sure you're okay with me running Fantasy and Filth? I know you said you were, but I need you to tell me again, and I need you to be honest with me. If you're not, then that's fine. We can work around that, but I don't want you to say you are and then get jealous or upset. I don't want whatever we are to be ruined by bad communication… at least, not again."

Gem chuckled. "I'm sure. I promise. Cross my heart and hope to die." He drew his hand across his chest. "I think it's really fucking sexy, and if you enjoy it, I want you to keep doing it. At the end of the day, nobody else knows it's you—"

"Except, er, for Chantelle… she was the one who encouraged me to do it," I said. "And some of my siblings… They came to check on me yesterday, and it sort of came out because they're all too bloody nosy to leave things alone and accept plot holes."

Gem stared at me, and for a moment, I wondered if that was too much. My family had never had much of a sense of boundaries, but I often forgot that not everyone else's family worked like that. Then Gem shook his head and grinned. "Okay then, well, none of your subscribers know who you are, and at the end of the day, I'm the one that gets to keep you. Plus, I'd be more than happy to inspire new scenarios… I'm very helpful like that." He leant across the sofa, and I mirrored him, our lips meeting in the middle. It was a kiss filled with sweetness and certainty. The sort that made everything a little better than it had been before.

"By the way," Gem continued. "I have to say that I'm

not surprised about Chantelle knowing. I doubt the two of you have many secrets."

"No, we don't. But I will say that I was very drunk when I first mentioned the idea to her, so we can totally blame drunk Finn for that. He doesn't really have a filter."

"I'll remember that for the future," Gem said. "I'm not surprised about your siblings either. They're an interesting bunch."

"They are, but I love them. They were all for grabbing torches and pitchforks and forming some sort of angry mob until I told them it was my fault we'd… Anyway, they're overprotective, but generally, their hearts are in the right place."

"They've always seemed that way."

"Is that why you messaged Lewis?" I asked, sliding slightly farther across the sofa.

"Yeah." Gem nodded. "I figured you'd want some space from me, but I didn't want you to… I don't know… blame yourself. I figured he'd be a good person to check on you. I didn't realise I'd be calling the whole cavalry."

"It's like a terrible summoning ritual," I said. "Or a bad deal in Tesco. Message one, get two or three extra for free."

Gem laughed, the sound beautiful and freeing. "I'll remember that."

There was a moment of silence, but it wasn't a weighty one filled with pressure and expectation. More one of peace.

"So, you're absolutely sure you don't mind me continuing with Fantasy and Filth?" I asked finally. "I know I've asked already, but I just need to make sure."

"I am. I want you to keep doing it for as long as you

want. I'd be a complete bastard if I stopped you doing something you loved because I had a problem with it, and given that I love it, it would be a dick move to say I did. You've always supported me in everything I've done, so it's my turn to return the favour, which means I won't be cancelling my subscription either." Gem slid across the sofa until he was pressed right against me. "And if that ever changes, then I'll talk to you. I promise."

"Okay," I said, nodding my head. Happiness radiated from my chest because never in my wildest dreams had I imagined things turning out so well.

"Good." He grinned at me. "Now I've got a question for you. What do you want this to be? I'm guessing since you're here, my declaration of love didn't totally put you off?"

"No. It didn't. Although I've never been called a bloody idiot in that way before. It wasn't quite the romantic moment I expected."

Gem threw back his head and laughed. "I'm sorry. Next time I'll include flowers or something."

"I don't want flowers," I said, reaching down to cup his jaw and bring him closer to me. "I just want you. I love you, Gem, and I have for a very long time. I never thought you'd want someone like me, but here you are. And I know I'll never love anyone the way I love you."

"I love you too." He kissed me softly, and when he went to pull away, I drew him in closer, pulling him onto my lap so we could make out lazily. My hands reached around him so I could squeeze his ass, and Gem chuckled. "Do you want to go into my room?"

"No," I said. "I want to stay here for a bit, just doing this."

"Okay. We can do that." His mouth met mine again, and I lost myself in our kisses. I'd never felt so relaxed and content.

"Can I ask you another question?" Gem asked several minutes later when we came up for air.

"Of course."

"What gave you the idea to start your blog? I know you've vaguely talked about it during Q&As, but I'm being nosy."

"You listen to the Q&As?" I grinned.

"I listen to everything."

That statement caught me off guard, even though it shouldn't have. Gem had already said he was a fan, but knowing he'd listened to all that work made me feel both pleased and vulnerable, probably because I'd never expected to meet any of my fans walking around in reality. "Well, er, let's see… It was a couple of years ago, and I was having a bad day. I was stressed and lonely and just feeling… Anyway, I thought it would be a brilliant idea to start drinking, and I have a ridiculously low tolerance, so about three-quarters of the way through a bottle of red wine, I decided I wanted to jerk off, and I ended up lying on my bed trying to find something that interested me when I stumbled across this guy's audio channel. The production values weren't great, and the audio quality was patchy, but it was… sexy. Very sexy. And this quiet voice in my brain suggested that I could do that too, only better."

"I like this quiet voice," Gem said. "He has good ideas."

"You can thank that voice for us too." I rubbed my hand over Gem's thigh. "It was the reason I suggested we first hook up."

Gem grinned and leant down to kiss me. "He has very good ideas, then."

I hummed. "Sometimes. Anyway, to cut a long, boring story short, I thought it would be a *brilliant* idea to send the channel to Chantelle, who agreed with the quiet voice. And I tried to deny it and pretend I hadn't said anything, but the idea wouldn't go away. So I ended up recording a couple to upload as a test. And that was that really."

"I'm glad you did," Gem said. "You've made me very happy over the past year. The way you just…" He let out a little moan and bit his lip. "You get me off every single time without fail."

I smirked as the little possessive symbiote in my chest purred happily. I always loved hearing from my fans, but this was truly special. "Every time?"

"Without. Fail." He ran his hand up my chest and slid his hips forward until I could feel the press of his erection through his jeans. He tilted his head until his lips were pressed against my ear. "I don't have just one favourite either. I have a list. But if I had to pick one… it would be the distraction one. Where you're working and I need you." He moaned again, starting to grind against me. I put one hand on his hip, holding him in place. It was fun watching him get so riled up, and after everything I'd done, Gem deserved a little fun. That still didn't mean he was in charge though. He was mine, and I was going to show him that.

"The one where you're a desperate, slutty boy for me?" I

asked. Gem groaned. I reached my other hand around and slapped his ass, not hard enough to hurt, more of a gentle reminder. "Answer me properly. And look at me when you do."

Gem sat up and nodded, but he didn't stop grinding against me. "Yes. That one… It's, mmm… It's so fucking hot. The way you make me suck your cock and take it all the way down my throat until I'm gagging. Telling me how, fuck, how good I am for you. And then… then working me open and fucking me… shit, making me jerk off and come for you so I can make you feel good. I want to make you feel good, Finn. I want to be good for you."

"Oh, baby," I said, unable to resist the desperation in his voice. "You're always so good for me." I leant up and kissed him, nipping his lip and claiming his mouth with my tongue. "Do you want to be good for me now?"

"Yes!" Gem groaned. "Please."

"Then get on your knees and suck my cock."

CHAPTER TWENTY-SEVEN

Gem

FINN'S COMMAND went straight to my dick, making it ache in the confines of my jeans. The temptation to keep grinding against him until I came was right there, but I knew if I did as I was told, the reward would be so much sweeter.

I climbed off Finn's lap and sank to the floor in front of him, watching as he unbuttoned his jeans and slowly pulled out his cock. I licked my lips, desperate for a taste, and Finn let out one of those dark chuckles that made my chest tighten. I loved that he knew exactly what I needed and that he was going to give it to me. The past few days had been rough for us, but this was the fun part of making up. Later, we could get to the detailed talking bit if we really needed to. Not that I thought we had much left to say.

"Do you want it?" Finn asked teasingly.

"Yes! Let me suck your cock." I leant forward opening my mouth for him, groaning as he playfully tapped his cock on my lower lip and outstretched tongue.

"Open wide for me." I stretched my mouth wider and looked up at him with pleading eyes. "Mmm, you look so pretty on your knees for me, baby. Such a beautiful little slut for me." Finn reached out a hand and gently gripped my hair, making pleasure shoot through me. "Do you like it when I do that?"

"Yeah, I do," I said. "Probably not much harder, but I… I like the idea of you controlling me."

Finn groaned and closed his eyes. It made me glow knowing I affected him so easily. "God, you're so perfect for me. I'm so lucky." He looked down at me with an expression filled with love and desire. It was everything I'd ever wanted. Then he pulled me forward and guided his cock into my mouth. "Now, be a good boy for me and suck my cock. Make me feel good. And if you do, then I'll give you what you need."

I was happy to comply. Wrapping my lips around Finn's cock, I flicked my tongue across the head to taste the salty-sweet precum gathered there before taking him deeper in my throat. One day, I wanted to take him all without gagging, but that was going to take time. I didn't mind practising though. Finn groaned, muttering filthy words of praise as I sucked him, pulling out every single trick I could think of while my cock strained against its fabric prison.

"You can touch yourself if you want," Finn said, a sweet

but dangerous edge to his voice. "As long as you don't come. And as long as you don't stop sucking me. Remember, you're supposed to be making me feel good."

I moaned around his cock, knowing I was stuck between a rock and a hard place. I desperately wanted to jack my cock, but I had to try to open my jeans and pull myself out without stopping what I was doing. One hand reached for my jeans as I used the other to steady myself on Finn's thigh so I could keep working his perfect length.

It took me a few minutes, but I eventually managed to pop the buttons on my fly open without changing my rhythm, and I was oddly proud of myself. I groaned when my fingers wrapped around my cock, slowly jerking it as I sucked Finn. He was my focus. I just wanted to stop my dick from feeling like it was going to explode. And not in the fun way.

"Mmm, that's it. I love seeing you like this," Finn said, tightening his hand in my hair and pulling me a tiny bit deeper. "I love it when you take what I give you because you're so good for me. And you'reit mine. All mine."

I groaned because those were the words I'd longed to hear. I'd been craving them for so long, and I knew they were real—they weren't just being thrown around in the heat of the moment. I was Finn's, and he was mine. The thought threatened to overwhelm me.

"Do you like that?" Finn continued. "Do you like that you're mine?"

"Y-yes," I said, pulling off his cock for a moment. "I love it. I want… Will you make me yours?"

Finn stroked my hair, then tugged me towards him. "Of course I will. Come here and give me a kiss, then go and get on your bed. I'm going to open you up for me and then fuck you slowly until you can't think about anything except me inside you."

I climbed to my feet and kissed him deeply, relishing every moment. When Finn released me, I raced off to my room, shedding clothes as I went. Behind me, I heard Finn chuckling and muttering something to himself about teaching me to be tidy. He could try, but I had better things to do right now than make sure all my clothes found their way into a neat pile or the washing basket. Grabbing the bottle of lube, I climbed onto the bed and presented myself to him face down, ass up.

Finn groaned as he entered the room, and the sound made my cock drip. "Fuck, baby, you look so good for me like that. So desperate for me." I twisted my head and watched him walk over to the bed, shivering as he ran a hand across my ass.

"Yes," I said. "Please, Finn. Fuck me. I need you."

"Be patient," he said, stripping out of his clothes and folding them neatly. "I promised you I'd give you what you needed, but you have to be good for me." Finn picked the bottle of lube up from beside me before leaning down to press a kiss to one cheek, then the other, and finally, my hole. I gasped, loving the way his tongue felt against the sensitive skin. My fingers grasped at the sheets as Finn began to tease my hole with his fingers and his tongue. I wanted so much more, but I knew begging would get me nowhere. Finn would not be moved, and he'd probably just draw it out further to remind me to be patient. With someone else, that would have driven me crazy, but with him… it just made me realise how much I loved him. He cared about me and my needs. He knew what I needed and what I wanted, and he'd make me feel more incredible than I had in my life.

I groaned as Finn's fingers breached me, opening me up slowly for him. "That's it, baby, nice and slow… Mmm, you have such a perfect hole. I can't wait to be inside you."

"Please… I want that," I said, turning my head to look at him. "Don't make me wait. Please, Finn."

"That's not your decision," Finn said pointedly. "But since you asked so nicely and you've been such a good boy for me, I suppose I can make an exception this time, my beautiful, desperate man."

"Thank you." I moaned as Finn pulled his fingers out of me and then slapped his cock on my hole before pushing it inside me. Fuck, he felt good! There was just the right amount of soft burn as I stretched around him, and Finn murmured soft praise as he slid deep inside me. He leant down and wrapped his hand around my chest, pulling me up onto my knees so my back was pressed against his chest.

"I love you," he whispered as he began to fuck me slowly, punctuating his words with deep thrusts and soft kisses to my neck. "You are so sweet, and sexy, and funny, and kind, and you are so fucking gorgeous. You are everything to me, Gem."

"I… I love you too."

"Good." Finn's hand gripped my hip, pulling me onto his cock. "Now touch yourself. I want you to come for me. I love feeling your ass tighten around me when you come. It... fuck... it always gets me there too. And... mmm, I know you want to please me."

I groaned and tipped my head back so it was resting on his shoulder as my hand reached for my cock. Finn was hitting my prostate with every deep thrust and grind, and my fingers on my shaft sent a bolt of electricity shooting through me. I jerked myself hard and fast, knowing I wasn't going to last long. "Finn... I'm c-close... I..."

"Come for me," Finn said, kissing my neck. It was like setting a match to tinder, and I cried out as my body tightened and my orgasm rushed through me, sparking off every nerve. Cum shot across my fist and the sheets, my ass tightening around Finn's cock and pulling him deep inside me. Finn let out a deep, rumbling growl as his fingers tightened on my hip. "You are mine," he said, his voice deep and possessive as he came deep inside me.

Our chests rose and fell together, and Finn pressed more soft kisses to my neck as we came down from the high of our orgasms. When he released me, I flopped onto the bed and laughed.

"You... you have got to stop turning my muscles to jelly," I said, rolling onto my back and looking across to where Finn was stretched out on the other side of the bed, carefully avoiding the wet spots of cum in the middle.

"You don't like it?" Finn asked, giving me a teasing smile. "Do you want to start having bad sex?"

"Fuck no… I just… Fuck, I have things I need to do today, and now I don't want to do any of them. It's really inconvenient."

Finn snorted. "I'm sorry?"

"You should be," I said. "Giving me all this good sex and being so nice to me. I'm not used to it."

"Maybe we should do it more, then?"

"But then we'd never go to work, and you'd have angry clients asking why they don't have audiobooks, and then we'd be poor and homeless, and that would be shit."

"Okay," Finn said. "Although I feel like that's a bit of an exaggeration. How much sex did you think I meant we should have?"

"I don't know, but if we do it more than… twice… or three times a day, I'm not going to be able to get out of bed." I chuckled. "Maybe I should start going to the gym? Build some stamina."

Finn laughed. "You could if you really wanted."

"Nah, that sounds like too much hard work." I grinned at him. "I love you, you know that, right?"

"I do, and I love you too. And I'm sorry for panicking and running away. I won't do it again." He slid across the bed and pulled me into his arms. "Thank you," he said. "For loving all of me. You're the only person who's ever seen all of who I am and loved me for it."

My chest tightened, because God, how the fuck could I not love him? "You are fucking perfect," I said. "And I'm so fucking lucky to have you."

"Not as lucky as me."

"Fuck off," I said. "We'll call it a tie."

Finn thought for a second, a rare glint of mischief in his eye. "I suppose that will do." He kissed me, and I melted into his arms. I knew I had stuff to do today—setting up the whole fucking shop for one—but that could wait just a little longer. I had more important things to do.

CHAPTER TWENTY-EIGHT

Finn

"RIGHT, you've all got your tasks. Does anyone have any questions?" I looked around at the motley crew of friends and family I had assembled to help finish setting up Gem's shop. Despite Gem's insistence that he could do it himself—with the help of a multipack of Red Bull—I didn't believe him. There was no way it was going to be possible for him to finish everything in twenty-four hours and still be standing at the end of it. So I had taken matters into my own hands.

Lewis stuck his hand up. "Can I take pictures and videos of all this for Instagram? Might be worth posting."

"Yes, but if anyone has any objections to being included, please let Lewis know," I said. "Anything else?"

"Do you have any materials in case I need to make signs?" Mimbles asked from the edge of the group. Since she was a school librarian and good at making things look eye-catching, I'd tasked her and Mum with setting up the window display.

"Yes." I pointed at a large, plastic tub on the counter. "I've got a tub of craft supplies there, but if you need anything else, someone can always make a run." Mimbles nodded and rolled up the sleeves of her jumper, ready to get stuck in. "Anything else? Good. Okay. Thanks for your help with this, everyone. I really appreciate it."

"Let's do it!" Eli called, and I laughed.

"Okay then, let's go." Everyone dispersed, and the shop was soon filled with chatter, laughter, and the sound of construction. Jules was helping Dad reaffix the last of the shelves to the walls while Lewis and Edward organised the storeroom. The stock had been delivered yesterday, and while Gem had made a start on sorting it, it wasn't as organised as it could have been. Lewis had practically begged to be allowed to get his hands on it, as had Edward, who'd grumbled about dealing with Jay's mess for years and that this would be different. Lewis had even come armed with stickers and Sharpies, and I got the impression the room would be ordered to within an inch of its life by the time they'd finished.

Mimbles and Mum were already working on the window display, and I watched as Mum pulled a sketch pad out of her large, sequinned bag and flipped through the pages, showing Mimbles various things. She must have drawn up some ideas last night after I'd messaged the family chat and asked for help. The fact that she'd done that made something clench in my chest because it was so typical of her and my family as a whole. We helped each other out whenever we needed it, no questions asked.

I turned and watched Richard and Ruby disappear up the stairs with dusters and cloths in hand to make sure everything was clean before the shelves were moved and filled. Oscar and Jason stood off to one side with their heads together, talking animatedly and occasionally pointing at things. I'd put them in charge of appearance and decoration since I wanted it to be tasteful, and I was pleased to see them getting on so well. Oscar came and went so much that it was nice to get to spend any time with him at all. I hoped before he jetted off on his next job we'd get to hang out and play games together, although I doubted his skills at *Mario Kart* had improved much.

The door opened behind me, setting off the newly installed buzzer, and I turned, frozen. Gem wasn't supposed to be here for another hour at least because he was working his very last shift at The Lost World. It was only Leo, though, and I exhaled loudly at the sight of the giant florist who was cradling an enormous bouquet of brightly coloured flowers in one arm with a glass vase clutched in the other hand. Angie, his beautiful, brindle Staffie, was with him and doing excited little tip-taps at the idea of having a whole roomful of people to talk to.

"Hey," Leo said when he spotted me. "I know the shop doesn't open until tomorrow, but I brought these."

"Oh my gosh, they're lovely!"

"Thanks. It's the same sort of arrangement I made Jay when he opened The Lost World. I figured they'd be good luck."

It was such an adorably sweet gesture that I couldn't stop myself from smiling. I didn't know Leo as well as I wanted, but I'd always gotten the impression he was a kind, gentle man who just happened to look like an enormous, tattooed Viking. The flowers themselves were beautiful, and it was easy to tell they'd been chosen and assembled with care and attention. "That's so kind of you. Gem will love them."

Leo looked away and then around at the shop, watching the hustle and bustle. "Is he still with Jay?"

"Yeah. Jay promised to keep him occupied for another hour and then bring him up. I don't trust Gem not to try to slide out early." I grinned, and Leo chuckled.

"Probably for the best that Jay isn't here too. I love him, but I don't think Gem wants half his stock dropped. Although he is getting better." From beside him, Angie let out a little huffed whine, and I bent down to fuss at her, laughing as she pushed into my arms. She was heavier than I expected and very determined to be cuddled. "Sorry," Leo said. "Just push her down. Angie, you can't climb on people."

"It's fine." I laughed. Angie licked my face. "Do you want to put the flowers on the counter? They shouldn't get knocked there."

"Sure. What else needs doing?"

"Er, we'll need to make a couple of displays and start stocking shelves. Eli and I were going to start on that since I have a rough idea of where Gem wants things, but it would be great to have another pair of hands. Especially because I'm not very good at making things look pretty."

"I can do that," Leo said. "What have you got in mind?"

Releasing Angie, I led Leo over to Eli, who'd joined Oscar and Jason's conversation, and the four of them started talking about displays and decorations. I gently gave them some pointers and let them know Gem's ideas for stock, but I soon got waved away. Despite my worries that this was going to get wildly out of hand, I realised that if Gem didn't like it, we could always change it in the morning. It wasn't as if we were gluing things down. This was more of a starting point to get us going.

The four of them moved towards the stockroom, only to be met by Edward. It appeared as though they had to negotiate for boxes.

I chuckled and turned away because I wasn't getting involved. I'd said I was going to help stock shelves, but maybe I'd wait until they actually started putting things out. I knew that if I waited, I'd feel less anxious because trying to help and being rebuffed or talked over was just going to make me feel awful. Plus, this way I could keep an eye on everyone else as well as watch for Gem. A nervous feeling was bubbling away in my stomach, and I was worried I'd overstepped. Perhaps getting everyone involved was too much.

"Are you okay, darling?" Mum asked when she spotted me lurking. She was carefully sticking some large dice transfers to the windowpanes, making it look like they were cascading down one window. I had no idea where they'd come from, but they were wonderful.

"Yes, just… nervous." I smiled, hoping it would make me feel better. It worked but only for a moment. "I like those." I pointed to the transfers. "Where did you get them?"

"Oh, I found the design online last night," she said. "And I found someone to print them this morning. I thought it would look rather sweet and whimsical, but in a good way, and I think it's worked."

I chuckled because that was so like her. Mum was the dreamy, impulsive one who only seemed to think things through afterwards. Luckily, Mimbles had always been there to catch her and check her ideas through before they happened. Mimbles watched her now, a soft smile on her face—the Disney smile, Chantelle called it. The one they always gave the hero when he was watching the princess when she wasn't looking. It was also the same look both Tulio and Miguel used various times during *The Road to El Dorado*, but that was a different can of gay worms.

Something inside my chest pinched, and it was both comfortable and not at the same time. I loved that Mimbles and Mum had found each other, that they'd made a life together after my dad's death and Mum's divorce—and it was obvious how much they loved each other even now. But sometimes I wondered whether Mimbles had ever looked at my dad in the same way and how different my life would be if he hadn't died.

I shook my head, and the moment of melancholy passed, just as it always did.

"I think they look beautiful," I said, clearing my throat with a little cough. "Thank you."

"You're so welcome," Mum said. "We're so happy for

the two of you. We always said you'd be great together, didn't we Ellie?"

"We did," Mimbles said. She'd acquired a pile of games from somewhere and was carefully arranging them on some shelving in the window so the cover art could be seen through the glass. "When you talked about Gem, you always seemed… happier. We just had to wait for the two of you to work it out."

"Th-thanks?" I stammered as I wondered just how long my parents had been taking bets on my love life.

"You're welcome," Mum said. She peered out the window as she stuck another die to the glass and smoothed it with one hand. "I think I see them. Gem has a tweed jacket, doesn't he?"

"Shit." I glanced at my watch. They weren't supposed to be here yet. The store wasn't nearly as ready as I wanted it to be. But we'd just have to roll with it. There wasn't time to tell everyone either. All I could do was hover awkwardly by the door and anxiously wait for Gem to appear, crossing my fingers that he didn't hate what we'd done and that I hadn't massively overstepped.

The door buzzed as it swung open, and behind me, I heard everyone stop moving to stare at the new arrivals. Gem had known I would be here since I'd asked to borrow the key earlier on the premise of making a start on the stockroom, but everything else was a surprise. And the stunned expression on his face as he looked around told me it had worked.

"What the… What's all this?" He took a step inside,

leaving Jay lurking in the doorway with an enormous grin on his face and Rupert at his feet.

"Surprise!" I smiled, trying not to let my worries show, even if all I wanted was to twist my hands together to calm the swirling storm of doubt raging inside me. "We thought you might like some help."

"This is… It's… Wow."

"Is it okay?"

"It's more than okay," Gem said. "I can't believe you're all doing this."

"You know," said Jules, twirling a screwdriver in her hand, "we didn't do anything. It was all Finn. He just told us when and where, and here we are."

"I didn't tell you," I muttered. "That makes it sound like I forced you."

"You didn't force us, you daft banana," she said with a wry smile. "We're here because we love you, and we wanted to help."

"Plus," added Jay from over Gem's shoulder, "we all know how tough this is and how hard you've worked. We wanted to make your life a little easier."

"You didn't do anything," Edward called from the stockroom door.

"I was running distraction," Jay said.

"He's not allowed to help," Lewis said, appearing at Edward's elbow and holding a roll of labels. "Not if Gem wants the stockroom to be usable."

"Mine's not that bad," Jay said. "I've not broken anything."

"Yet," Gem said. I chuckled quietly. "Seriously, though,

this is amazing. Thank you."

"You're welcome." He stepped close to me, pressing a gentle kiss to my lips. Someone made a whooping sound. Someone else *awwed*. And I felt like I'd never be able to look most of them in the eye again.

"Thank you," Gem whispered. "I love you so much."

"I love you too."

"I can't believe you did this for me."

"You're amazing, Gem," I said. "I can't believe you can't see it. I know you don't think you're special, but to me, you're the most incredible person in the world."

"You're going to make me blush."

I grinned. "Good. It was either that or tell you I only did this to stop you from drinking twelve cans of Red Bull and attempting to do it all in one night. I really don't think that amount of caffeine is healthy."

"It's not," said Eli, who'd suddenly appeared beside me. "Trust me—I tried it once at university to write a last-minute essay. Didn't sleep for three days. Never again, although I did get a first." Gem laughed. "Now, while I'm here, I'm just going to borrow your boyfriend. We want his opinion on our display ideas." Eli put his hand on Gem's elbow and began to casually steer him towards Oscar, Jason, and Leo. "By the way, if you felt very generous, you could order us all some pizza. I'm starving."

I watched as my boyfriend was stolen away, knowing I wouldn't get him back any time soon. I shook my head, a smile playing across my lips as I reached for my phone. "Okay," I said as loudly as I could. "What does everyone want?"

CHAPTER TWENTY-NINE

Gem

"I still can't believe you did that," I said. It wasn't quite midnight, and Finn and I were lying in bed, face to face in the glow of my bedside lamp. My arms were aching and sore from moving furniture around and helping put stock onto shelves, but it wasn't the bone-deep tiredness I'd been anticipating from the evening.

"Why not?"

"Because… I don't know." It was hard to put my feelings about the whole evening into words. When I stepped into the shop and saw everyone, I'd thought I was dreaming. I'd spent the whole day thinking about the long night ahead of me, trying to work out how long it would take me and Finn to get everything ready and wondering how much sleep I really needed to be functional. But seeing everyone at the shop, helping out and pitching in to make sure I didn't struggle, pushed on an old ache, deep in my chest I hadn't realised was still there.

Finn slid his hand across the mattress between us and gently brushed against my arm. "Do you feel like you don't deserve help?"

"Maybe?" I frowned. "I think somewhere along the line I stopped believing in myself, and I stopped believing that I deserved anything. It felt like… like there was something monstrous living in my chest I had to take everywhere with me. And every time I failed at something, it just got bigger and sank it's claws in a little deeper."

"I'm sorry," Finn said, interlacing our fingers together and squeezing my hand tightly. "I should have seen you were struggling."

"No, you shouldn't. That's not your job. You don't need to take on everyone else's problems and feelings, and you don't need to make everyone else happy at the expense of yourself." I lifted his hand to mine and brushed a kiss over his knuckles. "And don't tell me you don't because you do. I've seen you."

Finn smiled and dipped his head so I wouldn't see the blush spreading across his cheeks. "We're not talking about me."

"We will," I said.

"But not today." Finn looked up at me, warmth shining in his dark eyes. I'd never had anyone look at me like that before. "Tell me about this monster."

He shuffled closer until we were virtually nose to nose and there was no differentiation between where my body ended and his began. It was intimate in a way I hadn't experienced, and it was something I knew I'd come to crave. "I always expected so much of myself," I said. "That I'd be this mega successful game designer and have my own company or design something so popular it got bought by a huge studio, and I could basically just retire. I always knew it was just a dream, that that sort of thing only happens to a few people, but I held on to it for so long that every time something didn't happen, it felt like a failure, and I guess, over time, they just started adding up. And it felt like I had to carry those failures around with me, like, I don't know, like a pet I didn't want. One that kept getting bigger and feeding on all my failings."

"I'm sorry."

"You don't need to be," I said. "I probably should have let go of those things a long time ago."

"The dreams or the failures?" Finn asked, and I saw a wrinkle appear between his eyebrows.

"Both?" Finn's frowned deepened, and I couldn't help but chuckle. Despite his skills with dirty words and domination, most of the time Finn looked more like a grumpy kitten when he was annoyed. I leant over and kissed the wrinkled skin, and he huffed.

"Don't laugh at me. You'll pay for that."

"Oh? Will I?"

"Yes," he said, a teasing edge to his voice that meant trouble. "But it'll be so fun—for me at least—that you'll be thanking me for it." I swallowed as my cock jumped in my boxers. Finn let out a soft, pleased sound, and I knew he'd felt my dick respond. His fingers reached down to brush against me, and I gasped.

"I think you've forgotten that you're mine," Finn added. "And that I can do whatever I want to you because we both know you need it and love it." He tapped the head of my cock through the material of my underwear, smiling sweetly at me. "So you can tease me as much as you want, but remember I can do the same…" He pulled his hand back, and I knew at some point I was going to find myself being edged for hours, begging for release while Finn teased my cock and my hole. It sounded like a fun night. "By the way, you don't have to hold on to your failures, real or perceived. Learn from them, yes, but you don't have to carry them around with you. If you do, they'll eventually become so toxic that all you can do is focus on the negatives, and it'll stop you from ever doing anything. Everyone fails, it's part of life, but the real challenge is what you do afterwards. Do you sit around and let those things consume you? Or do you try to build something better?"

I reached out to caress the side of his face, bringing his lips to mine. "I love you," I said. "Thank you for looking out for me."

"You're welcome." Finn kissed me. "I know it's hard to let go, and it's hard not to be afraid, but I'm so proud of you for what you're doing."

"Thanks. I don't think I've ever had someone be proud of me before… well, not someone who wasn't my parents or family or something. And even then, it's been a while." It felt strange to admit that out loud, like it was something weird and forbidden. I was an adult, so surely I shouldn't need that praise, but I still wanted it. I still needed to know I hadn't totally fucked up my life.

Finn looked at me with an expression of sweet sadness and kissed me again. "Then I'll remember to tell you every single day because you deserve to know how wonderful you are and how proud you make me."

"How can you be proud of me when I haven't done anything?"

"But you have," Finn said. "You're opening a game shop by yourself." I opened my mouth to object, but Finn placed a finger against my lips. I decided not to argue. "And although you can say other people gave you the idea or helped you with it, at the end of the day, you were the one who decided to open the shop. Nobody else could have made that decision but you, and you've worked really hard to make it a reality."

"Thanks."

Another kiss. "Be proud of yourself. And if you can't be, then I'll be proud enough for both of us."

"I don't think I deserve you. How did I end up with someone so amazing?" I wrapped my arm around him to pull him into me. Finn's skin was warm where it brushed against mine, and our legs tangled together.

"I could ask the same question." We kissed softly, our tongues languidly exploring. My hand slid down Finn's back so I could squeeze his ass. He let out a little groan and pushed against me, and I felt his cock hardening through the thin material of his boxers. It was late, and we were both exhausted, but it didn't take much for us to get lost in the moment.

Finn's hand slipped between us, freeing his cock from his underwear and then doing the same to mine. He wrapped his hand around us as we rocked together slowly. There was no need to rush. We had all night. Finn gently nipped at my lip, and I groaned, pulling him closer against me. He rolled me until I was flat on my back with Finn between my legs. He released our cocks and put his hands on either side of my head, rocking his hips and frotting against me. It was a little dry and rough, but I didn't care. The moment was too good to break, and I needed the release.

"I love you," I whispered against his mouth. "So fucking much."

"I love you too." He kissed me again with a deep heat that seemed to burn me up from the inside out. "I'm proud of you, and I'm so happy you're mine."

"I'll always be yours." I groaned as precum dripped from my slit, adding a little slickness. "I'm so glad I found you, Finn."

"I'm glad you found me too."

There were no more words after that. Just soft groans and grunts as we ground against each other until we spilt our loads across our skin. Finn kissed me again, and I loved feeling the weight of him on top of me. It made me want to stay there forever, just the two of us, away from the rest of the world. But not even love could make time stop.

Finn rolled off me, and we shoved off our boxers and t-shirts that were now sticky with cum, too tired to care about doing any more clean-up than that. I flicked the lamp off and we lay curled together, Finn tucked tight against me.

"Can I ask you something?" I whispered into the dark. Finn hummed a quiet affirmative. "You've helped me with my dreams, but I never asked about yours. What do you want?"

There was a moment of silence, and Finn shifted in my arms. "I don't know anymore."

"Why not?"

"Because now that I've got you, I've got everything I've ever wanted." He reached for my hands and clutched them fiercely against his chest. "I don't need anything else. Just you, my family, my friends, and my job. I've got more than I ever could have hoped for. I'm the luckiest man in the world."

I kissed the back of his head, my whole body glowing with happiness. I swallowed, trying not to let my emotions show. "Seriously? You don't want anything else?"

"No. Should I?"

"You don't have to," I said. "As long as you're happy."

"I am. I've got you. That makes me very happy."

I squeezed Finn tightly, hoping he knew just how perfect he was. Even if he didn't, I intended to show him every day for the rest of our lives.

"Although," Finn said quietly. "Maybe…"

"Maybe what?"

"How do you feel about getting a cat?"

CHAPTER THIRTY

Gem

IT WAS three minutes and fifteen seconds until the door of Castle Games would open for the first time, and despite my promise to myself to stay calm, I felt like I was about to ride the world's most terrifying rollercoaster. My insides felt like they were full of snakes, and the toast Finn had forced me to have for breakfast kept threatening to make a dramatic reappearance. The only thing stopping me from hurling was the fact that I didn't want to ruin everyone's hard work.

The shop looked absolutely amazing from the colourful, eye-catching window display, to the shelves teeming with stock, to the bowl of dice on the counter alongside the enormous bouquet Leo had brought me. When I'd first stood in the tiny, dusty shop with nothing but a counter and some dingy paint, I'd never imagined it would look this good. Even through all my planning, none of the mental pictures I'd drawn up had looked anything like this.

For the first time, I felt pride in what I'd achieved. I'd made it this far, and I'd turned Jay's offhanded suggestion into a reality. Now all I could do was cross my fingers and hope people actually showed up. And kept showing up.

"Are you ready?" Finn asked, appearing from upstairs where he'd been doing a final check of the shelves.

"No. But I don't think I ever will be."

"It's going to be great." He smiled at me with the same quiet confidence he always had, and it was enough to slow my racing heart by a beat or two. Finn pulled out his phone and held it up. "Smile! You need a photo for Instagram."

"Says who?" I asked as I dutifully posed.

"Lewis," Finn said as he tapped something on his phone. "He'll be along in a bit, but he asked me to take some photos and videos for your Instagram. I think he's appointed himself your unofficial social media manager."

"He does realise he doesn't have to do that?"

Finn shrugged. "I know, but he's very keen. I did tell him you could do it, but he said you probably had better things to focus on today."

I chuckled and shook my head, leaning over the counter to grab the key to the door. "Well, I'm not going to tell him no. I'm going to get Jason to tell him."

"Good luck with that," Finn said. "My brother has his boyfriend wrapped around his little finger. Jason will never tell him no. Although, to be fair, Lewis doesn't really go over the top. He's pretty good at regulating himself. He just likes getting involved in new things."

"Okay, well, I…" My words trailed off as I reached the front door. "Shit."

"What's wrong?"

"There are people… outside." I stared, fumbling with the bolt at the top of the door as I stared at the small group of people waiting in the street. There were a few faces I recognised from The Lost World's game night along with some I didn't know at all. It felt a bit surreal, because surely they weren't there for me? I mean, logically they had to be, but it still didn't make sense.

Shoving the key into the lock, I finished unlocking the door and pulled it open. Someone cheered, and I recognised the instigator as Daniel, a frequent gamer and friend of Jay and Leo. He had a couple of children with him, and they bounced excitedly as Daniel winked at me.

"Hey, everyone," I said. "Sorry to keep you waiting. I didn't expect you to be here."

"Of course we're here," said Lila, who, as promised, was queued up to be first through the door. She had bright purple hair decorated with flowers and was wearing a long, leopard-print coat over a vintage jumper and jeans that looked achingly fashionable on her. "Don't be a banana. Now, let me in. I have money to spend."

I laughed and did a little mock bow as I waved her inside. She blew me a kiss as she walked past, then waved at Finn before gravitating towards one of the shelves that we'd stacked with large, new releases that each retailed for well over a hundred quid. I hadn't thought I'd sell any of those, but I was actively rethinking that sentiment.

More people poured into the shop with some even

heading upstairs to browse the larger collection. I still stood by the front door, a little stunned by everything. I'd *hoped* people would show up, but this many people so early in the day wasn't something I'd expected.

"Hello," said Izzy, Edward's partner. He grinned at me as he climbed the steps into the shop, carrying two large white boxes in front of him. "Did someone order some cake?"

"Cake?"

"You have to have cake," said Edward, appearing from behind Izzy with a third box. "It's a celebration after all, and what's a celebration without cake."

"Very boring?" I suggested as the two of them made their way over to the counter.

"Exactly, darling. Very boring indeed."

Izzy slid his boxes onto the counter, avoiding the bowl of dice, the vase of flowers, and the stack of promotional postcards for the shop that were placed neatly near the till so I would remember to put them in people's bags. "Okay, so," he said, "we weren't sure what you'd like or how many people there would be... so we might have gone a bit overboard."

"That's an understatement," I said. The boxes were huge, and Edward was still holding one. There was probably enough cake to feed a small army, regardless of what was actually inside.

"What's all this?" Finn asked, appearing from the stockroom with a large Descent: Legends of the Dark in his arms. I frowned at him, looking over at the shelves because there should have been a copy of that out already. Finn saw me looking and grinned. "Oh, Lila already took the copy you had out, so this is to replace it. But I think I heard Hayden muttering about getting a copy too."

"Seriously?"

"Yes, seriously," Finn said. "But you didn't answer my question about those?" He gestured to the boxes on the counter with a nod of his head.

"We brought cake," Edward said with a brilliant smile. Izzy lifted the lid of the top box to reveal an enormous chocolate cake that had *Congratulations* piped across the top with little chocolate stars scattered across the icing. It looked incredible.

"There's chocolate," Izzy said, moving the first box across the counter so he could open the second, which had bright pink pieces of freeze-dried raspberry artfully scattered over pale, yellow icing. "Lemon and raspberry. And that box"—he pointed at the one Edward was still holding —"has cupcakes. We got a mix of vanilla with rainbow sprinkles, salted caramel, and red velvet." Edward opened the lid with a flourish to reveal three rows of six perfect cupcakes, each with the Castle Games logo on top.

"Wow," Finn said. "They look incredible." He turned to me, and I recognised the look of concern on his face before he'd even spoken. "Do we have—"

"Knives? Plates? Napkins?" Edward asked. He slid the box of cupcakes onto the counter. It barely fit, and I was going to need to find somewhere else for the flowers and the dice at this rate. "I brought some with me. It would be terribly rude of me to expect you to have some, especially since the cake was a surprise."

He reached into the leather bag he had slung over his shoulder and produced several packs of dark red napkins, some matching paper plates, and a couple of sharp-looking knives wrapped in kitchen roll along with a silver cake server. "I thought this would make dishing up easier," he added. "Shall I cut some?"

"Er, sure," I said. "We might need to find somewhere else to put them, though, otherwise I'm not going to have a counter."

"Don't worry," Izzy said, making a shooing motion with one hand. "You go mingle. We'll sort the cake."

"Thanks." I gave the pair a smile then looked around the shop to see what was going on. There were several people browsing, and I heard the thud of footsteps and the hum of chatter from upstairs. I was torn between lurking down here by the till and heading up there to see if anyone needed anything. Despite the fact that I'd been working in retail for years, I suddenly felt like a fish out of water and was completely unsure what to do. I didn't want to appear overbearing or put people off by sticking my nose in where it wasn't wanted.

On the other hand, I didn't want it to seem like I didn't care. I wanted people to be able to ask me questions or talk to me about what they were looking for. I always loved giving recommendations, but shoving unwanted ones in people's faces was the last thing I wanted to do.

"Hey, Gem." I turned to see Blake, one of the regulars at The Lost World, giving me a little wave from over near one of the shelves, which I'd labelled Find A New Favourite and filled with the most popular games I knew. They stood with a couple of friends from university, most of whom I recognised from various board game nights.

"Hey," I said as I wandered over. "It's great to see you. Thanks for coming."

"No worries! We wouldn't have missed it." Blake smiled at me. "We're trying to decide what to get my sister for her birthday. I've played most of these before, but I'm not sure what she'd like best." Blake's sister was bestselling fantasy romance author, Annabel Monteforte, who'd once stopped by The Lost World and accidentally made it go viral. She was the one who'd first prompted Blake to come to Jay's game nights, and it felt like an odd full circle thing that Blake was now buying games for her birthday.

"I still think she'd love Azul," said one of Blake's friends —Hayley, I thought. "It's so pretty, and it's easy to play."

"Maybe," Blake said, not looking completely convinced.

"What sort of things does she like?" I asked. "Does she like more co-operative games? Things with a twist? Long games? Or something a bit more fun and light-hearted?"

"She likes… fun things. She's quite cute, but she can be pretty competitive and cut-throat," Blake said. "It's funny because Annie is so quiet, you'd think she'd love something collaborative, but she'll absolutely take you for everything you've got! She's vicious."

I laughed. "It's always the quiet ones that surprise you." I looked at the shelves, casting my eyes over the various boxes and tins. "I'd suggest either Sushi Go Party! or Takenoko. Sushi Go Party! is really fun. It's fast-paced, and you can change it up a lot, but holy hell, can you be mean if you play it right. Plus, the artwork is very cute, and you can vary the player numbers easily. Takenoko has gorgeous art. It's very visual because you have things to build, and it's got a cute panda, so that's a win. I'm not sure if you'd describe it as cut-throat because it really depends on what you draw card wise, and there's a random, dice-rolling element for one of the actions, but it's fun and fast-paced and well balanced. And both are great if your sister doesn't play many games."

"Cool, thanks," Blake said, looking at the two boxes I pointed out and picking up Takenoko for a closer look.

"No worries. By the way, if any of you want some cake, those two bought a whole bakery." I pointed at Edward and Izzy, who were chatting to Finn and Hayden who we regularly gamed with.

"Is that a 'please come take some cake'?" Blake asked with a wry smile.

"Yeah, it is. It's either you take it by choice, or I'll be forcing it on you when you leave."

"Don't worry," Hayley said, looking up from the box for Wingspan she was examining. "We'll take some."

I left the group of them looking at the shelves with a mention to let me know if they had any more questions. As soon as I stepped away, Lila grabbed me and began asking me questions about a couple of the new releases, and after that someone else wanted some help with some Dungeons and Dragons source books.

From then on, the day seemed to speed up as I zipped from customer to customer, answering questions, making recommendations, saying hi and thanking them for coming, and attempting to foist as much cake off on people as I could. I was ridiculously grateful Finn had volunteered to help staff the counter because it felt like I needed to be in three places at once. I assumed it was just because it was the first day, but if it was always going to be this busy, I was going to have to rethink my plans for hiring another member of staff.

I was glad my family wasn't coming down to see the shop for another couple of weeks because if they'd come today, I'd barely have been able to wave at them.

At about two, Finn forced me to retreat to the stockroom and shoved a bottle of water and a large slab of cake into my hand, forcing me to take a break for twenty minutes. "You need to breathe," he said. "Sit down, eat something, and just take a break. Nothing is going to burn down while you're gone."

I wanted to point out that I hadn't even realised what time it was, but I didn't. Instead, I sat on the old chair I'd shoved into the corner, munching on chocolate cake and scrolling through social media looking at everything Lewis had posted. I still wasn't sure where half of the videos and photos had come from, although I had seen Lewis and Jason briefly before lunch, so perhaps he'd taken some then when I'd been sucked into a long conversation about whether or not I was going to stock wargaming miniatures and if so, what armies and what accessories. The person had had very strong opinions, and it had taken me a while to extract myself.

As I flicked through the various stories and reels on Instagram, I realised Lewis had gotten Jason to film a little video and post it to his story while also tagging the shop. I doubted many of his fans lived in the area, but considering he had fifteen million followers, even just one percent of them checking out the shop's social media or brand-new web store would be incredible. I'd have to think of a way to say thank you, even though I knew Jason would just shrug and say something about it being what friends did.

Sometimes, it still blew my mind that Jason Lu was now someone I knew in real life. The world really was a small place.

"You have more visitors," Finn said, sticking his head around the door with an almost apologetic smile. I heard a loud swell of voices behind him, and I chuckled, already knowing who it was.

"They didn't have to come."

"They insisted. You're one of us now," he said, then blushed furiously. "If you want to be that is. I mean that in a totally non-creepy way."

"It's fine." I stood and walked over to him, ignoring the ache in my muscles. I kissed him gently. "I love you, and that means I love them too."

"You might regret the second part of that sentence."

"Never." I watched a smile blossom on Finn's face, wishing I could stay here with him for just a moment longer. But duty called.

I emerged onto the shop floor to find the downstairs packed with Finn's entire family, including Lewis and Jason who'd obviously returned. They were all browsing, and I noticed Tristan already had an armful of games while Richard and Ruby were perusing a little display under the label Games for Two that Leo had suggested. Jules was halfway up the stairs with Oscar in tow, and Terry and Paul were looking over the favourites section Blake had been perusing earlier. I noticed it already needed a bit of a restock, and I made a mental note to grab some more games for it.

Miranda and Mimbles stood near the counter, waiting for me, and Miranda pulled me into an enormous, floral-scented hug as soon as I was within range.

"This place looks amazing! You did such a wonderful job," she said.

"Well, I couldn't have done it without you. Thanks again for all your help yesterday."

"Nonsense," said Mimbles from behind her wife. "You'd have done splendidly."

"Thanks." I tried not to let my face show how much their words meant to me, but I knew I'd failed. They both beamed at me. It was funny how much their quiet sincerity seemed to settle in my chest, adding another layer of pride to my achievement. I didn't get to spend much time with my own family, and the fact that Finn's had welcomed me with open arms meant more than I could say.

"Now," continued Mimbles, "I want to get a few things that the four of us"—she gestured to Miranda, Terry, and Paul—"can play during the week. Nothing too boring, please. We're not that old, and I'm sick of playing Scrabble."

"I thought you liked Scrabble?" Miranda said.

"Yes, but you're all terrible at it, and I'm tired of winning all the time," Mimbles said, and Miranda laughed softly.

I grinned. "Fancy a legacy game? Something you can build on each week? It'll mean each session has an effect on what happens later, even if you don't know it at the time."

"Perfect. Show me what you've got." I led Mimbles over to a nearby shelf and started to explain her options. Over her shoulder, I saw Finn holding a cupcake covered in sprinkles and giving me a fond smile.

People had said the store was my success, but that was only partly true. I wouldn't have taken the risk if it wasn't for Finn. He'd changed everything for me. This success was ours, and I would hold on to that forever.

CHAPTER THIRTY-ONE

Finn

"Ready for round two?" Gem asked, grabbing the keys from behind the counter and heading over to the door. "There's no queue today if that helps."

I chuckled and sipped the large mocha I'd acquired from a nearby coffee shop, wrinkling my nose at the taste. I didn't usually drink coffee because I generally found the taste quite overpowering, but today was an exception. If it was going to be anything like yesterday, I was going to need the caffeine. "It does."

"Thanks again," Gem said as he straightened a box on one of the displays. "For helping me this weekend. You didn't have to."

"I'd be a pretty rubbish boyfriend if I didn't." I reached for one of the leftover salted caramel cupcakes, hoping the addition of sugar to my system would help give it the kick it needed. I hated being tired. "Hopefully after this weekend it will settle down and become a little more manageable for you."

"Fingers crossed. I want a steady stream of customers and orders, not so many I'm drowning but enough that I can afford to keep a roof over my head."

"That sounds like the perfect balance," I said, handing Gem a cupcake of his own. We'd managed to get rid of most of the cake yesterday, despite the vast quantities Edward and Izzy had brought, but there'd be enough to get us through today for anyone that really wanted some. "Yesterday was a good start though."

Gem nodded. "Better than I'd anticipated. And I had a couple of people say they'd seen the little ad I put in *Game and Geek*. I didn't think the next issue was out until next week, so that was a nice surprise. I think it's mostly going to be word of mouth, and hopefully we'll build up a steady stream of regulars. Jay's already agreed we can co-host the game nights, and I can hand out little prizes or vouchers." He began to pull the cupcake apart. "I was thinking of setting up a league or something for a couple of games. Just something casual that we can run for a couple of months. Something to think about." He shoved half the cupcake into his mouth just as the door buzzed and a couple of people entered. Gem's face screwed up in annoyance, and he glared furiously at the rest of the cupcake while I laughed behind my hand.

After that, there was a steady stream of people in and out of the shop. Some had known we were opening, some had just been passing by and been curious, and some had been sent by other people. Two had come up from The Lost

World after chatting with Jay, and another group had come all the way up from the centre of town and the little board game café on Cornhill. Apparently, they'd been playing a couple of games there and two of them had been looking to get a copy of their own. Since the café didn't keep a ton of games in stock to sell—usually only their most popular loans or the latest releases—they hadn't had any, but they'd been kind enough to mention that Gem might.

I was pleased to hear that. We'd gone down during the week with a little stack of postcards, unsure whether they'd be open to the idea of another game shop opening, even if the market wasn't quite the same. Gem had done a wonderful job of introducing himself and had framed the conversation in such a positive way that it had made me realise just how amazing he was with people. I'd always known he'd be good at the personal aspect of owning a customer-facing business, but watching him chat away with the café owner about games and the perils of opening a small business just hammered home how perfect he was at this. There was something warm and approachable about Gem. It was what had drawn me to him in the first place. Gem could make someone feel like they had known him their whole life after just five minutes, and he'd made me feel safe and listened to. Like I could be myself around him without any fear of repercussion. It was why I'd fallen for him so hard.

It was why I kept falling for him.

Every day, I felt myself falling a little bit more in love with Gem, and I hoped that continued for a very, very long time.

"What're you thinking about?" Gem asked as he emerged from the stockroom with a stack of games in hand. "Anything fun?"

"Just about you, actually."

"Oh? Good things I hope." He leant over and pressed a quick kiss to my cheek before heading to a shelf.

"Of course," I said, smiling as I watched him. "It sounds cheesy, but I was just thinking about how much I love you, and how lucky I am to have you in my life."

"Aww." Gem grinned at me cheekily. "You're a soppy bastard."

"I am, and you love that about me."

"That I do," he said. He shoved a copy of Carcassone into place, then opened his mouth to say something else but was cut off by the door opening and two familiar figures bursting through the door, accompanied by one unexpected one.

"Gem!" Kelsey hurtled across the floor and flung herself at Gem, who threw the last game onto the shelf at light speed before scooping Kelsey up into his arms.

"Hey, Kelsey," Gem said. "I didn't know you were coming today." He turned to me and gave me a pointed look, but I shrugged because I was as bewildered as he was. I'd spoken to Chantelle yesterday morning, and she'd said nothing about making the trip. Chantelle stood near the door, grinning and looking as fabulous as usual with Jules standing next to her. Jules was also smiling, but at Chantelle rather than me, and a note of suspicion lodged itself in my brain.

"Surprise," Kelsey said, waving her arms around. "Mummy and I wanted to surprise you."

"Congratulations," Chantelle said, walking over to give Gem a hug as Kelsey slithered out of his arms and went to talk to Jules. Chantelle muttered something to him that I couldn't hear, and Gem burst out laughing.

"What are you two conspiring about?" I asked, moving around the counter. "And how come Gem gets a hug first?"

"There's no conspiracy," Chantelle said. "And stop pouting. You'll get your hug."

"Good," I said as I pulled her into my arms. "Otherwise I might get jealous."

Chantelle snorted. "You couldn't get jealous if you tried. You're too sweet." From behind us, Jules made a choking sound, and I felt my face heat. Chantelle raised an eyebrow and looked between the pair of us. "Do I want to know?"

"Probably not," Jules said, and Chantelle hummed, a mischievous grin on her lips. I'd told Chantelle what had happened with Gem and how that had led to my siblings finding out my secret, but Jules didn't know that. There was the strong potential for this to blow up in my face, but that would mean Chantelle and Jules talking to each other…

But they must be in some sort of communication if Chantelle had organised this visit in secret, and Jules had come with her. I'd seen them chatting when Chantelle had been up and we'd gone for lunch with my family, but I hadn't thought anything of it. It felt like I was missing something, and I had an uncharacteristic urge to know what it was.

"So," I said quietly as Kelsey began asking Gem questions about some of the colourful boxes on the nearest display. "You and Jules?" I was taking a wild stab in the dark, but the flare of Chantelle's eyes and the pink tint under her make-up suggested I wasn't far off. Interesting.

"It's nothing serious. We just got chatting when we were over at your parents' for lunch last time I came to stay, and then she followed me on Insta when I got home, and it just went from there." I hummed quietly, and Chantelle smacked my chest playfully. "Don't be a dick and ruin this. Your sister is really sweet."

"I'm not saying a word," I said, pretending to zip up my mouth but unable to stop myself from grinning.

"Good."

"I'm happy for you."

"I thought you weren't saying anything."

"Technically, I'm not saying anything about your relationship—friendly or otherwise—with my sister."

"Don't get fucking technical with me," Chantelle said. She looked over at Gem and Kelsey, who were heading upstairs. Kelsey was holding Gem's hand and chattering away while Jules followed them with a soft look on her face I'd never seen before. I logged that away for later, but I'd be good and wouldn't tell anyone. I wasn't my brothers and didn't need to put Jules in the spotlight in the family group chat. *If* there was anything going on, Jules would tell us when she was ready. Besides, Chantelle lived in London and had Kelsey, so there would be more complex things for them to navigate, and they'd all be easier without my family breathing down their necks.

"We're just friends," Chantelle added.

"I've heard that one before. A note of advice, it never works out the way you think it will."

"Oh, please. You were in love with Gem before this whole friends-with-benefits thing even started. You were practically dating just without making it official."

I opened my mouth but realised I couldn't argue. "Point taken."

"Besides," Chantelle said. "We live so far apart, and I've got Kelsey, and I'm not sure Jules would be interested in someone like me… I'm a hot mess. Plus, I've never dated a woman before."

"What about that girl at uni? Nina?" I vaguely remembered the two of them being very cosy during our second year.

"Er, that was just a bit of fun." Chantelle blushed. "We were just fooling around."

"Well, take it from someone who's just done the whole terrible communication thing—"

"Against my advice," Chantelle said with a pointed smile.

I ignored her and continued. "Just be open with Jules. That's all you can do. Talk to each other, please."

"Don't do a Finn. Noted."

"You're so sweet." I pushed the box of leftover cake towards her. "Have a cupcake."

There was the thundering of feet on the stairs and Kelsey appeared, clutching a My Little Pony role-play starter book. "Mummy! Can we get this please? I can be a pony and have adventures, and Gem said he'd teach me how to play!"

"It's designed for kids," I said. "It's a starter RPG. It's cute and very simple. We can play over Skype or Zoom or something."

"I'll play too," said Jules, coming down the stairs behind Gem. "I like My Little Pony."

"Oh, will you now," I muttered, ignoring Chantelle's glare.

"Finn," Kelsey said. "You know how last time you said Gem wasn't your boyfriend?"

"Yes…"

"Is he now? Mummy said he was and that you…" She scrunched up her face. "You finally stopped being a 'nana."

I chuckled as Chantelle put one hand on her face. "Yes, Gem is my boyfriend."

"Okay. Does he make you doughnuts now?"

"Er, no," I said.

Kelsey sighed and gave me a pitying look. "I'm sorry. I don't think it's worth having a boyfriend if you don't get doughnuts."

Behind her, Gem burst into raucous laughter. "Don't worry, Kelsey. I'll learn to make some."

"Good," she said with a nod as if she'd just righted one of the greatest wrongs in the world. "Mummy, can I have doughnuts now? I'm hungry."

"How about," Jules said, coming up behind Kelsey, "we pay for your book and then we go and get something to eat. Do you like pizza?"

"Yes! Let's go!"

We arranged for them to come back to mine later for dinner, and Chantelle gave me another hug. Jules insisted on paying for Kelsey's book, and when they left, I noticed Kelsey holding her hand. I hummed and watched the three of them walk down the street from the upstairs window while filling some of the shelves.

"So…" Gem said when I came down. He was stacking one of the cases near the door. "They're banging."

I snorted. "Chantelle says they're just friends."

Gem scoffed. "Yeah, but we said that too, and look how that turned out."

"That's what I said." I walked up to him and kissed him quickly. "And I'm very glad it did. I love you."

"I love you too." Gem shoved the last box onto the shelf. "You're the best thing that has happened to me."

"I could say the same to you too," I said, my heart so full of happiness I thought I might burst. If this was going to be my life, I couldn't wish for a better one.

EPILOGUE

TWO YEARS LATER

Finn

"Are you ready?" Gem asked me, sticking his head around the door of the hotel bathroom as I adjusted my tie in the enormous mirror over the sink. He grinned and shook his head. "Your tie is crooked."

"My fingers won't stop shaking," I said, giving him a wry smile. "I'm so nervous, and I'm not even the one getting married."

"Yeah, but you're giving the bride away, *and* you have to make a speech. I'd be nervous too." Gem's fingers found mine and began gently adjusting the knot of my tie until he was convinced I looked presentable. "There. Very handsome."

"Thanks." I leant over and kissed him gently. It was something that always gave me comfort. "What would I do without you?"

"I don't know." He grinned. "Be less awesome?"

295

"Definitely." I kissed him again, my hand finding his and squeezing it gently. "You know, when this is all over, we should get married."

"Is that a proposal?" Gem asked with a raised eyebrow.

"No," I said. When I did propose, I was going to do it properly. Unless Gem got to it first. And now that I'd mentioned it, it was a distinct possibility. Still, I had the whole of today to plan something because I knew Gem wouldn't do anything today if he wanted to live. You didn't propose at another person's wedding, no matter how well you knew them. It just wasn't done. "It's more of a casual suggestion for you to think about. When I do ask, you'll know."

Gem grinned at me mischievously. "I'll hold you to that." He gave me another lingering kiss. "Okay, you better get going! I'll see you downstairs later."

"Don't forget the gift," I said as I walked out of the bathroom. "It's still in the suitcase."

"I won't forget. You can't forget something that fucking big."

I snorted, then patted my jacket pocket to make sure my speech was in there for later and headed out of the room. The hotel's patterned carpet was plush underfoot, and it only took me a couple of minutes to get upstairs to one of the suites where my charge was waiting. I knocked on the door and heard a flurried cry of voices before it swung open. I grinned as I looked down at the beautiful little girl in front of me, her dark hair threaded with baby blue flowers that matched the ones on her dress.

"Hey, Kelsey. How's your mum doing?" I asked. Kelsey sighed dramatically. She was seven going on seventeen.

"She's worrying again. Can you go and tell her to stop because it's very annoying. She's supposed to be happy today."

"Sure, bub. I'll try."

"Good. She might listen to you," Kelsey said. "Also, can I have some cake? Uncle Edward brought us some cupcakes when he brought Mum's dress over, but apparently I have to ask first." She did not look impressed by this fact, but at least she had asked rather than just helping herself. Although, when I walked into the suite, I realised the reason Kelsey had asked was because someone, probably Edward, had put the cupcakes on one of the shelves in the little kitchenette, well out of Kelsey's reach, and all the chairs around the little dining room table were either occupied with fussing bridesmaids or covered in stuff.

"Okay, first let's get cake," I said, retrieving the box of lemon and blueberry cupcakes. "Then I'll help Mum. But you have to promise to go sit down and eat this nicely and not get any on your dress. Do you promise?" I held out one of the cupcakes to Kelsey who stuck out her little finger in return.

"Pinky promise."

"Done." I handed her the cake, then walked over to the bridesmaids and put the box on the table.

"Finn? Is that you?"

"It's me." I turned to see Chantelle emerging from the bedroom and my mouth dropped open, my breath catching in my throat. Chantelle was always beautiful, but today she looked like a literal princess. The bodice of her dress shimmered as the little sequins sewn into the lace caught the light. The skirt was made of soft pink tulle and seemed to cascade like a waterfall. It couldn't have been any more perfect if Edward had worked on it for a thousand years. "Wow."

"Yeah? Do I look okay?" Her hands brushed over the skirt nervously. "It's not too much."

"No." I shook my head. "No, it's perfect."

"Thanks." She smiled and let out a deep breath. "God, why am I so fucking nervous?"

"Mum!"

"Sorry, baby," Chantelle said, looking over at Kelsey who sat on one of the sofas, eating her cupcake with the tiniest bites possible so she didn't drop any of it. "Where did she get cake?"

"Edward brought it."

"Oh, that makes sense. He spoils her."

"He's like that. He's like the kind of gay uncle who'll never have his own kids but dotes on everyone else's whether he's related to them or not."

"He's an angel." Chantelle smiled fondly at her daughter. "How long have we got?"

I looked at my watch. "Registrar will be here in fifteen minutes. Ceremony starts in thirty. Are you ready?"

"Bit late now if I'm not." I laughed, and Chantelle shook her head. "But, yeah, I am. I can't believe this is happening. I never thought I'd get something like this… and yet, here we are."

"Here we are," I said. "And now you get to be my sister

for real." I closed the gap between us and pulled her into a gentle hug, pressing a soft kiss to her cheek. "I love you."

"I love you too." Chantelle stepped back, the biggest smile on her face. "Let's get this show on the road."

Thirty minutes later, we stood at the entrance to the hotel's conservatory, waiting for the music to begin. The room in front of us was packed with guests, and late-spring sunshine streamed through the windows onto the aisle that was lined with chairs, each with bouquets of trailing flowers tied to the ends. At the front of the line stood Kelsey, armed with a basket of petals, followed by several bridesmaids and then Chantelle's mum with Chantelle and me at the end.

I'd been surprised when Chantelle had asked me to walk her down the aisle instead of her mum, but I'd been absolutely honoured.

As the music struck up—"Who Is She" from *Cinderella*—Chantelle squeezed my arm, and I felt tears start to prickle my eyes. The doors swung open, and the bridesmaids began their slow walk. Everyone in the audience *aww*ed at Kelsey, and I was sure she was loving every moment of the attention.

"Ready?" I asked, my voice catching again. Chantelle nodded. We took a step forward and swept down the aisle together.

At the end, I saw Jules waiting for us, looking resplendent in a dark blue suit with Eli beside her. Tears dripped down her cheeks as she watched us, and I couldn't blame her. Out of the corner of my eye I saw Gem standing next to Lewis, Jason, Edward, Izzy, Leo, and Jay. Every single one of them looked ready to burst, and as we walked past, I couldn't stop myself from mouthing, "I love you" to Gem.

When we reached the end of the aisle, I brushed a kiss against Chantelle's cheek before taking my seat with the rest of the bridesmaids, digging my handkerchief out of my pocket to wipe my eyes as gracefully as I could.

As the registrar started talking about love and marriage, I realised how much had changed over the past couple of years. It seemed like only yesterday I'd introduced Chantelle and Jules and then teased Chantelle about them being "friends" when she'd appeared at the opening weekend of Castle Games. Chantelle had said it was nothing, but everything had fallen into place so quickly after that weekend that from the outside it had seemed so beautifully easy.

When Lewis stood up to read a poem, I turned my head to look at Gem. We'd been together for over two years now, and I couldn't imagine my life without him in it. Sure, there had been bumps in the road, but every couple had those, and ours had never been that serious. Mostly it was just one of us getting annoyed at the other for working too much.

Castle Games had gone from strength to strength ever since it opened, and Gem was starting to wonder whether it might be worth looking at larger premises. The only thing stopping him was the idea of moving, which we'd both agreed would be a nightmare. Setting up the shop the first time around had been draining enough, and doing it again sounded like torture. Although, I wouldn't necessarily be against more mid-painting, stockroom blow jobs if the opportunity ever arose.

Gem had hired a second member of staff, which, to my surprise, had turned out to be Link, the guy Jesse had left him for. I sometimes wondered whether I should thank Link for gifting me Gem, but that would probably be very awkward. Link was very sweet, if lacking a smidge of common sense at times, but he was a hard worker, and everyone liked him. Link, Gem, and I had done a big board game show together last summer, leaving the shop in Lewis's and Jay's hands for the weekend, and it had been fun if exhausting. Link's natural exuberance had helped make it less torturous than I'd been expecting.

Gem had even started designing games again after seeing the testing tables at the show, and now hosted monthly play test nights in the basement of The Lost World for local creators to come and experiment on willing participants. Seeing Gem do both made me happy in a way I couldn't explain, but I was so proud of him for never giving up on his dream—even if the execution looked slightly different from how he'd first imagined it.

My narration work had continued to grow, and I'd even won a couple of awards last year. It meant I had more authors and recording companies interested than ever, but I was getting better at managing my diary now. I was careful not to overbook myself because I actually had a reason to stop working in the evenings. I continued to run Fantasy and Filth too, and my fears that Gem would get jealous and want me to stop had never materialised. Instead, he was more than happy to help me with scenarios and scripts, and I was all too happy to have his assistance.

When the ceremony ended and Jules and Chantelle filed out as wives, I clapped so hard my hands started to hurt. Gem found me afterwards and kissed me softly. "That was beautiful," he said. "They look so happy."

"They do." I handed him a packet of confetti from a little basket on a nearby table. "I love you, you know that, right?"

"I love you too." Gem slipped his hand into mine and led me outside. "By the way, Blake sent me a photo of Pip asleep on Merry's head." I chuckled as Gem pulled out his phone to show me the picture. Pippin and Merry were a pair of kittens we'd bought not long after we'd moved in together eighteen months ago. They were both adorable, if incredibly troublesome, but I loved having them around. Gem and I had already decided that once we bought a house, which was the next thing we were aiming for, we were going to make sure there were lots of things for them to sit on and in because they adored climbing on everything, even if it wasn't designed for climbing.

"One day, Merry is going to lose his patience with his brother," I said.

"Probably, but Pippin still won't learn boundaries. He thinks Merry's personal space is his too."

I laughed and handed Gem back his phone before looking around at the assembled guests. "Come on. You can help me round everyone up for the confetti tunnel."

"Fine, but I want two envelopes," he said with a grin. "And a kiss."

"Done." I kissed him deeply and squeezed his hand. I was the luckiest man in the world. I'd found the man of my dreams, the man who'd seen me for who I truly was, and he had found me. And my life couldn't be more perfect.

The End

ACKNOWLEDGMENTS

Finn and Gem have been a long time coming for me. Gem first appeared as a small, side-character way back in *Natural Twenty* and casually made himself part of the family, and originally I thought he might be book four in that series… until I created Finn.

Finn was always going to be a fun one from the moment his side-hustle popped into my head, and it was fun to let my imagination run wild! I absolutely adore these two together, and I hope you have too.

As with every novel I write, I am supported by a wonderful group of people who I'm incredibly grateful for.

To Carly, who has always encouraged me, cheered me on, and never let me talk shit about myself. Thank you for everything.

To Charity, who read through my early draft and poked me to keep going. Thanks for being the best PA and friend, and for putting up with me on a daily basis.

To Susie, who continues to believe in me when I don't believe in myself.

To Toby, Ali, Rosie, and Jayne for always being there.

To Natasha, for creating such beautiful covers.

To Lori, for all the stray typo hunting.

To my husband for continually providing me with love,

support and chocolate. And to my beautiful Biscuit puppy for making me smile.

And last, but never least, to you, my fabulous readers. Whether I'm new to you or you've been here since the start, I am grateful for you love and support.

If you enjoyed *Finding Finn*, please consider leaving a review. Reviews are invaluable for indie authors, and may help other readers find this book.

Until next time.

ALSO BY CHARLIE NOVAK

Forever Love

Always Eli

Finding Finn

Oh So Oscar

Heather Bay

Like I Pictured

Like I Promised (July 2022)

Roll for Love

Natural Twenty

Charisma Check

Proficiency Bonus

Kiss Me

Strawberry Kisses

Summer Kisses

Spiced Kisses

Off the Pitch

Breakaway

Extra Time

Final Score

The Off the Pitch Short Collection

Off the Pitch: The Complete Collection (Boxset)

STANDALONES

Screens Apart

SHORT STORIES

One More Night

Twenty-Two Years (Newsletter Exclusive)

Snow Way In Hell

AUDIOBOOKS

Always Eli

Finding Finn

Natural Twenty

Charisma Check

Proficiency Bonus

Strawberry Kisses

Summer Kisses

For a regularly updated list, please visit:

charlienovak.com/books

charlienovak.com/audiobooks

CHARLIE NOVAK

Charlie lives in England with her husband and two cheeky dogs. She spends most of her days wrangling other people's words in her day job and then trying to force her own onto the page in the evening.

She loves cute stories with a healthy dollop of fluff, plenty of delicious sex, and happily ever afters — because the world needs more of them.

Charlie has very little spare time, but what she does have she fills with baking, Dungeons and Dragons, reading and many other nerdy pursuits. She also thinks that everyone should have at least one favourite dinosaur…

Website: charlienovak.com
Facebook Group: Charlie's Angels
For day-to-day-musings, giveaways and teasers.

Plus sign up for her newsletter for bonus scenes, new releases and extras.

facebook.com / charlienovakauthor

twitter.com / charlienwrites

instagram.com / charlienwrites

bookbub.com / profile / charlie-novak

amazon.com / author / charlienovak

Lightning Source UK Ltd.
Milton Keynes UK
UKHW011941180522
403172UK00004B/437